JACK SLATER:
A LONG YEAR IN
OUTLAW COUNTRY

JACK SLATER: A LONG YEAR IN OUTLAW COUNTRY

JOHNNY GUNN

THORNDIKE PRESS
A part of Gale, a Cengage Company

Copyright © 2018 Johnny Gunn.
Thorndike Press, a part of Gale, a Cengage Company.

ALL RIGHTS RESERVED
Thorndike Press® Large Print Softcover Western.
The text of this Large Print edition is unabridged.
Other aspects of the book may vary from the original edition.
Set in 16 pt. Plantin.

**LIBRARY OF CONGRESS CIP DATA ON FILE.
CATALOGUING IN PUBLICATION FOR THIS BOOK
IS AVAILABLE FROM THE LIBRARY OF CONGRESS.**

ISBN-13: 978-1-4205-1935-8 (softcover alk. paper)

Published in 2024 by arrangement with Wolfpack Publishing LLC.

Printed in the USA
1 2 3 4 5   28 27 26 25 24

JACK SLATER:
A LONG YEAR IN
OUTLAW COUNTRY

[1]

"You just grew up too fast, Jack. Never learned how to play." Cactus Jack Faraday, that wild east Texas cowboy, Jack Slater's ranch foreman, was giving the boss what for. Faraday was rambunctious and slightly wild most of the time while Jack Slater was a bit withdrawn and quiet. Working a herd of cattle, training horses, chasing strays, they were a perfect pair.

"You're probably right Jack." The two men were working with a colt in a corral turned into a round pen. Jack Slater, twenty-two years old and owner of the ranch had come west many years ago on what was called an orphan train after his parents were killed in a buggy accident. Jack was ten at the time and had to grow up fast.

Jack was a big boy, even at ten he was usually thought to be twelve or so and grew into a large man who stood about six feet four inches and weighed a solid two twenty.

He wondered about that comment from Cactus about not learning how to play.

"I'm sure Mims would agree with you. When I look back over these years, all I see is me trying to get something done or somebody straightened out. Without Mims, I would not have survived at Jablonski's farm."

In the mid to late 1800s, boys and girls, orphans or throw-aways, were sent to families on the frontier by the Children's Aid Society. Most of the families were loving, warm, and welcomed the additions to their homes. Jack, unfortunately, ended up on a farm near Fargo in the Dakota Territory run by a ruthless old man named Pete Jablonski.

An orphan girl named Mims was living there, and the two became excellent friends. Jack ran away as soon as he was able, Mims ended up with serious problems when the Aid Society took the rest of the children from Jablonski.

She was abducted and raped by a gang of outlaws and came away from that miserable ordeal with a baby girl. She searched for Jack Slater, they ended up finding each other, and they were now happily married these last two years. Jack had adopted the little girl, and there was one other child on the ranch.

"On the other hand, Cactus Jack Faraday, if I hadn't had to grow up all tough and mean, you wouldn't be working for me."

The two big men were laughing and punching each other on the shoulder, dancing away from punches, feigning jabs and whops, working their way from the training corral to the main ranch house on the Slater family ranch. "That colt is gonna be one fine stock horse," Slater said, "if you would just learn to stay in the saddle long enough to teach him proper manners."

"Maybe, I'll just let you ride him after dinner," Cactus Jack laughed, brushing dirt and dust from his chaps. "Something smells mighty good in the kitchen."

It was late spring, the calf crop was doing well, the grass was growing tall, and the men were discussing how involved in raising ranch horses they should become. The army always needed horses, but it was the proliferating of ranching in northern and eastern Nevada and western Utah that had their attention.

"Most horses can be trained to work stock, but if we breed into the traits we're looking for, I think we'll find an open and ready market." Slater had learned while working on Henry Rupert's big ranch in Wyoming just how vital a good horse was on the open range.

"When they talk about open range, this is open range country, Mr. Faraday, and we have an opportunity here."

Slater's ranch was in the flats just west of the towering Ruby Mountains in eastern Nevada. The valley was often referred to as The Meadows and featured good grass, mountain-fed streams, and natural springs. He owned two sections of land and grazed his cattle on open range as well. A lot of the deeded property was used for growing grasses to be used as winter feed.

"You boys put work aside for an hour now and concentrate on Sandra's roast pork dinner." Mims brought a cast iron Dutch oven to the table and Slater remembered the times back in Fargo. It was a perfect picture of little Mims, twelve years old, running the farmhouse kitchen and taking abuse from Jablonski.

"Here," he said, "let me help you with that."

She handed off the heavy kettle and laughed out loud. "Pete Jablonski wouldn't like that," and Jack had to laugh right along with her.

"No, he wouldn't. How did we survive those years? Well, Mrs. Slater, our kids won't have those kinds of stories to tell."

Mims looked at him with just the slightest smile. "You already know?"

"Know what?" Jack asked, looking to their cook, Sandra, and to Cactus Jack.

"We're going to have a child of our very own, Jack. Just in time for Christmas."

The period of silence was less than two seconds, and everyone started talking at the same time, all saying about the same thing, and all of it very positive. "Well," Cactus Jack said with a grin. "I'm glad that's over. I'm hungry."

Sandra Gomez had called everyone in, and the table filled quickly. The hands working cattle carried what food they wanted in saddlebags, but one or two were around the barns and scurried to the kitchen. Sandra's son, Robbie, joined young Maybelle Slater, roiling in from the backyard.

Great slabs of roast pork, platters of potatoes and bowls of beans were passed around along with baskets of freshly baked bread, and for the first several minutes there was no conversation. "When it gets quiet like this, it must mean I cooked this mess pretty good," Sandra Gomez joked. Even that didn't bring much response. They were just too busy enjoying the bounty of the ranch.

■ ■ ■ ■

"Don't know why I eat that much, Jack," Cactus said, rubbing his distended stomach. "I was totally against you raising hogs on this place, you might remember, but when a kettle of roast pork is put down next to me, I want to demand that we increase the herd."

"You did take care of your fair share, Cactus Jack." Slater looked out across the large ranch at some dust half a mile away. "Looks like we might have some company coming in. Maybe Valley Paddock bringing in the mail?"

"I'll be in the barn watchin'," Cactus said, loping off. Jack knew he would get his rifle and keep a close eye on the rider. Jack Slater had his ranch burned out once, and he vowed it wouldn't happen twice. The rider loped into the large yard area between the ranch house and barns and corrals.

"Well, Jimmy Delgado, what brings you out here from Skelton's neighborly warmth?" Slater asked, taking the reins as the Elko County deputy sheriff dismounted. "A friendly visit, I hope?"

Delgado was a skinny man with narrow shoulders, no hips, and big feet. He stood almost six feet tall but probably didn't weigh one fifty fully dressed. His long stringy brown hair hung loosely about his shoulders, some of it held in place by a floppy and ancient sombrero. A thin beard, rather scraggly, clung tenaciously to his face, and his piercing gray eyes shone brightly.

His looks were deceiving and had cost more than one man his life. He could pull that big iron and put two slugs in a man so fast it sounded like one shot being fired. He was deadly with a knife, and his long arms had the strength of a much larger man.

"Actually, I'm here on business, Jack. Can we talk?"

"Tie your horse at the corral, Jimmy, and let's find a cup of coffee in the kitchen. Might have some roast and biscuits left if Cactus didn't eat everything." He waved at Cactus Jack to say everything was okay and headed for the kitchen door. Delgado picked up on the wave and gave Jack a smile.

"Bad times in the Ruby Valley, Jack," Delgado said, taking coffee from Sandra and nodding thank you. He offered a generous smile and doffed that sombrero. "You don't look well, Sandra. Are you all right?"

"Just a little tired, Jimmy. Thank you for asking." Her smile back to the deputy should have told him that he could visit

13

anytime he wanted. In her heart, she was afraid that he wasn't wise enough to understand. "Will you want anything else, Jack?

"No, you go rest, Sandra. I can take care of anything else we might want. You go rest."

Sandra Gomez, like Jimmy Delgado, was thin as a rail and suffered from tiredness most of the time. Slater was fearful of her health, and he and Mims had talked about it often. "She's one of those people that won't slow down," he said after she left the kitchen. "I'm sure there's something wrong, but she won't go to the doctor, either."

He took a chair across the table from the deputy. "So, Jimmy, how are these problems in the Ruby Valley affecting us?"

The Ruby Mountains, high and rugged, separated the Ruby Valley from Skelton and The Meadows, with just one pass through the range, Harrison Pass, connecting the two. There was very little socializing between the areas, mostly due to the long distances and rough terrain.

"Sheriff wanted me to let everyone know there seems to be a gang of outlaws attacking ranches in the valley. They've hit a couple over there, killed some people, and stole their stock and possessions."

"And Bill Connors thinks they might

14

come into our little valley? Did he mention any names, Jimmy?" Slater's eyes narrowed into slits; his jaw visibly tightened thinking about such a thing, remembering some of the wicked men and outlaws he'd had to face just a few years ago. Those that did their best to kill him in Deadwood and then on Rupert's Wyoming ranch. An entire family of outlaws.

After the former Elko sheriff was killed during a bank robbery, foiled by Slater, the county elected Bill Connors who carried the moniker of Wild Bill from his days along the Arkansas/Texas border, and a few years fighting outlaws in Missouri. Bill Connors was a good lawman, big and tough, and had the respect of the ranching community in the county.

"Seems as though a feller named Jake Reynolds and his kid brother, Sandy, have at least three others riding with them. The sheriff wanted you particularly and the other ranchers in the area to know about this. He's putting together a posse to chase these men down.

"I'm going to stay in Skelton as the resident deputy and he's got another deputy setting up camp in the Ruby Valley. With the telegraph, we can get word to the sheriff if we see or hear anything."

"That's a good idea, Jimmy. Thank Wild Bill for thinking of us and thank you for bringing us this awful news. Is Valley Paddock looking to put together any kind of posse in town?"

"Just a loose group that can ride at a quick notice but won't be out searching or nothing." He wolfed another biscuit, grabbed one for the saddlebag, and they walked out to his horse. The wind had picked up and before he could get that sombrero settled in, his hair seemed to take a life of its own, flying in every direction. Jack smiled and noticed that he paid no attention to brushing it back with his fingers, just plopped the old hat on his head and scrunched it down some.

"Tell Sandra she needs to see a doc. She just doesn't look well." He rode off at a gentle lope, and Slater walked back to tell Mims what the deputy had said.

[2]

"Sure, as I'm sittin' here, that fool sheriff is gonna be comin' down on us, Jake. We should have killed that old man. I knew right at that minute, leavin' him lie there in the mud was wrong. Shoulda shot him dead." Henry Coates had ridden into the outlaw camp just minutes before, after spending a day at Halleck, a railhead community on the intercontinental railroad.

"Tell me what you're grousin' about, Henry," Jake Reynolds said, holding Coates' horse. Reynolds was short, skinny, half bald, with a bad attitude toward everyone and everything. "You angry at me, say so," he snarled, letting the big Coates know he would pull his gun in a flash. "You angry about something else, don't gripe at me about it."

"Ain't angry at you, boss," Henry Coates said, tying his big gelding to a rail in front of a rundown cabin in a canyon north of

17

Halleck. "Me and the others raided that ranch along the emigrant trail last week, found some good stock, too, but didn't kill the old man when we left.

"Guess the Kid thought he'd die, but he didn't, and now Connors is putting together a posse to chase us down." Coates was shaking his head in anger and frustration.

The Kid that Coates was talking about was Sandy Reynolds, Jake's younger brother, as much of a hothead as Jake, and equally dangerous. He was called Kid more often than Sandy but didn't have the smarts that his older brother had. He wore his blond hair long and it hung in waves and curls. He had a wispy mustache and steel gray eyes. He preferred shooting a man in the back to standing up to a fight.

"So, you boys rode off and left a wounded man behind? That's the most stupid thing you could do, Henry. I should just shoot you where you stand," he growled, and almost pulled that heavy iron.

"No, boss," Coates almost yelled. "It was the Kid's decision. He was running the game and he said leave the fool sprawled and bleeding in the mud, that he'd be dead in an hour. He was gut shot, Jake. He should have died, but the Kid wouldn't let me kill him off."

Jake Reynolds eased his hand away from the big Colt. He wondered about whether Coates could be called off by his kid brother but didn't say anything. Is Coates getting soft? Why would he let himself be called off on something that important? Or is Coates playing a game, maybe lookin' to get between him and the Kid.

Jake's anger about the situation grew as his thoughts about it rumbled through his less than intelligent mind. "Just ride off and leave a wounded man to talk all about you?" He was cussing a blue streak, turned, and stormed into the little cabin. The rest of the outlaw gang was sitting around a large table passing a bottle back and forth, playing a hand or two of poker.

"Tell me about this foray of yours a couple of days ago," he snarled at his brother. "I don't remember sending anyone out. I don't remember seeing any gold coming in." His eyes were narrowed down, his feet spread slightly, and his hand close to his weapon.

"We had a good time, eh boys?" Sandy Reynolds said, laughing some. "Found an old ranch off a creek that feeds the Humboldt River. Some old geezer and his wife. Whoooeee, their stock was all penned up and ready for us. Old Simon Scruggs would have bought those steers in a flash. We had

19

us some fun, then the old guy and his wife got all scared and started screaming and all, and we shot 'em dead."

He was laughing and thumping the table, nodding at his brother and the men around the table. They nodded back at the Kid, laughing right along with him.

"Didn't finish the job, Kid. You rode off and left one alive." Jake Reynolds was glaring at his brother. Those at the table got very quiet and Sandy Reynolds fists tightened.

"Who told you that?" Kid Reynolds jumped to his feet, looking around the table, at his brother, then let his eyes fall on Henry Coates. "You tell him that?" His hand hovered close to his sidearm, fingers stretched out and ready to take that handle in quickly.

"Damn right, Kid. I told you then he should die. Instead, we rode off, the sheriff rode in, and now they be looking for us." Coates was fast with his revolver, but stood tall, looking the Kid in the eye, just waiting for the slightest movement. "I just got back from Halleck, Kid. The whole damn town's talking about our raid. Even describing you and your golden locks. Better cut your hair and dye it black, boy."

Nobody in the gang had ever called the

Kid boy, ever. Along with the Kid, there were two others at the table, and they slowly moved back away from what was sure to be a loud death scene. The Kid was standing, his legs spread, hand quivering near the weapon's handle, eyes glaring at Henry Coates. Coates was a mirror image of the Kid and it took an accidental scrape of a chair leg for the two to draw, almost simultaneously.

Sandy Reynolds was thrown back ten feet, slamming into the wall of the cabin, and onto the floor. Coates was flung back and crashed through the partially open door of the cabin, into the dirt off the porch. There was silence and the aroma of gunfire and blood in the cabin for a full ten seconds before Jake rushed to his brother's side.

"Kid," he said, holding his bloody body. Sandy Reynolds wasn't dead and moaned as Jake helped him onto a cot. The bullet sliced through some meat along the side of his chest, just under his armpit, nicking a rib but doing a considerable amount of damage to muscles in his chest and back. There was heavy bleeding that Jake was having trouble getting under control.

Coates, on the other hand, suffered a gunshot to his lower left leg that was bleeding heavily. The bullet went right through the leg, tore up some meat, didn't touch a bone, and he sat in the dirt, wrapped the wound, and got up. He limped back into the cabin, his weapon still in hand and glared at Jake and the Kid.

"You ever so much as look at me sideways, you little fool, I'll kill you," he snarled. He walked up to the pair and got right in Jake's face.

"You're sittin' next to that lying fool. You ask him. He told us not to kill that old man. Ask any of the others." Coates was ready to kill, his leg hurt, he had been called a liar, and he didn't give a hoot who might die next. Both men were known throughout the area for their gun work, fast, accurate, and with short fuse tempers. Both now suffering gunshot wounds because of their speed.

"Did you tell them not to kill the old man?" Jake demanded, sitting on the cot next to the groaning Kid. "Did you?" He whacked him on the wound bringing a cry of pain from the outlaw. If that old man did live and could identify any of his gang, they would be attacked and soon. Jake wanted to just shoot the damn fool.

The Kid groaned something, and Jake slapped him across the side of his head, hard. "I can't hear you, Kid. Did you?" he got right down into the Kid's face, sat back, and slapped him again, almost driving him off the cot.

Jake got up and walked over to the stove, poured half a cup of coffee, filled the cup up with whiskey and paced around for a minute. "No more raids on any ranches unless we are all together from now on. I'm the boss, and anyone don't like that, make your move right now." He looked around the one-room cabin, eye to eye with each man, including Coates and the Kid.

"We hit these ranches because they have money on the property. If they have cattle or stock we can dispose of quickly, that's just a little extra for us, but what we're after is the money. If you fools made this raid without me, where is the money? Where is the stock?" There were no answers, and all the eyes were looking at the dirt floor.

"Get that idiot patched up," he said, nodding at the Kid. "You okay to ride, Coates?"

"Yeah, boss."

"Pack it up, then. We got to find a new home for the Reynolds Gang."

"I can't ride like this." The Kid whined.

Jake spun on him and said, "If he ain't on his horse when we ride out of here, kill him." Sandy Reynolds' eyes widened in horror, knowing his brother would do just that.

"I don't understand, Coates. If there was

stock, did you sell it to Scruggs? He buys most of the stock we steal. And if there was gold or cash, where is it?"

Coates said something about brotherly love, spit some tobacco juice into the dust and walked off shaking his head. *These boys are not as smart as I was led to believe.*

"I can't answer those kinds of question, Mr. Lee." Sheriff Connors was standing next to Lee's hospital bed in Halleck. Lee was in critical condition with a gunshot wound to his midsection. The doctor had doubts the man would live. In a quavering voice just barely audible, the elderly rancher had asked the simple question, 'Why?'

He and his wife lived peaceably on their ranch north of the Humboldt River, running a small herd of steers, a few sheep, keeping three men and one woman on the payroll. "Why did they do this?" he asked again. Lee had the stock in and ready for shipment and gave his employees a couple of days off before the drive to the railroad stockyards.

"We're supposed to be a civilized society and those men were worse than animals. What makes a man act like that? You asked, and I can't answer," Bill Connors said quietly. "Not just a lack of respect for life and property, a lack of respect for the whole human race."

Connors was shaking his head not willing or able to answer Lee's questions. A man, belly shot and left to die in a mud puddle, his elderly wife abused and then killed, in her own kitchen. For a few lambs, a few steers, a goat or two?

"The crime, compounded by the malicious, demeaning violence of their actions is beyond comprehension, Mr. Lee. I'll catch 'em, you can bet on that, and they'll die for their crimes, and you can bet the wad on that one, but it won't be enough, will it?"

Connors had no answers for Orion Lee, and worse, none for himself either. *This is the second raid on a ranch and I don't know why the raiders act like they do . . . Stealing stock is one thing but killing the man's wife while she was busy in the kitchen, and then shooting Lee and leaving him to bleed out slowly was far beyond rustling. They tore that little house apart looking for money and property and didn't need to hurt or kill anyone!*

Connors was large, bull-headed, prone to act before thinking sometimes, and a long-time lawman. He was elected sheriff in Elko County following the downfall of Sheriff Cyrus Simpson.

Simpson tried to run the county his way

and became an outlaw himself. It was Jack Slater who finally brought him down during an early morning bank robbery.

Connors believed in the law, demanded justice, and was considered fair in his handling of those accused of crimes. This crime against the Lee family was the worst he could imagine. Lee's wife murdered before the old man's eyes, and him, shot and left to bleed to death in the pig sty. *They stood that old lady up next to her stove and shot her dead right in front of her husband. Miserable animals.*

It was only because one of Lee's ranch hands rode back to the ranch to fix a broken saddle cinch that the old man was found at all. Slick White brought Lee to Halleck, a hard five-mile ride, otherwise it would have been that many more hours before the crime would even have been known. Coates was in the saloon when White rode in and knew the gang was in trouble.

When Connors and his deputies rode in from Elko, miles away, any indication of which way the outlaws rode was gone. He told his chief deputy, Eli Reardon, that every community in the county needs to have its own deputy, a resident deputy. "You know what's wrong with that plan? I'll tell you. If that plan was in effect, old Mr. Lee would still be suffering; his family would still be dead.

"But we'd have a slight advantage in that at least we'd know which way those men rode. I feel like a complete failure, Eli. I was elected to protect these people, and I've let them down, horribly. I can't help old Orion, can't bring his wife back, but I can work my butt off to not let this happen again." Eli Reardon had seen his boss in a twit before, but what he saw at that moment was rage and knew those outlaw's days were numbered.

Connors rode back to Elko the next day and called in some of the outlying deputies from around the large county. "This attack on the Lee family north of Halleck is not the first. Last winter you might remember the attack on the Chapman ranch in the Ruby Valley, and there have been some stagecoach attacks during which any stock or valuable property that was around was taken and whoever was present was murdered. They have left no witnesses until this attack on the Lee place.

"Why these men are acting this way isn't our concern, despite the articles you'll read in the newspapers. Men have been criminals for thousands of years. It's wrong, we know it's wrong, any decent man knows it's wrong. We'll let the newspapers ask why and we'll catch and kill these barbarians in Elko County."

He sent local deputies to Halleck, Wells, the Ruby Valley, Skelton, and to Indian enclaves along the northern border with Idaho. Orion Lee had given good descriptions of the men, in particular, the one who seemed to be in charge. He wore blond hair that hung long, had a thin mustache, and his eyes seemed to bore into you, filled with hatred as he attacked.

"This is a big county and our ranchers need to know they are safe living here. I want these men dead, gentlemen. Return to your communities and make sure everyone is aware of these outlaws and keep our people safe."

Connors rode north of town the next morning to talk with Ted Wilson at his ranch. He outlined what had happened to Lee's family and reminded him of the Chapman attack the year before. "I remember the Chapman family massacre, Connors," Wilson said, "but I hadn't heard about old man Lee. Those are rotten animals. I'm not sure how I can help you, though?" he asked.

Wilson had a large cattle and sheep ranch and had many hired hands. There would always be men around the barns and corrals, around the bunkhouse and main house. His family was probably more secure than most in the county.

"I want to ask if you would be able to put some of your men into a posse if I get a handle on where these outlaws might be holed up. And ask if you know of ranchers like yourself who have a few hands who could also help? I'd like to have men ready to ride here in the Elko area, in the Ruby Valley, near Skelton, and probably in Wells."

"That's a big order, sheriff. You can count on me and my men, and in Skelton, I'm sure you can count on Jack Slater and Cactus Jack. Maybe old Ike Jackson in the Rubies."

"That's good, Ted. I'll get with them right away. I knew I could count on you and we'll get this ordeal over with as quick as possible. And without any more men and women killed."

The five-man Jake Reynolds gang had two wounded when they rode into the marshes deep in the Ruby Valley. The Marshes was an area ranchers shunned, and it saw few visitors other than water birds. Jake Reynolds and his brother Sandy had come west from Missouri along with childhood friends

Peter "Rowdy" Simmons and his brother Clyde usually called Doc.

Kansas outlaw Henry Coates had joined the gang while running away from a bungled bank job in Salt Lake City. The Reynolds and Simmons boys were the next generation after the war between the states. Their fathers and uncles had ridden for the Confederacy and were never able to accept the defeat of the south. The boys were raised to enjoy hate, violence, and depravity. Money was to be taken, and women were to be used.

Jake Reynolds' father never raised an animal nor planted a crop. He stole what he needed and taught his boys to do the same. Jake spent his first night in jail when he was eight-years-old, accused of stealing a pig. It was said in the Missouri Breaks that Reynolds killed his first man on his tenth birthday and killed his first lawman when he was twelve.

Coates, on the other hand, was well educated, he simply didn't believe in authority or the rule of law. They were a good fit, the Reynolds boys, Simmons boys, and Coates. The group rode up and down the long valley, spent more than five days searching out a good place to build their headquarters, their hideout. The ranchers wouldn't miss a young steer and the gang ate well.

"Don't really know why we need a permanent place." Rowdy Simmons was nursing a cup of whiskey by the fire. "That old cabin was okay, I guess, but so is what we're doing right now."

"We're gonna lay low for a few weeks, and then when we do make some moves on ranchers or banks or saloons or whatever, we need a place to hide and keep our loot safe. Get up in those hills along these marshes, and nobody will ever find us," Jake Reynolds said. "It's gotta be off any main trail, in the woods, and out of sight. We need to look like a ranch, so when we bring stock in, it will look natural. In the morning, let's find a place, and then we can spend a couple of weeks looking for the kinds of ranches we like to attack."

"Yeah," Coates said. "Those with more than one pretty girl." General laughter echoed through the trees for a few minutes. The leg wound had festered some the first day, but liberal splashes of whiskey cleared that up and he could walk and ride with little pain.

The Kid, on the other hand, was in constant pain and spent most of each day whimpering as they rode through rough country. "I need a doc," he said more than

31

once, only to be told to shut up and ride. "It hurts, Jake. It hurts real bad." The wound was infected, a fragment of the bullet still stuck into a rib bone, and the whole mess bled continuously.

Clyde Simmons' nickname was Doc, because once when he was nine or ten, he tried to fix a dog's broken leg. The dog lived, and his friends figured he was responsible. Simmons liked to dress the part as well and was used often when they were checking out banks and other businesses.

Doc Simmons strutted around in a filthy white shirt and string tie, wore a frayed frock coat and told Jake that what he wanted most in life was a brocade vest. Neither of the Reynolds men had spent a day in school, Rowdy Simmons made it through the third grade and Doc didn't bother.

"I'd a had that bullet out the first day, Jake, if you'd 'a asked." Clyde Simmons in his white shirt, nice wool vest, and frock coat frowned at Sandy. "Now, it's all infected and nasty. I can get it, though."

"Let Doc pull that bullet, Jake. Please."

"Maybe. We'll find a hideout first," he said and mounted up. "Let's ride."

[3]

Robbie Gomez was fourteen, working on fifteen, and becoming a fine hand around the ranch. He was working with Cactus Jack, learning how to rope, move cattle, and read terrain. He was a skinny little boy when Jack Slater brought him and his mother to the ranch and hard work with good food and fresh air was the best thing that ever happened to the boy.

Sandra had stayed at her job in Skelton when Jack and Mims brought the boy to the ranch and it took some long talks to convince her to leave the café and come be the ranch's cook. Robbie and Jack had become close during that time.

"He's a bit like we were, Mims. He does have his mother, though. The boy was seriously lacking in education and we corrected that." Over the two-year period, Robbie Gomez has blossomed, as a student, as a young boy learning how to have fun, and as a buckaroo under some excellent tutelage.

"That boy's in the saddle all day every day," Sandra commented often. Cactus Jack and Robbie rode across a broad pasture toward the ranch house late one afternoon. "That was good work, Robbie. We got those steers and heifers moved nice and easy. Don't want to get 'em all riled up and runnin' around. They're on good grass now and the grass where they have been will grow back up nice and sweet, too."

The western alluvial front of the Ruby Mountains was filled with rich grasses and with two sections of pasture, Jack Slater was able to rotate his herds between pastures and open range grazing. Moving the herds and protecting them from predators were the jobs that kept the buckaroos busy most of the time. Wolves, bears, coyotes, and lions knew a good thing when they found it and Slater kept one man busy as a hunter most of the time.

Spring was calving time and buckaroos were constantly being called on to help. The first-time heifers had trouble delivering more than the veterans. "You gotta be careful with helping, Robbie. Sometimes old mama cow doesn't know you're helping. She is gonna protect her young'un and you look like a villain." Cactus Jack chuckled and then got serious. "Those calves are why we're here. They are our main business, old son, and it's our job to keep 'em in good shape."

Cactus Jack Faraday noticed a quietness in the boy he hadn't seen before. "Is your mama still feeling sickly?" Sandra Gomez missed breakfast, complaining of stomach cramps and a headache. Mims told her to stay in bed and took care of the morning chores, feeding the crew and taking care of the kitchen garden.

"She won't go to the doctor, Cactus, but she needs to," Robbie said softly. "She's really afraid of doctors."

They rode up to the barn and took care of their horses and walked across the large yard to the main house just as Mims came out on the porch and rang the big bell announcing suppertime. "Nice timing, boys," she chuckled walking in with them. "Wash up good; you've got enough Nevada landscape on you to plant corn."

Jack Slater came in from the office with a scowl on his face. "After supper, you and Robbie take Sandra into Skelton, Cactus. There won't be any arguments from her or either of you. Mims, do you have her things ready to go with her?"

"I do, Jack, but she's gonna put up a fight.

She don't want to go."

"She's scared," Robbie said. "That old doctor in Denver really hurt her when she broke her leg." This was the first time anyone had heard this, and Mims jumped when Robbie said it.

"What happened?" Mims asked. "I haven't heard about that. Did you know that, Jack?" He shook his head just as several hands came into the kitchen for supper.

"Settle in, boys," she said. "Here's a platter of fried chicken, mashed up taters, and a gallon or two of gravy. Bread'll be up in a minute. Hope you're hungry."

"I could eat a whole buffalo all by myself," Robbie said and several of the men suggested he better leave a bite or two for them. After everyone was settled and had their plates full, Mims asked again about Sandra and her broken leg.

"She was walking across a street in Denver, it was when we had to wait for a train to bring us here, and a horse went crazy and started bucking and kicking and mama couldn't get out of the way. She was trying to protect me, and the horse kicked her really hard. I think I was seven or eight.

"Anyway, I could see the bone and men grabbed mama and me and took us to the doctor's and he was really mean. Just jerked her leg and I could hear the bone ends scraping together." That distinctive sound was well remembered by several of the buckaroos sitting at the table. More than one scowled at the memory. "Mama was screaming in pain, and then he wrapped it in something and told her she owed him fifty dollars. He said some nasty things about Mexicans that I still don't understand."

"My God!" Mims all but cried. "That's terrible.

"We didn't get to eat on the train ride after that because that was all the money mama had, and her leg was really sore. A doctor in Elko fixed it right, but that hurt very much too. When it's cold, you'll see mama limping just a little bit, and sometimes she cries at night when it hurts. She's really scared of doctors."

"No wonder she doesn't want to see the doctor," Slater said.

"I still don't know why the doctor was so angry with Mexicans. Mama is from St. Louis. Her father is French, and her mother is Spanish. And, even though I don't know him, my father was a Spanish diplomat from New Orleans. Mama speaks French, Spanish, and English, and so do I. Do you understand why the doctor was so upset and called mama a Mexican? She's never even been there."

"It has a great deal to do with ignorance and stupidity, Robbie." Jack looked around the large kitchen table at his ranch hands, all seeming in awe at Robbie's story. "We'll talk more about that after we get your mama well."

"Jack, let's you and me take her into town after supper," Mims said. "It would be better, and we can stay with her overnight. Cactus, Robbie, is that all right with you?"

"That's the best idea I've heard," Cactus Jack chuckled. "I ain't the best nursemaid. You stay with her, and the boys and I will keep the ranch in one or two pieces 'till you get back."

Platters of fried chicken along with bowls of mashed potatoes and gravy disappeared in quick order. "You boys will be on your own for breakfast," Jack said. "I'm sure we won't be back until sometime tomorrow."

"I don't think we should do this, Jack, now that I've thought about it. That five-mile ride in the wagon will be too rough for her. You need to ride to Skelton and bring Doctor Fowler back here."

Jack scowled a bit. "This is the third change. Good thing nobody's moved on the first two ideas." He thought about what she said and got a little smile cooking. "Just lettin' my head talk instead of my heart," he said.

"I like that idea," Robbie Gomez said. "Mama's really sick. I know she'd put up a real fuss if you tried to take her to town."

It was a fine late spring evening when Jack Slater rode off the ranch for the short trip into town. "I'll be back as early as I can get that crabby old man moving in the morning," he chuckled. Mims had her arm around Robbie, feeling him shake a bit, holding back his tears and hiding his worry.

"That's all I know, Doc," Slater said, sitting in a warm kitchen in Doc Fowler's home in Skelton. "She's just too sick to bring to you."

"That's fine, Jack. I think you did the right thing not making her come here. We'll leave first thing in the morning. You say she has stomach cramps, headaches, and can't keep anything down? Nasty for her. Okay, I'll see you early in the morning."

He told Valley Paddock that it was just too easy convincing the doc to make the ride back to the ranch. "That old guy will argue about walking across the street, Valley, and he said, be here early so we can get underway. Amazing."

Paddock laughed pouring each of them another cup of boiling coffee. "Want a taste of good bourbon in that?" Slater nodded, and Paddock continued. "Doc Fowler used to have moon-eyes for Sandra Gomez when she cooked for Irene. You called him an old man, but he isn't really. He looks it sometimes, but he's not yet forty. He wasn't happy when you took her out of that kitchen.

"Being a doc in a small community like this is hard on a man. Every little thing is a crisis and after a time, all that takes its toll. He's probably looking forward to putting a shine on his smile seeing Sandra again."

"What do you know about that?" Slater chuckled. "He's got some competition then. Deputy Jimmy Delgado has eyes on the lady, too."

"I'm glad you brought up his name, Jack. Have you talked with Delgado? There are some nasty things happening around this county. He told me about Orion Lee's family being raped and murdered, and there was another ranch that was raided like that, the Chapman's place, last year. I didn't know Lee or Chapman, and I surely wouldn't want something like that to happen around here."

"Jimmy came out to tell us about that,"

Slater said. "Seems as though the voters did the right thing bringing Bill Connors in as sheriff. I've got Mims and Maybelle and, of course, Sandra around the house every day and what Delgado said, that's what these men were looking for.

"God help the man who goes after Mims," he growled, his eyes narrowed, and his fists doubled up.

"Jimmy said the sheriff wants to come to Skelton and have an open town meeting next week. He wants you to be there. I was gonna send one of the boys out to tell you. Wild Bill Connors sometimes shoots first, but maybe that isn't all bad in situations like this."

"I'll be glad to talk with Connors. Cactus Jack and I have discussed keeping at least one, maybe two hands around the home place at all times, just in case. They come around my place lookin' for trouble, they'll get it. We had dealings with rustlers at that ranch in Wyoming, you might remember, and we won. They killed Oak Blossom and I'll never forget that."

Jack had been remembering those times ever since Delgado brought the bad news and made up his mind it would never happen again. *I'll not lose Mims or Maybelle and I'll not let ugly men take my stock, either. I guess I've loved Mims from the first day on that old farm in Fargo. No man will ever violate her or take her from me.*

"They called this the Mound Valley a few years ago, Jack. Your ranch sits on some of the best grass in this part of Nevada." John Fowler, M.D. was driving the buggy with Jack Slater sitting alongside. Slater's horse was tied on behind. The ride out of Skelton and into the broad alluvial valley took them through stands of hardwood, pine, even aspen along with cottonwood anywhere there were springs or water, and there was lots of water this spring.

"You've been around these parts for a long time, eh?" Jack said. "I know I plan to be."

Fowler chuckled at the young man's enthusiasm. "I came west right out of school, Jack. Grew up in Boston, you know. My father was just as snotty as all the rest of them. I had to get out," and he laughed right out loud. "Thought about Kansas City or Dodge but just kept right on coming west. Spent six months in Elko and moved down here when some of the citizens asked me to. Been right here ever since. Fifteen years now, Jack," he said, keeping his fine bred trotter moving along briskly.

"Has anyone mentioned Sandra's encounter with a doctor in Denver when she suffered a broken leg?"

"No," Fowler said. He scrunched around in the buggy seat. "Something bad happen to that charming lady?"

"I'm afraid so. We just heard the story, from Robbie, last evening. Seems she had a compound fracture, the bone coming right through the skin, and the doc was rough and almost mean-spirited setting it.

"Robbie says ever since then she's been scared to death of doctors."

"I imagine she has," he drawled in his finest Boston way. "That answers a few of my own questions," he murmured. "Probably shouldn't talk about this, so let's just keep this between us, Jack." Slater smiled and nodded.

"I asked the young lady to attend a dance or two before you absconded with her to these hinterlands you call a ranch. Her reaction was unsettling, and maybe I just found out why. She was afraid of me because I'm a doctor, a healer, one dedicated to doing good, and she's afraid. That's sad, Jack." He was shaking his head back and forth as if he couldn't really believe it. "I can't imagine being mean to someone as sweet and lovely as Sandra Gomez. Particularly a doctor, for heaven's sake."

The last mile into the ranch was quiet, both men simply enjoying the sights and letting their own thoughts rumble through their heads. Doctor John Fowler was giving serious thought to seeing to it that Sandra Gomez was no longer afraid of doctors. *One in particular.* He smiled, keeping the horses at a solid trot.

Jack Slater had other thoughts on his mind, thoughts of outlaws roaming through the countryside attacking ranches, killing, rustling stock, and committing other atrocities. Would Bill Connors be able to find them and stop the attacks? What would he do if his family and ranch were attacked? Would his men, hired to run the ranch, stand and defend the ranch and the Slater family?

"You know Doc, my ranch was attacked once before, burned to the ground, and my foreman seriously injured. It was Sheriff Simpson did that the first year I was here. But that attack is different than what's being discussed with this gang that killed the Orion Lee family."

"I've never encountered these kinds of attacks, Jack. Animals. That's what they are. Animals," he said again. "I've read the stories about the gangs of men that swarmed through Missouri and Kansas after the war and their vicious attacks on anyone and everyone, but even they were nothing like what Jimmy Delgado described."

"I'm looking forward to whatever Sheriff Connors has to say next week." Jack sat back in the seat seeing the ranch slowly come into view. "Hope Mims has plenty of coffee boiling. Valley Paddock's idea of breakfast was skimpy too. I might have to have dinner a bit early today."

The two men were still chuckling when the buggy came to a stop in front of the ranch house and Robbie Gomez came running out to help with the horse. "I'm glad you're here, Doctor. Mama's really sick."

[4]

Jake Reynolds was standing alongside a large pine tree on the ridge several hundred feet above the Ruby Valley, watching two riders wend their way toward the outlaw camp. The camp was set back several hundred feet from the ridge on a plateau and tucked into a stand of aspen trees. A small creek meandered across the plateau and splashed down the mountainside into the marshes in the valley.

"I hope at least one of them is Henry Coates," he murmured. "That would mean the other would be Hickory Slim Obregon." Reynolds had a Winchester rifle at his side but did not have a telescope and couldn't make out just exactly who the riders were.

Doc Simmons walked up and said, "Looks like old Henry made it back okay. Hope he brought a couple of jugs with him."

"Yup," is all Reynolds said, thinking that the young Simmons' eyes must be really good. "Haven't met or even heard of this Obregon before Coates brought his name up."

"Coates said he's really good with locks on bank safes. You and Coates working on a plan that me and Rowdy don't know about?" Doc Simmons was young, aggressive, and had more of a friendship with Sandy Reynolds than with Jake.

Reynolds turned to the young man. "Nope," is all he said and walked back toward the lean-to the men had slapped together. He stopped suddenly, whirled with that Colt in his hand, the hammer pulled back and aimed at Doc Simmons' chest. Simmons never moved, and Jake laughed watching the stain form in the young man's crotch.

"Don't ever cross me, Doc."

Reynolds was still smiling when Coates and Obregon stepped off their horses and tied them to a crossbar laid between two trees. "Glad you made it back, Henry." He turned to the tall Mexican wearing his weapon in a cross-draw holster high on his waist. "You Obregon?"

"Jake Reynolds," Henry Coates said, "meet Hickory Slim Obregon. Slim, say hello to Jake."

The two men stood about six feet or so

apart, sizing each other up as men tend to do. Reynolds saw a tall muscular man with a massive mustache and long coal black hair waving in the wind as he doffed his floppy sombrero and knocked trail dust about. He carried a finely braided rawhide quirt that hung on a loop from his wrist and wore silver engraved spurs with large pointed rowels. While Obregon seemed to be smiling, his eyes were not. Neither man offered a hand to shake or a word to warm.

"Let's talk," Reynolds said turning to walk to the fire where some logs had been brought up. "Bring us some good news, Henry?" Coates gave him a nod taking saddlebags from his horse.

Obregon pulled a bedroll and saddlebags from his horse and walked to some trees to lay out his bedroll.

"I think I said, let's talk," Reynolds said, turning to glare at the Mexican.

"Be right with you, Jake, soon's I get my horse taken care of. Taking care of a good horse is like keeping a good woman." He pulled a long thin cigar, bit the end and stuck a flame. He pulled the saddle and blanket and stood them near his bedroll, and then seemed to saunter back to the horse to pull the bit and reins.

"Had sweet Charity here for most of ten

48

years now, Jake. Fast as lightning, mean as the devil's daughter, and the only love of my life." He saw to it his tack was in order, took a long drag on his cigar and walked over to the fire. "Kind of an ugly little camp you've got here."

Jake's anger was building with each trip Hickory Slim took to his horse, with each drag on his cigar, and with every comment the man made. "You're just a couple of seconds from bein' not welcome here, Mexican." He hadn't yet sat down, had his legs spread just a bit, and his hand slowly moved toward the big revolver.

"Well now, see, there you go, Jake, making life hard for yourself. You know, I remember my pa said that when he was a younger man, riding some long trails following the cattle north out of Texas, he'd run into a man now and then didn't have much for manners. One of 'em said some nasty things about my mother once. Called her a whore just cuz she was married to pa.

"That's when I took her name for my own. See, Pa's from Kentucky original like, named Sinclair, but after he carved that old Texas rat into little pieces, I kinda liked the name Obregon."

All the time he was talking Rowdy Simmons was moving slowly in behind the tall man and Henry Coates could see nothing but trouble. "How about we get a pot of coffee boiling and get to know each other," Coates said.

Jake Reynolds realized he'd just been lectured and humiliated in his own camp and only Rowdy was willing to stand with him. Coates was Obregon's friend, young Doc Simmons was probably still changing into dry trousers, and this Mexican just openly challenged him.

"I don't think so," Reynolds said, making a lightning move for his heavy iron, feeling the sting of rawhide slicing through his cheek, almost taking out an eye. Reynolds screamed in pain letting the revolver fall to the ground.

Obregon spun and slashed Rowdy Simmons across the face before the big Missouri farmer turned outlaw could move. "Ya see, boys," Obregon said quietly, "I am half Mexican even though I was born in Texas as was my mother. I'm also half Kentucky wildcat with a father who drove cattle more miles than you know how to count.

"Henry, you said one of these gentlemen is called Doc. If he's only part doc, maybe he could help keep some of that blood from dripping into the dirt. I'll make the coffee."

Not one of the men present would ever

forget the scene they just lived through despite the humiliation and pain inflicted. Jake Reynolds was holding his neckerchief tight against his cheek, keeping the skin from flapping in the wind and the blood from flowing. The rawhide thongs on that long quirt opened his face up like peeling an orange, and the pain was searing.

Rowdy Simmons was on his knees in pain, bent over, holding one ear close to where it belonged, and stopping the blood from flowing out both sides of his cheek, that is, onto the dirt and into his mouth. That was how deep the quirt cut.

"Who's doing all the screaming?" The Kid climbed out of his bedroll inside the lean-to and hobbled out toward the fire pit. "What the hell? Who did this?"

Before anyone answered, Doc Simmons came running up from the ridge where he'd had an encounter of his own. "Rowdy, what happened?" Doc said, kneeling next to his older brother. "Who did this?" he demanded, taking off his bandanna and handing it to Rowdy.

Only the clanking of a coffee pot being set on a hot rock in the middle of the fire pit could be heard. Henry Coates was standing in the same spot as before the festivities and Hickory Slim was busy with the coffee pot.

The only sound was the two men moaning in pain.

"You the one called Doc?" Obregon asked, getting a nod from young Simmons. "Looks like you got some work to do. Who are you?" he asked, looking into the angry eyes of Kid Reynolds.

"Name's Reynolds, Kid Reynolds," he said. It was too late he realized he didn't have his gun belt strapped on. "What the hell have you done?"

"Sometimes even a grown man needs to learn his manners, sonny. Why don't you help your friend the doc there with these fine gentlemen while us grownups have some coffee, maybe with a dash or two of whiskey floating about."

Coates, the Kid, Rowdy, Jake, and Doc had never run into the likes of Hickory Slim Obregon and hoped that he would leave just as quickly as he had arrived. *People don't talk like that, and surely don't carry whips around with them.* Jake Reynolds was ready to kill anyone who moved the wrong way or said the wrong thing. The only problem was, Obregon had his pistol and he was having a hard time seeing things right. How could this man ride into his camp, whip members of his gang, whip him? *This is my camp, my gang. I'm gonna kill me a Mexican.*

The hatred boiled deep in Jake Reynolds, his mind could think of nothing but the painful death of this Slim Obregon. Jake Reynolds made the first three grades of school before his father jerked him out, more school than any other members of the Reynolds clan, and that was probably the socially acceptable highlight of Jake's life. He was an ego-driven and ignorant fool. Every time Doc Simmons touched the deep slashes to stem the flow of blood or try to cleanse the wound, the pain seared through the man.

He watched this Obregon fellow walk in and demolish his gang, humiliate him, and swagger about like the winning cock at Saturday's fights. While some of Jake's blood was spilling onto the ground, the rest of it boiled in a cauldron of hate. "Somebody get me a drink," he said through bloody lips.

"Let's you and me talk about this so-called gang of outlaws you've invited me into, Señor Coates." Slim Obregon used a rag to pick up the coffee pot and pour each about a quarter cup of the stuff while Coates filled each cup to the top with whiskey.

"I think it's time, Hickory Slim, I really do."

"Gimme some of that whiskey," Jake Reynolds demanded.

"Speak when you're spoken to, Reynolds." Obregon laughed, flicked that nasty quirt onto his high boot, and turned his back on the man.

"Some of what you've told me about raids on ranches and the like grate like sand in the coffee, Henry. To be looked upon a man needs to do his job with some finesse and killing women in their ranch house kitchen is not how a real man does his work." Obregon looked over to where Sandy was sitting in the dirt, moaning.

"That was a very stupid raid, and you, boy are a very stupid idiot. When one robs a bank, takes a strong box from a coach, or opens a safe in a Wells Fargo rail car, it must be done with finesse.

"What I'm seeing, Henry is pitiful. You're riding with the lowest form of outlaw rubbish a man could find." Hickory Slim spat into the fire and jerked a thumb toward Kid Reynolds. "Is that the scum that shot the old lady and left the witness?"

Kid Reynolds got to his feet and took a step toward Obregon, the quirt flashed, and the Kid was on his knees holding his hands to his face, crying in pain and humiliation. "Yup," is all Henry Coates said, a smile spreading slowly across his ugly face.

"You men listen to me," Obregon commanded. He took a long pull on his cup of mostly whiskey, took a long drag on his cigar, and flicked that quirt a time or two. "Each of you can ride out of this miserable little camp at any time. If you don't, you will then do exactly as I say. If you ride with Hickory Slim Obregon you will have gold in your pockets, women in your beds, and posses on your trail." He chuckled and walked about the men lying about in the dirt, moaning from ugly deep wounds.

"And you won't be killing old women standing next to their cook stoves, you won't be terrorizing farmers and ranchers for five cows and a goat, and you won't be leaving witnesses who hate your very feces."

The only sound was sobbing and moaning from those bleeding, and a wry snicker from Henry Coates. *I'm going to be rid of these back-country fools and ride with a real outlaw. I made the right decision finding old Hickory Slim.*

The tall broad-shouldered Mexican turned his back on the members of the former Jake Reynolds gang and poured a splash of coffee in his tin mug, took a bottle from Henry Coates and topped the cup off. "Any questions?" He looked first to Jake

Reynolds who was howling in pain as Doc Simmons tried to sew up his cheek. "No?" Obregon asked. He flicked that quirt viscously against his boot top, making it almost crack and turned his gaze to Rowdy Simmons and then to Kid Reynolds. Nobody said a word.

"Whoever is still in this camp tomorrow at sunrise rides with me and takes orders from me. I will not tolerate fools or cowards." He drank the cup empty and turned to Coates. "Let's you and me have a nice long conversation, Henry. There are some banks in this country that need tending to, and I believe Wells Fargo moves considerable amounts of cash and coin through the area as well."

Eli Reardon's horse was covered in sweaty foam on a cool and breezy late spring afternoon when the Elko County Chief Deputy tied him off in front of the sheriff's office. "Looks like you've 'bout wore that critter out, Eli," Wild Bill Connors said. "Come on in and tell me all about it."

"You were right sending me to Winnemucca, but it was in Golconda that I got the information about this outlaw gang that attacked Orion Lee."

Golconda was a busy little community

with operating mines, big cattle, and sheep ranches, and a railroad switching, coaling, and watering station. It was on the emigrant trail as well. "Several weeks ago, they killed a rancher and his wife and got away with about fifteen head of steers. They forced the rancher to sign off on a bill of sale for the steers and then killed him. They sold the cattle right here in Elko. There's a fella named Scruggs that buys and sells stolen stock.

"Funny, ain't it, Bill? Had to ride all the way to Winnemucca to find out we had a man named Simon Scruggs right here in Elko known for buying and selling stolen stock."

Reardon caught his breath as they slipped into chairs in the office. "I just came at a high lope from the feedlots and have good descriptions of several men. You were right thinking it was that lout Jake Reynolds, his kid brother, and the Simmons brothers. There was a fifth man that nobody seemed to know. We've got posters on all the Reynolds' gang.

"What they did to Lee is a mirror image of what they did in Golconda, and the descriptions all fit. They need to hang, Bill."

Reardon wrote out the descriptions of all five men, put names to four of them, and

Connors said he would have flyers made and distributed right away. "This is three attacks on ranchers that we know of," Connors mused. "All relatively isolated. Ike Jackson has the largest ranch in the Ruby Valley and Jack Slater has the largest near Skelton."

"What are you thinking, sheriff?"

"I'm thinkin' you need to ride into the Ruby Valley and I need to ride into Skelton, Eli. These ranchers need to fort up, I think, and I want to give them as much help as I can. Ted Wilson has the north of us under control. No gang would take on his crew, so we need to build some defense south of us."

[5]

"Jack, bring Mims and join me for a little walk around your garden," John Fowler said. He had spent more than an hour with his patient and it was obvious that he was not a happy man. His eyes were downcast, and he was sweating profusely, walking from Sandra Gomez's bedroom.

Sandra Gomez was more than a patient, a lovely lady that the good doctor wanted to see on a more personal basis. He had been under the impression that she was not of the same mind, that the possibility of romance was out of the question, and that bothered him. To discover that this charming lady had a desperate fear of doctors should never have been in the discussion. Now, he also feared for her life.

Fowler was a sensitive man, held his patients in the highest esteem, and sometimes gave the appearance of actually feeling their pain. Slater and Mims, already worried about Sandra followed the good doctor into the kitchen garden. "Is Sandra's sickness as serious as your face makes me believe?" Mims asked. She had a strong hold of Jack's hand and he could feel her worry.

"I'm afraid it is, Mims. She has an internal infection of some kind that I've not seen before, and her temperature is such that she may not be with us much longer." He wiped perspiration from his forehead and stood near some poles that would soon hold many pounds of green beans. "She may last two days, she may last two weeks, but I can tell you for certain that she will not last long."

Mims took in several quick breaths, squeezed Jack's hand even harder, and cried out, "No." The two women had developed a strong relationship during the last two years, far beyond employee/employer, and with the pending birth of her child, Mims was looking forward to having an ever-closer relationship. "My heavens, doctor, no," she almost whimpered.

"Is there anything we can do?" Jack asked. "She's always looked frail but seemed strong up until just recently. Is this something we should fear?" Jack immediately thought of Mims, Maybelle, and Robbie, of Cactus Jack and the crew. "Is what she's suffering from catching?"

"No, I don't think that's a worry, Jack. She's developed an internal infection, somehow, like blood poisoning, and it's spread rapidly through her system. Has she been in any kind of accident?"

"The only thing I know of is that broken leg that Robbie told us about." Jack looked at Mims to see if she had heard of anything.

"Check her feet, doctor," Mims said. "She's always running around barefoot, and I've noticed that she started limping slightly the last week or so."

Doctor Fowler said a quick thank you and almost ran back to Sandra's room. Jack Slater looked at Mims and quietly said, "Lockjaw." Mims started crying, threw her arms around the big man and squeezed hard. "I've seen her around the hogs, in the barn and near the corrals without her shoes."

"Will Doctor Fowler be able to help her?" Mims cried. "I really love that girl, Jack. Her life has been so much like ours. Her family ripped apart, her fighting her way across the country with her baby, and always being looked down on." She let go of Jack and turned toward the house.

"I've got to be with her, Jack. Find Robbie and be gentle with the boy, like you were

with all of us when we were all little kids."
She jumped back into his arms then walked
toward the house, wiping a flood of tears
away.

*I'm the luckiest man in the world to have a
woman like Mims. I can remember her coming out of the kitchen door that first day at
Jablonski's farm. Ten years old, and just as
feisty then as she is today. You take charge,
Mims, and Sandra Gomez might just live
through this.*

Jack went looking for young Robbie
Gomez with a black cloud following over-
head. He was very aware that few people
survived tetanus infections. "She must have
cut her foot on some rusty old metal somewhere, and then, with all the animals, the
infection set in quickly," he muttered. He
found Ornery Pound in the barn, who told
him that Robbie was riding in the south
pasture with Cactus Jack. The buckaroos
called entire sections, six hundred forty
acres of pastures.

Slater saddled up and loped out of the
large ranch yard toward a one-hundred-acre
grass and brush area to the south. He rode
over a rise and looked down on a small herd
of cows and calves, spotted his foreman and
Robbie, and rode toward them. "What the

heck am I gonna say to this kid?" he muttered.

"Hey, Cactus," he called. "I need to steal Robbie from you. It's important." He smiled at Robbie as he pulled his horse to a stop. "Should I send someone out?"

"No, it's fine, boss. I'll make another turn around these critters and then I'll be coming in too," Cactus Jack said. "We have a fine little herd of young-uns, Jack. Minimal loss so far this spring." Jack nodded thanks, motioned Robbie to come with him, and started back to the ranch at a slow walk.

"Got some bad news for you, son," Jack said.

"Mama's real sick isn't she," he said. "I didn't want to leave this morning, but she made me go. What did the doctor find out?"

Jack knew the boy wasn't as strong as he should be, what with the life he and his mama had before coming to the ranch, but also knew that he had to tell the truth. "Doc Fowler thinks she may be suffering from a tetanus infection, Robbie. He and Mims are with her right now."

"Tetanus," he whispered. "Oh, Jack," he said, his voice breaking some, tears beginning their long streak across his high cheekbones. "Is she . . ." and he couldn't finish the question.

Jack Slater set his jaw, kept his horse at a slow walk, and looked at the boy, thinking back to that time in 1872 when, at ten-years-old, he had become an orphan. This boy wouldn't face those problems but the problems he would face would be just as bad. "We don't know, Robbie. Your mama isn't very strong, and the doc says the infection is bad, all through her body. Whether or not he can do anything, I just don't know.

"One thing I do know, son," he said, giving the boy a quick glance, "is your mama is going to want you to be as strong as possible. You know Mims and I love her very much, and I hope you know we love you very much, too. Your mama is gonna need you to be with her and to be as strong as you can."

"I know, Jack," Robbie Gomez said, sitting at a slump in his saddle, crying softly as they rode up to the barn. "I will be, Jack. I will," he said. He straightened up in the saddle, his mouth grimmer than Jack had ever seen, but his eyes were downcast and very wet.

Jack stepped off his horse and took the reins from both horses. "I'll take care of the horses. You go see your mama." He could see so many of the little orphans from his past watching Robbie walk across the yard.

He remembered Mims as a survivor, more than anything else. She worked so hard to see to it that the others got fed properly, despite the efforts of Pete Jablonski.

This boy is gonna need Mims to get him through this. She never knew her parents, never even knew her own real name, but knew she would win the game of life. He'll need her in every way, just like I did and still do.

"Mama's a little better this morning, Mims," Robbie said coming into the kitchen the next morning. His face was drawn, his cheeks stained with tears, and he really tried to offer a smile. "She's in so much pain." He broke into sobs, wrapping his arms around Mims. "I can't do anything to help her."

"Being with her is the best help she can have, Robbie. Why don't you sit down and have some breakfast and I'll fix a small bite for Sandra. Did you get any sleep, young man?"

"I'm not hungry, Mims. Mama said she just wants a piece of a biscuit. I'll take it to her."

"No, no, Robbie, you must eat. We can't have you down too. You eat your breakfast and I'll take care of Sandra." Robbie tried to get a little grin on his face when Mims tousled his hair and gave him a peck on the cheek. "I pounded a piece of beef and fried it up, there's gravy for it, and plenty of biscuits. You eat, little man."

He didn't think he was hungry until he took that first bite of meat drowned in a rich gravy. His mind was on Sandra the entire time he spent at the table. *Mama always said that all we had in the world was each other. When that ugly old man threw us out of our home in Chicago, calling us Mexican tramps. Mama took care of me and we made it all the way across the country.* He remembered every day of that trip, and every minute Sandra spent mothering her boy. The meat, biscuits, and gravy were gone amidst a flood of tears and warm memories.

For two days Robbie spent every minute he could sitting next to his mother, watching her slowly fade from this existence. He tried to get her to eat, and it wouldn't stay down, he mopped her head and body with cool and damp towels to ease the fever, to no use, and slept on the floor next to her bed, in fits and pieces.

Mims fed him, tried to feed him as much as he would eat, took long stretches at a time sitting with Sandra when the boy finally drifted off to a fitful sleep. Jack felt

66

terribly helpless and devoted all his time to taking care of Maybelle, a little cherub that could get into more mischief in ten minutes than he and Mims could in two hours back in Dakota Territory. Jack left the running of the ranch to Cactus Jack and a good crew of buckaroos.

He sat at the large kitchen table sipping coffee and watching Maybelle down two large pancakes dripping with butter and peach syrup. He walked into the living room and brought one of the books he and Mims bought for her. "Want to hear a story while you have breakfast?"

"I'll read it to you daddy," she squealed, grabbing the book. She opened it up and started reading to his complete dismay.

"When did you learn to read?"

"Mama and I read to each other every day," she said, her big brown eyes scanning the pages.

"I taught your mama to read, did you know that? You're four-years-old, little one and you read very good." *I wonder if Robbie knows how to read or do his numbers? I forgot what I knew when I was twelve. I need to catch up around here.*

On the third morning while Jack was sitting at the kitchen table with the crew and Mims finished serving their breakfast, there came a long, sorrowful cry from the back of the house. Jack, Mims, and Cactus Jack were down the hallway in half a second and found Robbie lying across Sandra's body, sobbing.

"She looked at me and smiled for the first time in days, and closed her eyes," he cried, not moving from hugging his mother. "Oh, God," he cried, over and over. "Mama," he whimpered, "is gone."

Word was sent to Skelton, to Doc Fowler, and Robbie helped Mims prepare Sandra's remains. That was when all the doubt started, the fear settled in, and the understanding that he was now alone in the world. He remembered all the stories that Jack and Mims told of that horrible Pete Jablonski and his treatment of the orphans. Robbie Gomez understood that now, he was an orphan, alone, and with nothing in the world to call his except what he was wearing.

Most of the town of Skelton along with many friends from Elko and the Ruby Valley turned out for Sandra Gomez's burial on the Slater ranch. After her husband ran away and left her and the baby, all the people in Chicago were willing to see was a destitute Mexican woman desperately trying to survive in an area filled with desperation. She knew her background, knew she would fight her way to survival, and packed the two of them off to the west. To the West, where they could start over.

When she and Robbie settled in Skelton, the real Sandra Gomez surfaced, the warm and loving mother, the best cook in town with the delightful sense of humor, the lady who would give you what you needed when you needed it. For many, the funeral seemed to be the right time to pay long due respects.

Robbie, Jack, Cactus Jack, and several of the buckaroo crew served as pallbearers, and Valley Paddock officiated. It was a quiet dignified ceremony, over with quickly.

Town women had been at the ranch for two days preparing food for the occasion, and the group walked down from the hillside area Jack had set aside for the family burial grounds, looking forward to platters of fine eating. The recently dedicated cemetery was a sunny knoll, filled with trees and grasses, some brush, and no sage or cedar bushes. Late afternoon sunshine splashed across Sandra's gravestone and the group left after singing a hymn or two.

Mims had her arm around Robbie's broad shoulders, humming softly. She wondered when he had gotten so big. She couldn't help remembering just how big Jack was as a boy back on the Dakota farm, how strong and brave he became at such a young age. *This boy is going to be big and strong, too, and like us, will grow up without his own parents. He will grow up being loved like Jack and I love each other.*

"She didn't suffer too much, did she?" he asked through tears.

"You're such a brave little man, Robbie. You're a lot like Jack was at your age." She had a hanky out and wiped his nose, smiling deep into his big brown eyes. "I don't think Sandra knew just how serious her infection was. She was in pain, though, we can't hide that. Tetanus is more than just a simple infection as we can testify."

"What happens now, Mims? Do I have to leave?" He almost bawled the question out and Mims stopped dead in her tracks, gathered the boy into her arms and hugged him as close to her as she could. She nodded to Jack to come to her.

"My God, no! You will stay right here, with Jack and me. No!" she exclaimed again, hugging Robbie tight. Jack walked up hearing Mims comments almost shouted out.

"What's the problem?" he asked.

"I don't want to leave, Jack. Don't make

70

me leave, please. I love you, Jack."

"It would take more than an act of Congress to force you off this place, Robbie. You will be welcome here for as long as you live. You put those fears away, boy, and know the Slater family is your family." Jack put his arms out and Robbie unfolded from Mims and jumped into Jack's. They hugged for a moment and Jack, with Robbie on one side and Mims on the other, walked them off the little hill and down to the house.

"I have to be in Skelton tomorrow and probably the next day, too," Jack said. "Sheriff Connors is coming to talk about this outlaw gang. Cactus will keep things going and Ornery Pound will always be near the barn or the house."

[6]

Never missing the chance to give a little speech before the town folk, Valley Paddock strode to the front and called for order. The meeting was in blacksmith Jesse Winthrop's barn and there were about twenty men scattered about, sitting on stall fences, barrels, hay bales, or just squatting up against a fence post. Connors and his chief deputy, Eli Reardon sat on chairs waiting for Paddock to get through with his flowery oration.

"Nice to be here," the sheriff said when finally introduced. "What I'm gonna say ain't nice at all. Our county is filled with people ranching, mining, and doing business, being prosperous and successful, and that picture, as pretty as it is, has drawn some ugly people into our midst. I'm sure by now, you've heard many stories, and most of them are probably true." He got some guffaws from that.

"This animal, Jake Reynolds, leads a group of outlaws that have committed barbaric crimes against some of our ranchers, killed innocent women and children, and stolen livestock, money, and other personal possessions. If I'm gonna catch these rotten vermin, I'm gonna need some help."

Most of the men in attendance responded, some loudly, that they were ready and willing to help. Skelton's town folk were families, in business or working for a business, and would stand together for protection. They had done so in the past and would do so again. Many could remember a flu epidemic that swept the community not too long ago, with several deaths, and many unable to work, whether it be at a store or a ranch.

Unlike many of the early mining camps in the west, these little towns that were built up to serve surrounding ranches were dominated by families, not single men.

"It's been a couple of weeks since their last attack," Connors continued. "That was on Orion Lee and his family, north of Halleck. I've placed deputies in each of our communities around this huge county, but they will need help if that gang strikes. Jimmy Delgado is the resident deputy here in Skelton and he's taking names of those he can call on for help if a problem develops around here."

Discussions about what to do and when to do it went on for an hour and the sheriff said he wanted to meet privately with Paddock and Jack Slater when the meeting broke up. "Let's take our little group to the Alabama House Saloon, sheriff," Valley Paddock said. "Free lunch and cold beer."

Horseface Hawkins, probably near seventy years old and a veteran of the war between the states and the Mexican war, ran the Alabama House as a true son of the gilded south would have if there had been a gilded south. Hawkins limped from a shattered bone in his leg, could only see out of one eye because of powder burns in the other, and couldn't hear out of one ear from the effects of canon muzzle blast. "Other than that," he would proclaim to all newcomers to his saloon, "I'm doing just fine, thankee."

Nobody is willing to dispute the man when he tells of wearing a union army uniform when he was fifteen years old, rising to the rank of sergeant before the onset of the problems between the states. "You betchy, boy," he'd cackle, "I was a sergeant in both armies. Jist not at the same time. Not a'tall," he'd drawl out.

Hawkins had a wild sense of humor and loved to tell tales of his past, real or otherwise. There were battle flags from both sides hanging with dignity in his big building, mementos from the big war, from Mexican battles, and from the Indian wars, and Horseface Hawkins had at least one story for each memento.

Connors, Reardon, and Delgado sat along one side of two tables pulled together, and Valley Paddock, Jack, and Doc Fowler took up the other side. Each had a plate of smoked meats, some cheese, and assorted fruit in front of them, and great mugs of cold beer, brewed in the basement below.

"You fine gentlemen want anything, just holler loud and strong," Horseface yelled over his shoulder walking back behind his rather ornate walnut bar. "The pleasures of the Alabama House are yourn."

"I like that old codger," Wild Bill Connors said. "I bet he was a fine soldier in his day." He put some roasted venison between the split halves of a biscuit and took a big bite, chewing slowly, knowing he had never had venison that tender and tasty. "He must smoke his own meat. Why in Elko he'd have 'em standing five deep at the bar for this stuff."

"We'll have a taste or two of his own

whiskey after, Bill. Got a still along with his brewery downstairs. The man's amazing," Paddock said.

"Well, I could talk about this for a long time, but let's get down to business. Slater, Paddock, has there been any indications of this Jake Reynolds gang around Skelton? Don't know where they hide out, nor why they're attacking ranchers when the banks are doing so well." He chuckled, thinking an outlaw should look to banks full of gold before stealing cattle and sheep.

Jack looked to Valley and Doc Fowler before saying, "No, Connors, there hasn't been any indication that they might be around this neck of the woods." He was shaking his head slowly. "Are you anticipating an attack around here?"

Connors gave a quick no to that and continued. "I'm depending on you, Jack, and you, Valley Paddock, to back up my deputy, Delgado, if something should happen. I know your reputation, Slater, and I know I'm kinda pushin' on you, but it's important that I can depend on you." Jack's cheeks reddened a bit, he would defend his ranch, his wonderful Mims, and children, he knew. But could he leave them to defend this little village five miles from his home ranch? Could he justify riding off from the home place?

It didn't take the big man long to understand his position. He nodded to the sheriff. "I'm not alone when I say I would have a lot to lose if my outfit were attacked, my wife and children, my home, my herds, and my employees. Every man in the valley could say that, Reardon.

"I also believe I have a responsibility to my community, to these fine people with their homes, families, and businesses, so yes, you can depend on me. I'll do whatever is necessary to end this threat." Slater also had the question in the back of his mind, what would Mims say or think about that answer?

"These men are more violent than any criminal gang I've ever run up against. They don't just kill, Jack, they torture first. They must be stopped at all costs."

"You can depend on us, sheriff," Valley Paddock said. "Now, let's have a taste of some fine whiskey to top off our meal." He waved to Horseface Hawkins to bring a jug of his best to the table.

Horseface Hawkins brought the jug over and included glasses for the men as well as one for himself. "Takes a spell for the good taste," he said pouring true sippin' whiskey. "One of my relatives worked for George Washington at distillin' Virginia rum, and all us Hawkins have been making good whiskey for years.

"Now, Jack Slater, I heard what you boys have been chawin' about over here, and I want you to know that even though I might be gittin' a bit long in the tooth, I can still fight with the best of 'em. I'm a growly old dawg when I fight, and what I heard that Reynolds did to old Orion Lee's wife makes my Virginia blood boil, it does." Hawkins had his fightin' face on, not the friendly local barkeep face, and Slater thought he could actually hear a snarl, like a mean dog after a fast rabbit.

Wild Bill Connors jumped to his feet, clapping his hands. He reached down and grabbed his glass, raised it, and proclaimed to all in Skelton, "I'd be honored, sir, if you would accept the position of honorary special deputy for this district. I want men like you to represent the Elko County Sheriff."

Horseface Hawkins was never a bashful man and he jumped to attention, almost clicking his heels, raised his right hand up quickly, and said, "I do," which brought laughter from everyone in the Alabama House Saloon. "This son of the south will be proud to be in your regiment, sheriff."

The conversation at the table never did get back to anything more serious than just how good that sippin' whiskey was.

Hickory Slim Obregon and Henry Coates were walking through the tall pines in one of the canyons above the outlaw camp discussing what they would be doing as spring slowly became summer in eastern Nevada. "That mine south of Skelton receives its payroll in gold and paper each month by way of an armed courier from Elko," Coates said. "It's been hit before, but not for some time."

"That has to be on the menu," Obregon laughed. "The banks in Elko, Winnemucca, and Reno have to be there as well. What we need to know, Henry is whether Reynolds and those boys are up to it. Sandy Reynolds and Rowdy Simmons are idiots, and Jake isn't much better.

"We need a test, Henry. Something simple for good outlaws, but that might challenge the likes of those boys. Is there a small bank or something like it in one of these Podunk towns that we could hit?"

Coates had spent a lot of time in eastern Nevada, southern Idaho, and the Salt Lake area, and was giving the question some good thought. "The banks will take a lot of planning, Slim. And Reynolds' gang isn't up to a good bank. A nice fat mercantile business though, usually has plenty of cash on hand along with merchandise like guns and ammunition, not to mention dynamite and blasting caps."

"Sounds like you have somewhere in mind, old friend," Hickory Slim said. "Tell me all about it as we head back to that miserable camp. We gotta do better than that camp, and we gotta do better on the lousy food Reynolds thinks is fine dining."

"It's time we talked with Robbie about his future. I want him to be our son, Jack, and I want you to adopt Maybelle as we have already discussed. You knew and loved your parents and I don't even know who mine were or even what my original name might have been. You are the only love I've ever had." Tears streamed as at spring thaw, she had to blow her nose a couple of times, and Jack sat on the sofa next to her with a big smile.

The living room, Jack called it the great room, always with a chuckle, had a high ceiling with open beam construction. One wall included a massive stone fireplace complete with iron hanging rods such as would have been used a hundred years before. There were large south facing windows that let in light and warmth during the cold winters, and Mims had braided rugs spread about covering hardwood floors.

Most of the furniture came from local artisans and was large, fitting Jack's large presence, and featuring lots of natural wood and leather. Tiny little Mims would almost get lost snuggling into one of the overstuffed chairs near the fireplace. She could hide inside a buffalo robe on the coldest days.

"As far as you and I being adopted, we didn't have much choice in the matter," he said. He slipped his arm around Mims and drew her in close. "I think it's only right that I adopt Maybelle. She is so much like you, so feisty, so much fun to be around, like you," and she gave him a little poke in the ribs, crying and laughing at the same time.

"Robbie is growing up fast and has not had the best life so far. His father ran away, his mother now gone, too. He's been called ugly names he doesn't understand at all. I would be proud to have him as a son, but I think he's old enough to understand what his life might be in the future. I think we should talk about what's in his future and ask if he would like to be our son. Nobody ever asked us those kinds of questions.

"Maybe I'll not let him have supper tonight and Maybelle can hide some biscuits for him out in the barn," he said, laughing aloud.

"How many biscuits and chunks of sliced meat did I bring out to you in that cold old barn?" Mims was laughing too, and threw her arms around Jack, kissing him. "I'm teaching Robbie and Maybelle how to read just like you taught me, and they get along just like brothers and sisters should. Robbie has had some schooling, but not as much as he should have for his age. We'll talk with Robbie tonight after we feed the crew."

[7]

It was a Monday morning just after sunrise when Doc Fowler spotted the two men riding into town. The June warmth brought people out of their homes, gardens were showing the benefits of that warmth, and there hadn't been any bad illnesses in town all winter. Fowler nodded as the two-rode past. *That's a nasty scar on that man's face. Looks to be a recent wound, too. I wonder if he can even see out of that one eye?* Miners from the south of town and itinerate cowboys coming through town weren't unusual, but men with serious wounds would catch the good doctor's eye every time.

Jake Reynolds and Doc Simmons rode slowly down the main street, stopping in front of the Skelton Mercantile and Farm Supply business. They tied off their horses and walked up on the board walkway, turning toward the café farther down the street. "That's the place, Doc," Reynolds said. He had a sneer on his face pointing toward the large store with his battered chin.

"I don't much care for working for Obregon," Simmons said. "I'd like to just kill him and go back to you runnin' our outfit."

"Maybe I will, Doc," Jake said. They took a table near the front window and ordered breakfast. "As soon as we get back, I'll just pull and shoot, and I'll never let Henry Coates ever tell me what to do again." Anger had been building in Jake Reynolds since the fracas with Hickory Slim Obregon. "You back me up when we get back to camp, Doc."

"I will," Simmons said, "and you know Rowdy will, too. Just what are we supposed to be doing here? Obregon told you but didn't say anything to me. What are we doing, buying something?" Obregon was very clear when he outlined what Jake and Simmons were to do, but Simmons was too busy playing smart Alex with his brother and missed it.

Jake Reynolds stiffened up when Simmons reminded him of why they were here. Jake would have liked to just ride on out, but Hickory Slim Obregon pulled a fast one on him. The words still hurt as Jake sat in the café. "That man is going to kill Sandy and Rowdy if we don't do what we've been told to do," Jake snarled, trying to keep his voice as low as possible.

"We're looking to see how easy it will be to hold up the store," Reynolds said. "I think it's darn stupid, myself, but that's what Obregon wants and if we don't bring all the information to him, our brothers are dead."

The impact of Reynolds words, as usual, didn't filter through Simmons slow mind. "What are we gonna steal, an ax?" Simmons chuckled and watched the woman bring their breakfast out of the kitchen. "Or maybe some hammers and nails." Reynolds had to snicker at his long-time friend, and just shake his head slowly.

Valley Paddock's mercantile business served the entire ranching community as well as providing supplies for the town and several small mining operations to the south. He had built it into a thriving business that brought considerable money into his coffers. The store also acted as a bank in that he had a large vault built into the west wall and kept money and valuables for many in the area. Whether or not Slim Obregon knew that wasn't known, but he did know how busy the operation was.

By the time Reynolds and Simmons finished their breakfast and paid their bill, the town was coming alive. Paddock's boys had the doors opened and lamps lit inside, Horseface Hawkins had the Alabama House Saloon open, and Jesse Winthrop was busy getting his forge hot and his tools spread out. The greening of the landscape and the streams running full of snowmelt brought a lot of life to the broad valley.

"We'll just walk in and look around to see where that fat old man keeps his money and whether he has any decent guns on hand. We don't need to buy anything or do any talking unless we have to," Reynolds said.

"Still seems kind of stupid to steal stuff like that," Simmons said.

"Mornin' to you," Paddock said when the two walked in. "Looks like you been on the wrong side of a mean tiger, mister. You lookin' for a doctor?"

"No," Reynolds snapped. "It's bein' tended to." He scowled at Paddock and walked toward the counter to look at revolvers in a glass-topped display case. There were rifles and shotguns displayed along the wall behind the counter.

Paddock had seen nasty wounds before and knew this one had never been tended to by a real doctor and that more than anything else caught his attention. "Take your time, gentlemen. If you have any questions I'll be right here." *I wonder what Doc Fowler would say about those wounds?*

"Ah, there you are, Valley," Horseface Hawkins said. "Heard anything on my shipment of barley and wheat? Lot of them yahoos gonna want good beer, old man."

"Last word still stands, Horseface. That wire said next week and that's when it'll get here. Fifty burlap bags of each are on a fast freight from Nebraska."

"Just wanted to make sure, Valley, don't get yerself in a twit." He was chuckling as he said that, and Paddock realized he may have been a bit quick with the old soldier. "Whoooeee, who took the whip to you?" Hawkins said, looking at Jack Reynolds.

"Mind your own business, fool," Reynolds said, letting his hand move quickly toward the handle of his big revolver.

"Ain't meanin' to be pushy or git in your craw, mister, but I know whip wounds when I see 'em, and those are infected besides. You're lookin' to die here, mister if they ain't looked to." Horseface Hawkins, his cane in one hand and his other resting on the top of the counter wasn't packing any kind of weapon. Everyone in town knew he never did.

"You threatenin' me old man?" Reynolds snapped. The big Colt flashed out of leather and just as quickly went sailing across the floor. Reynolds howled when the cane smashed his wrist then came down across the side of his neck, sending a shockwave through his nervous system. His knees became pudding and Jake Reynolds slowly fell to the floor.

Paddock grabbed up the gun and aimed it at young Simmons. "Don't," is all he said, seeing Simmons's hand quivering near his weapon. "Pull it with two fingers and let it fall to the floor, boy. Nice and slow." Reynolds was on his knees, holding his wrist, which was probably broken, and whimpering some from the pain.

"Jake, are you okay?" Simmons asked. He looked at Horseface, standing quietly by the counter that wicked oak branch he called a cane, ready for more action if needed. "You're gonna pay for hurtin' my friend," the boy said.

"He's hurtin' and you're about to be," Hawkins said quietly. "Who is this fool that tried to pull a gun on me? All I wanted was to get him some help. Who is he?" he snarled. "I heard you call him Jake. Jake who?"

Simmons didn't say a word, but Valley Paddock did. "Are you Jake Reynolds?" he asked. Hawkins jabbed Reynolds with his cane. "Are you?" Paddock asked again, and Reynolds didn't answer. "Better go get Delgado, Horseface, I think if he's not here quickly we might have a couple of dead outlaws on the floor of my emporium." He waved the weapon, moving Simmons over next to Reynolds and told the two to sit on the floor with their backs to the display case. "Right now, even a cough'll get you shot," he said. Paddock took a casual stand, leaning against a stack of heavy boxes, the outlaw's Colt cocked and ready for action.

"I'm on my way," Delgado said. He was eating breakfast in his little cabin when Horseface Hawkins barged in. Half the cabin was living quarters while the other half was office and one not entirely secure cell. "Better roust the doctor out and bring him down, too." Delgado strapped his gun belt on and strode down the main street from his office/jail/cabin to Paddock's mercantile store. Horseface hobbled the other way toward Fowler's home to bring him down.

"Horseface isn't one to jump to conclusions or just say something off the top of his head," Delgado murmured. "If this really is Reynolds I better make sure I'm ready to face that monster. The way those ranchers and their wives died, I'm walking into a mighty dangerous situation." He checked his rifle and sidearm twice before reaching the big store.

"What have we got here?" Delgado said, seeing Paddock holding a gun on two men sitting on the floor. He kneeled to get a closer look at the men. "Wow, somebody don't much like you," he said. "Ain't seen someone whipped like that since I left Virginia." He saw the other man was younger and just as filthy. Both men had mean eyes that told the deputy each would kill at a moment's notice.

"Think the man with the torn-up face might be Jake Reynolds," Valley Paddock said. "The young one called him Jake when Horseface clubbed him. Do you recognize him?"

"Never seen Reynolds or this man." Delgado looked hard into angry eyes and asked what his name was. Reynolds didn't answer, just held his wrist and glared at the deputy. Delgado asked Simmons, "What's your name, boy."

"I ain't no boy, mister. Don't call me boy."

"And I ain't no mister, boy. I'm Elko County Deputy Sheriff Jimmy Delgado and the two of you're under arrest."

"Under arrest?" Simmons shouted. "I ain't done nothin'." He started to jump to his feet and Delgado slammed him across the side of his head with his pistol. Simmons howled in pain as the blood flowed down onto his shirt.

"Tried to pull a gun on me, you did," Paddock said. "And old Jake there did pull a gun on Horseface Hawkins." Delgado nodded. That was all he needed to hold these two for the sheriff.

Paddock was about to say more when Hawkins limped in with Doc Fowler right behind. "Well, I'd say you're lucky that you made a stupid move on old Horseface here, mister. Another week and you'd be a dead man." Fowler wasn't going to get anywhere near either man until they were bound up, but he could see the serious infection that Reynolds was already suffering from. "Some kind of pig butcher tried to fix you up, it looks like to me."

"I ain't no pig butcher," Simmons piped up and got a jab from Reynolds. "Well, I ain't. I've fixed your wounds before Jake, and you know it."

"Shut up, you fool," Reynolds snapped.

"Looks like back in sixty-four, Doc," Horseface chuckled. "Or maybe it was Mexico City I saw this much blood." He was cackling, trying to dance on his one good leg, and threatening everyone with his cane.

"I'm too young for any of your wars, Horseface, but we do have a mess here." Doc Fowler was getting his kit open and Valley Paddock was getting upset at all the shenanigans going on in his store. Doc smiled at the storekeeper and said, "It's only Monday, Valley, you'll have the whole rest of the week to make money." Paddock har-rumphed some, Fowler chuckled, and Reynolds whimpered when he moved his broken wrist.

"Get 'em bound up Delgado, Paddock send one of your boys to get Jesse Winthrop and a wagon to drive the bunch of us to Elko." Fowler took command immediately. "Can't do nothing for this feller here and he ain't gonna die from a broken wrist. Horseface, get over to the telegraph office and send a wire to the sheriff that we're on our way."

Within half an hour, Winthrop driving the team and Horseface Hawkins riding shot-gun, the wagon was filled with Deputy Del-gado, Doctor Fowler, Simmons, and Reynolds, and they were on their way to Elko. Valley Paddock sent one of his boys along as an outrider and another to the Slater ranch to spread the word. Was this really the killer Jake Reynolds and part of his gang? Paddock remembered that even Connors said he didn't know for sure what Reynolds looked like.

"I better not find out that your brother has run out on me, Sandy Reynolds, or I'll carve your face up worse than his." Obregon whapped his high-top moccasins with that ugly quirt to make his point. "He's been gone nine days; Sandy and we know it doesn't take nine days to ride from here to Skelton and back." He smacked that quirt again, a little harder. Reynolds, still in pain from the infected gunshot wound, cowered back against the tree he was leaning on.

"Jake wouldn't run out on me," he almost cried.

"Or me?" Obregon watched the pitiful show for a few seconds. "If your brother ain't back by this time tomorrow, I'm gonna hang you up by your heels, naked, and whip every ounce of meat from your filthy body." He walked back toward the fire with a slight grin on his face. *I love to say things like that. That boy won't sleep a wink tonight.*

"Rider coming," Henry Coates said from his lookout on a high escarpment above the little camp. "Looks like Rowdy Simmons."

Simmons rode in slow knowing several

weapons were aimed his way. "It's Rowdy," he hollered coming around a large rock formation and into camp. "Jake and Doc are in jail in Elko. I heard that Jake tried to pull a gun on some old codger who whipped him good with his cane, and Doc tried to help."

"Help the old codger or Jake," Obregon laughed right out loud. "Well, okay then, I guess we can forget them. Henry," he called, "come on down here, we got some plannin' to do."

"What do you mean, forget them? That's my brother you're talking about," Rowdy Simmons said. He was still stepping off his horse and glared at Hickory Slim. "I ain't gonna ride off and forget my brother."

"He ain't much help to us, now, is he? He'll rot there along with Jake while we see if we can make some money around these parts."

"I think we ought to bust 'em out," Rowdy said.

"I think you'd best keep your stupid mouth shut." Obregon motioned to Henry Coates to join him by the fire. He swaggered toward the fire, slapping that quirt with each step and chuckling to himself.

Rowdy Simmons walked toward the lean-to where Kid Reynolds was slumped. "He's just gonna leave Doc and Jake to rot in jail. We gotta do something."

"I'm burnin' up with fever and we can't fight those two. I'm gonna try to keep from dying here and you'd best start thinkin' the same way. They're plannin' something over there and wantin' to leave us out. Get over there, forget about Doc and Jake, and find out what's goin' on. That's the only way we're gonna live until we can get away from them."

The Kid knew he was in more than just bad shape with the infection from the bullet wound burning him up with fever. He'd been shot before but had been patched up by a real doctor and what Doc Simmons did wasn't working. Considering the filth the gang lived in, how the wound was treated, most doctors would find it surprising that The Kid was still alive.

Rowdy's very slow mind wrapped itself around Sandy's little speech until the lamp got lit, and he casually walked over to the fire. "So, I guess it's just us now," he said to the two. "Gonna miss Doc's gun."

"That's better," Hickory Slim Obregon said. He spit a wad into the fire and poured whiskey into his cup, offering the flask to Rowdy. "We'll take a little ride to Skelton come morning."

[8]

"Who was that, Jack?" Mims was kneading dough for bread when Jack walked into the kitchen. "I heard a rider but couldn't walk away from this mess." She laughed softly showing Jack her hands, all floured, and a large ball of dough on the massive cutting board Jack had built for her.

"Valley Paddock sent one of his boys with a message for me. Seems they think this Jake Reynolds may have come to Skelton, got stupid with old Horseface, and is in custody and on his way to the Elko jail. I don't think I'd want to tangle with Horseface Hawkins and that oak cudgel he calls a cane."

"Reynolds? Is that the man who's been raiding some of the ranches? Oh, dear," she said.

"If it is, no worries now. I'm gonna take Robbie for a look at the critters in the north pastures and talk to him about what we decided. Okay with you? And then we'll come back here for some fresh hot bread and your sweet butter."

"Good. He needs to know this is his home, we are his family. I think Roberto Hernandez Gomez-Slater is a good name for a young man." He kissed her on the cheek, patted her on the bottom, and slipped out to the barn to find Robbie.

To think I almost lost that man when I was so young. I seemed to know when I was ten years old that he was just what a girl like me needed. And then when we all got separated and those horrible men attacked me, I thought it was the end of my life. Mims chuckled right out loud. "Jack Slater, I love you," she said. Even with her well-floured hands, she grabbed little Maybelle and hugged her close.

"You're about to get a big brother, my little May flower. Grab those bread pans for me while I shape these loaves." *The most terrifying time of my life and what came out of it is adorable. Those vile men, their foul odor, and what they did to me, and I got Maybelle. Life is full of little puzzles, little intrigues.* Maybelle banged the bread pans together and giggled when Mims jumped.

"You scared me," Mims said bringing more giggles from the little girl.

■ ■ ■ ■

Ornery Pound came running out of the barn just as Jack got to the big doors. "Better come quick, boss. Robbie's been hurt."

Jack rushed into the barn to find young Robbie sprawled across the floor holding his leg and breathing hard. "What happened, boy?" Jack said. He kneeled to find Robbie had a badly broken leg.

"Old Dough-boy kicked me, and I fell on the rake. It really hurts, Jack."

Jack hadn't seen that Robbie had two tines from a hay rake stuck in his back. Blood was flowing freely. "Ornery, get Mims and bring towels. After you do that, harness the team to the surrey. I've got to get this boy to Doc Fowler as fast as possible."

Ornery Pound raced off for the house, no cussing, no arguing, no back talk at all. Jack eased Robbie onto his side. "You're bleeding some, probably cracked a rib or two, but I don't think you stuck that old rake into your lung. This is gonna hurt, son," he said and pulled the rake tines out in one quick move.

Robbie howled in pain but didn't try to jerk away. "That hurt worse than falling on it," he said, moaned just a bit, and slumped down, not quite unconscious. Mims came in at a run, holding Maybelle in one arm and a bunch of toweling in the other, and got right down on her knees to help.

"I'm right here, Robbie. We'll get you fixed up," Mims said. Jack grabbed Maybelle and watched as Mims got the blood from the back wounds under control. "You hold that bandage in place, Robbie, while I rip some of this to wrap it in. Can you reach it? What's wrong with his leg, Jack?"

"Looks like a bad break, Mims. Old Dough-Boy kicked him while he was raking the stall. Ornery's getting the surrey ready. We'll take him into Doc Fowler's as soon as you're ready. I'll ride my horse and you can sit with Robbie and Maybelle while Ornery drives."

"Get me something to use as a splint for the leg," she said. Jack was surprised when she pulled a fair-sized knife out of her dress pocket and cut Robbie's pants away. "You're right, it's a bad break. Robbie, this is gonna hurt some," she said.

"You guys gotta quit sayin' that." He tried to chuckle and instead groaned when Mims tied the splint to both sides of the break. "I'm too young to cuss, but I sure do want to," he said.

"You're one tough little hombre, son."

Mims leaned down and kissed the boy on the forehead. "Let's get you wrapped in some blankets and in the surrey. I've got a story to tell you on our way to Skelton, about your pa and me."

The five-mile ride was slow and easy, and Mims spent the time telling Robbie all about how she and Jack lived as youngsters and why they wanted to adopt Robbie. She talked about love, responsibility, dedication, and more love. By the time they pulled up in front of Doc Fowler's place, Robbie knew the story about how Jack outsmarted old Jablonski and how Mims got food to him out in the barn every night. How Jack stood up to every mean thing that farmer tried to do and how he took care of Mims and tried to protect little Jason.

"We'll be so proud if you'll be our son," Mims said. Jack picked the boy up, as gently as possible, and carried him toward Fowler's office/home.

"If it's all right with you two, I want to call you mama," he said, trying to smile through the pain, "and, Jack, you're my pa from now on." They watched the tears flow down the boy's cheeks and knew most of them were from joy. Pain was also part of the picture. "I was afraid you'd send me away," he blubbered.

"What have you done to yourself, son?" Fowler had him on the table, his shirt off, and got the bandage pulled away from the two deep wounds in the boy's back. "When these heal, they're gonna look like bullet wounds, Robbie. Better get a good story put together," Doc chuckled. "Fell on a rake? I bet that hurt. I'm gonna put some medicine deep into these wounds, son, and it's gonna hurt."

"There you go again," Robbie said, grimacing as the pain shot through him from the antiseptic. "Oh, oh, oh," he said, several times.

"That rake has probably carried some foul loads, pal," Jack said. "We don't want a bad infection to take you out. We have plans for you, Mr. Slater."

Robbie's eyes got huge when Jack said that, and he laid back on the table, closed his eyes and replayed the words several times, the grin on his face getting bigger and bigger. "I like the sound of that. Mr. Slater."

"Mims, you have Ornery drive you and Maybelle back to the ranch." Jack turned to Fowler. "How long will you keep Robbie?"

"At least three days, Jack. I can set his leg and get it in a cast quickly, but I want to keep a close eye on those puncture wounds.

101

I've got some crutches here that should fit him, too. Three days for sure."

"I'm gonna stay at least overnight, Mims, and if longer, I'll get word to you. Have Cactus Jack keep the ranch in order." They hugged and kissed, Mims gave Robbie another kiss on the forehead and headed out to find Ornery Pound.

"I'm gonna go see Horseface Hawkins, then check in with Valley Paddock, and I'll be back to have supper with you, Robbie. That is if Doc will let me."

"Of course I will, Jack. Me, Hawkins, and Paddock rode back into town about an hour ago. You can bet that old Horseface will tell you all about capturing the fiendish outlaw Jake Reynolds," he chuckled. "I've heard the story ten times, so far."

"I'm looking forward to it," Jack said.

Wild Bill Connors had Clyde Simmons in his office, away from the cellblock and Jake Reynolds. "They call you Doc, eh? From the look on your partner's face, he needs one. You want a cup of coffee? Old Chief Deputy Eli, there, makes a fine pot." Connors had every intention of making young Simmons believe that he was the best friend he could have now. He'd used that technique many times and planned to know everything about this Jake Reynolds gang before nightfall.

Doc Simmons didn't know what to make of that. "Well, uh, yeah, I would. I haven't ate since breakfast." It was breakfast the day before, but Simmons didn't have any idea of time since his capture. *This boy is a complete dunce. I'll bet he's never had a day of school,* and Connors gave him a nice smile.

"Well, we'll have some coffee, a nice chat between the two of us, and then we'll see about getting you some good food." He looked up to Eli Reardon and nodded. "How was it that you were in Skelton, uh, Doc? Is it okay to call you Doc?"

"Yeah, sure," Simmons stammered. He took the coffee from Reardon and almost gulped the first drink. "Hot," he said. He looked at Wild Bill Connors, knew he was the sheriff, knew he shouldn't trust the sheriff. Jake always said it was his responsibility to hate lawmen. "This is good coffee," he said. "Thanks."

"I'm glad you like it," Connors beamed. "Your friend might be in a little trouble, but I don't think you are. Why were you two in Skelton?"

"Jake kinda got angry at that old man. He gets angry some fast, you know. He didn't mean no harm."

"Well, we'll talk about that, maybe during breakfast. It isn't nice to pull a gun on somebody, you know." Connors gave the young man a big smile. "Skelton ain't a very big town. Why were you there?" He knew the boy would be dumb enough to just blurt something out if he kept pressing.

"We wanted to see what was in that big store. Hickory Slim Obregon said he wanted us to bring him a detailed list of specific things we should look for. We're gonna be building a new cabin, is what we were gonna get stuff for."

Connors almost jumped straight out of his chair at the mention of Hickory Slim Obregon, and he saw Reardon stiffen up like a rake handle. "So, you and Jake Reynolds work for this Hickory Slim feller?" Connors knew it was time to be very careful with how he asked the questions of this stupid young man.

"Well, old Henry Coates brought him into camp and he kinda took over. That's how Jake got hurt so bad. I tried to patch him up, but I'm not a real doc. Jake's gonna die, isn't he?" It was as much a statement as a question.

"No," Connors said. "We ain't gonna let your friend die. One of our town doctors is on his way over to see Jake Reynolds right now." When the sheriff called the outlaw by his full name the young man didn't correct him at all. *I gotta sit down alone and get all this straight. Holy cow, Obregon and Coates teamed up? And with idiots like Simmons here?*

"Have some more coffee, Doc, and tell me about what you were looking for at the mercantile store in Skelton. Old Valley Paddock has just about anything you'd want to build a cabin."

"Yeah," Simmons said. He took another cup from Reardon who was still trying to tie Obregon to Reynolds. "I've never been in a store like that. Hickory Slim gave us a list to look for, but neither Jake or me can read, so he just shoved it in his pocket. We saw lots of rifles and bullets, and some dynamite. Hickory Slim said to look for where they might keep their money, too."

Connors stood up. "Well, we better get you back in your cell, so you can have your breakfast." He nodded to the jailer standing near the door to the cellblock to take Simmons back. "Reardon, let's you and me take a little walk."

They were out the door and walking fast toward the telegraph office. "Obregon has taken over this Jake Reynolds gang and I'll put my reputation on him hitting Valley Paddock's place, and I mean soon."

"I can be there in just a few hours or so," Reardon said.

"Take two or three men with you. I'm sending a wire to Delgado to form the town up and be prepared. This Obregon is the meanest man I've ever known, will inflict horrible wounds instead of killing outright, and then deny medical help and watch somebody slowly die. Ride hard, Eli, I'm sure Obregon's already on his way."

Build a cabin is less likely than anything I can imagine. Guns and ammunition, and dynamite. Banks in eastern Nevada won't be safe if they get their hands on that stuff. I wonder how someone like Obregon could get tangled up with the likes of Reynolds and Simmons. Simmons is the most ignorant man I've ever met.

"You're just a little sissy coward, Sandy Reynolds. Your name shouldn't be The Kid, it should be Baby Sandy." Obregon was towering over the huddled Kid Reynolds, whacking his boot with that ever-present quirt. "We ride in ten minutes. If you're not in the saddle, you die," Obregon said.

Reynolds went back and forth between pure terror, extreme pain from the infected wound, and hoped that he could actually get in the saddle. He made it to his feet for the first time in two days and got to his horse, almost passing out once. The raging fever was affecting more than his body. More than once during the night he was sure he heard Jake talking to him, telling him to get away. *I'll kill that man if it's the last thing I do. Then I'll find Jake and Doc.*

Coates, Rowdy Simmons, and Obregon were on their horses, ready to ride out from their miserable little camp. Obregon told Rowdy Simmons that he tried to help Sandy, he'd kill him slow and easy. "You comin', Baby Reynolds? If not, you die," Obregon laughed. "We're going to Skelton and make some money. You comin'?" His taunts drove boiling oil through Reynolds. The Kid hadn't eaten for two days, wouldn't drink any water, and was suffering an extreme fever.

It took two tries with anguished cries before Kid Reynolds got up on his horse. "I'm comin'," he said, nudging the gelding alongside Rowdy Simmons' horse. "Let's go." Simmons nodded as if to say that he would do his best to help his old friend.

It was late spring when the group made the ride toward and over Harrison Pass in the Ruby Mountains. The pass challenged ten thousand feet and was still clogged with snow and ice as they neared the summit after a hard six-hour ride from their camp. Reynolds was having a difficult time staying conscious, almost fell from his horse several times, but Obregon refused to slow down or stop.

The trail was narrow and steep, clogged with downed trees and drifted snow and Rowdy Simmons did his best to help Sandy Reynolds. He noticed that Obregon kept an ugly leer on his face anytime he looked back at the two. "Don't let Baby Reynolds fall off his horsey," he called back more than once.

Rowdy didn't know if Kid Reynolds could even hear what was being said, but he could, and he wanted to kill Obregon with every little comment. Why didn't he? Rowdy Simmons was older than Doc Simmons, had killed more than one man, in fact was good with his guns. Obregon would win this round simply by intimidation. That quirt. Rowdy had seen what it could do, felt it every time he moved.

He let his horse slow just a bit, let Coates and Obregon get somewhat ahead of them, and as they rounded a bend on the steep trail, just yards from the summit, Rowdy Simmons pulled his revolver and cocked it, leveling the sights on the middle of Obregon's back. He felt the bullet rip through his chest before he heard Henry Coates's pistol.

Simmons was flung back off his horse, crashing into the rocky trail. "Thanks, Henry. He's a dead one, let's keep moving," Obregon didn't even look back, just nudged his horse some. "I think this old gang of ours is gonna end up just you and me, Henry. Course, that's the way we wanted it anyway, isn't it?"

Night was coming on and with it freezing temperatures and the always-present Nevada wind. "We'll make camp under those trees. Get a fire started Coates, help Reynolds get that lean-to up."

"Ain't gonna get any help from him," Coates laughed.

"You're the one what shot the little baby. Should have had better aim, Coates."

Coates was laughing as he pulled the tarp off the packhorse and dragged it over to the tall pine trees off the main trail. The Kid fell off his horse and just laid on the ground near the trees, moaning in feverish gibberish. Coates ignored him, got the horses taken care of and started gathering what wood he could find for a fire.

"I want that fire started now," Obregon snarled. "Baby Reynolds can die for all I care. Get that fire going."

Coates was cussing under his breath when he dumped a load of wood. "Might help some, Slim. Just you and me now and I ain't no slave." Obregon ignored him.

Supper was chunks of stale meat held over the fire on a stick and coffee. "You sure tangled yourself up with a pod of idiots, Henry. What were you thinkin'?" Obregon had ridden with Henry Coates in Kansas and Nebraska and came west when things got hot following a botched bank job. "I thought you were smarter than this."

"Jake Reynolds told a good story, Slim. I contacted you when I knew what a fool he was. You aught to just put that kid out of his misery. It'll just be us taking that store in Skelton. We should head west after and look at the banks in Winnemucca and Reno."

"My plan exactly. You got that flask of yours?" He had no intention of putting Kid Reynolds out of his misery. He was enjoying the show too much for that to happen. It didn't take either man more than five minutes to fall asleep alongside a good fire. The Kid hadn't yet moved.

Coates got the fire up and burning just as the sky lightened some. Obregon came out of the lean-to just minutes later. "Looks like

Reynolds kicked it off sometime during the night. He would have died from that wound anyway. We don't need that pack animal and all this crap, Henry. Let's coffee-up and ride hard for Skelton."

[9]

"You look tired, Mims." Cactus Jack was worried about the large amount of work Mims had to do around the ranch, the baby coming on fast, and her getting little help. "Why don't you let me, and boys take care of our own breakfast." Sunrise on the Slater ranch on a warm and delightful June morning found Mims at the kitchen stove and Cactus Jack Faraday leading the ranch hands in for a hot breakfast.

"I'm more worried than I am tired, Cactus. Robbie hurt himself bad when he fell on that rake." She set out a platter of biscuits followed by half a side of hog called bacon. She poked Cactus with her big fork when he went for the bacon first. She chuckled and watched him jump away. "I'll be okay."

She didn't want to think about the Slater cowboys messing up her kitchen trying to fix food. "I need to keep you boys well fed so you keep me and Maybelle safe and sound." There had been definite changes in the way things were done since the death of Sandra, and now with both Jack and Robbie gone, there would be nobody around the big ranch house during the day.

"When's the boss due back?"

"Not for a day or two, I think." She waved her arms about and got the crew in and settled. They were watching her and listening instead of eating. Platters of bacon, biscuits, and scrambled eggs were passed about quickly. "Cactus, let's have a little chat after you get the crew lined out."

Big, strong, young men who spend hours every day in the saddle doing hard work need lots of food and eat fast. Fifteen minutes after they walked in the kitchen they were gone and so was every scrap of food from the table. What few biscuits that may have been left found their way into pockets or saddlebags for munching later. Most pockets also held an assortment of jerky or other dried meat that holds well. Just brush off some pocket lint, a piece of alfalfa, and it's fine.

"Are you worried about something, Mims?"

"I am, Cactus. These stories about this gang of killers attacking ranches around the

113

county really bother me, and with Jack in town for a couple of days, I'm even more worried." She knew what outlaw gangs did when they abducted young girls and vowed many times over the years that it would never happen to her again.

"It's just me and Maybelle here at the ranch most of the time, Cactus. With Jack and Robbie gone, and now Ornery Pound riding with the buckaroos, I'm scared."

"I'm so sorry, Mims," Cactus Jack said. "That one got right by me and I'll get it corrected immediately." He was almost shaking in embarrassment, knowing he had promised Jack Slater that he would keep his family safe and then let the whole crew just ride off to play with the critters.

"You'll have two men with rifles in and around the barnyard as soon as I can ride out to the herd. If Jack doesn't fire me for this, he sure as all get out should. Please, Mims, forgive this old piece of Texas rot, and I won't let anything hurt you or Maybelle."

Storming out the door, Mims heard Cactus murmuring to himself, "oh, my God," over and over, and had to smile hoping she hadn't hurt the man. She wanted to tell him that she wasn't accusing him of anything, just asking for protection, but also, she knew, Cactus would have the strongest of his crew and the best shots protecting her and Maybelle.

From the time she could remember, right up to when Jack Slater came to live at the Jablonski farm, she had taken care of herself, fighting off Pete Jablonski's incredible meanness toward the children, even stealing food for Jack and the other children. But after being abducted and sexually tormented by that gang, she understood how vulnerable she really was.

Mims walked into Jack's office and got his fowling piece, a double-barreled shotgun that she knew would bring a man down. She trooped into their bedroom and found the Remington handgun he had given her, thought about strapping it on and had to laugh right out. "Now wouldn't that be a sight. Dusting the tables while armed to the teeth."

With the loaded shotgun near the door and the little Remmie sitting close at hand in the kitchen, Mims felt much better. "You bring Robbie home safe and don't you ever leave me again," she said as if Jack was standing next to her.

"I think we've got that infection pretty well under control, Jack." Doc Fowler and Jack were standing at the foot of the bed where Robbie was tucked under a wool blanket. "Puncture wounds are the worst for some reason. Whatever punches the hole in the body brings all kinds of filth in with it and it's hard to cleanse properly. Did you know the Indians do that with their arrowheads, with poison and filth? Well, I think Robbie's shirt and jacket must have cleaned up that rake a bit," he laughed.

"I'm glad to hear that, Doc. Are you saying I can take my boy home?"

"I'm gonna clean the wound one more time, put another dressing on, and he can go home.

"I'll send some medicine home with you and Mims will have to change that dressing at least twice a day for the next few days. If it infects up, you hustle me out there right away. You'll need to bring him back in a few weeks, about three, so I can change the cast on his leg."

"Can he ride with that cast? His horse isn't here, and neither is one of our buggies. That wasn't very smart of me, not having Ornery bring a horse or buggy back."

"He can ride nice and slow. No bucking shows and no racing," Fowler laughed. "How many times has Horseface Hawkins told you the story of capturing the Reynolds gang?"

Slater had to laugh right out at the question. "I've heard it from Horseface, from Valley Paddock, and from Jesse Winthrop. At least Jimmy Delgado admits that all he did was put the handcuffs on the two. That one man's face must have really been a mess."

"I've seen men's backs whipped so hard the bones show, and that's what I saw in that outlaw's wounds. Somebody whipped him right across his face, and I mean more than once. The infection was serious, and it was the weakness from that, that probably allowed old Hawkins to cane the man into submission."

"Man that did it must be some kind of cold-blooded."

Well, I'm gonna go round up a horse and tack for Robbie." He gave his boy a big smile. "I'll be back in an hour or so to bring you home, son."

Jesse Winthrop had a gentle old mare for Robbie to ride home on and Jack wanted to stop by Paddock's on the way out of town. "That feller in Elko is supposed to have my new saddle done. Hope it's already here."

"It's going to be a slow ride home, Jack," Robbie said. "Can't get my other foot in

117

the stirrup. Yeah," he chuckled, "no bucking show today." They tied their horses off in front of the mercantile just as two other men rode up, one tall and dark, carrying a braided rawhide quirt with long tails. The other man was shorter but heavier and carried a shotgun as well as a sidearm.

Jack let the strangers go in first since Robbie was still learning how to make those crutches work for him. They were almost laughing when they got all the way in the store after Robbie took an accidental turn into a display shelf. "Mornin' Valley," Jack hollered. "Pecos send that saddle yet?"

"Be with you in a minute, Jack. Need to talk to you. Let me take care of these gentlemen first. Mornin' to you, strangers. What can I entice you into buying today?"

Before Hickory Slim Obregon could answer, Horseface Hawkins and Jimmy Delgado hurried in. "Jack Slater, I'm sure glad you're here. I think we may have a problem coming our way."

Delgado looked around the store and spotted Obregon who in turn spotted the big tin star on Delgado's wool vest. Coates saw the problem before Obregon and pulled that shotgun up only to have it knocked out of his hands when the shaft of a heavy oak cane broke one of his arms.

Obregon was faster getting his weapon drawn and took two quick shots as he raced for the front doors of the emporium. Delgado fell back into a shelf of canned goods, holding his leg, Hawkins whipped Coates across the head three or four times, and Jack Slater, revolver in hand shoved Robbie out of the way and made for the door.

Robbie crashed into a shelf and went down in a heap.

Obregon was on his horse and riding west as fast as the animal would go. Hawkins was on the porch alongside Jack in a moment. "That road leads to my place, Horseface. I've got to go now. Tend to Delgado and raise a posse to follow me."

"I can ride, Jack, and fight. Paddock will take care of that stuff. Let's go." Horseface Hawkins limped faster than Jack had ever seen him move and jumped on his horse. The two went out of town at full speed toward the Slater ranch. After ten minutes they had to pull their horses back to a walk or kill them.

"That man's called Hickory Slim Obregon, Jack. The sheriff sent a telegram about him. He's taken over the Reynolds gang. He's the man what whipped Jake Reynolds' face into ground meat. That's what we came to tell you. Eli Reardon is bringing a posse

119

down from Elko right now." Horseface
Hawkins face was alive, his eyes shining like
a panamint ball, telling the story.

"You got a lot of grit in that craw of yours,
Horseface. Besides that wicked cane of
yours, do you have any other weapons with
you?" He was amazed that this old veteran
of two wars was so quick to jump into
danger. "You probably saved a lot of lives
back there, Mr. Hawkins."

"Sure, you bet I carry weapons, Mr.
Slater." He reached back and pulled a
Winchester rifle from its saddle scabbard,
then tucked it back. Then he opened his old
army jacket and Jack saw a Colt Peacemaker
tucked in a shoulder holster. "Got a Bowie
on my belt, too, Mr. Slater. When I go to
war, I go to war," and he laughed and
wheezed and laughed some more.

Despite the situation they were in, Jack
found himself laughing right along with the
old saloonkeeper. "One amazing man, Mr.
Hawkins. I'm proud to fight alongside you.
We'll be coming up on the ranch road
shortly. I hope this trail we're following
doesn't turn in there."

They were within half a mile of the ranch
when they heard heavy gunfire coming from
that direction. "Let's go," Jack yelled, put-

ting the spurs to his horse, Hawkins right alongside.

Ornery Pound wasn't happy about being pulled off the buckaroo crew but when Cactus Jack told him why he changed his mind. "I love that little girl, Cactus, so, you bet I'll ride shotgun on her. Anybody want to hurt Mims Slater or that baby girl, well they better be ready to talk to Ornery Pound."

"I want you to grab Phineas Cassidy and bring him up to date. At least one of you must be on the porch of that big house at all times. If the other is doing a chore or something, he must be fully armed. Ride hard, Ornery," Cactus Jack Faraday said. Pound rode off to find Cassidy. Cactus Jack wondered if maybe it should be him instead of one of those two at the ranch.

It was a full half an hour later that Cactus Jack finally quit arguing with himself, told one of the hands to finish with the cattle. Cactus rode toward the ranch at a fast trot cussing himself out the whole way. "That's what's wrong with riding for a brand like this one. The people are too nice, the work ain't the least hard, the food is excellent. A man loses his edge. Two years ago, I would have had my rifle cocked and my Colt at hand if I thought Mims was in trouble.

"Just look at yourself, Cactus Jack Faraday, you're a mess. Old Ted Wilson would have fired your skinny frame at the breakfast table this morning." He rode into the barnyard, walked his horse into the barn and unsaddled it, grabbed the rifle from the scabbard, and headed for the big house.

"Where's Ornery?" he muttered. "I don't see Cassidy either." He checked the rifle's receiver, pulled the hammer back on the old Winchester, and started for the house when a sting on his arm knocked the rifle free. The quirt lashed out once more but tangled in a barn post.

Cactus Jack rolled to the ground, his arm in flaming pain, pulled the Colt and fired twice at where he thought someone might be standing. He heard a grunt, knew he hit the man, and scrambled as fast as he could into the protection of one of the stalls. "Good thing it's empty," he chuckled.

The rawhide strings on the quirt ripped right through his heavy denim shirt and tore a gash in his arm. He was about to strip his shirt off to rip it up for a bandage when he spotted Hickory Slim Obregon run toward the front of the barn. He snapped off a quick shot, leaped from the stall and chased out the door after the man.

Obregon was suffering from a wound in his hand. One of Cactus's shots went right through the hand, breaking bones and tearing meat. He ducked behind a cottonwood tree, spotted Cactus Jack and fired twice in his direction. Cactus flung himself to the ground and fired once more at Obregon.

Obregon's horse was a goner from the hard run from Skelton, but he knew Pound's horse was just ten yards away and made a dash for it. The cottonwood shielded him well and he was in the saddle and at a fast gallop down the ranch road toward the main road. Cactus Jack jumped to his feet and raced to the big house and was almost shot by Mims who recognized him just in time. All Cactus saw were two black holes from the barrels of that scattergun pointed at his midsection.

The blast from the shotgun would have all but cut that Texas cowboy in half, but she pulled it away as she squeezed the trigger. "Oh, Cactus, oh," she cried. Half the door-frame was in splinters and the kitchen was filled with the acrid smell of gun smoke. She saw Cactus's bloody arm and was sure she had shot her own ranch foreman. "Let's get that fixed. I'm so sorry," she cried.

"You didn't do this, Mims. It's okay. Where's Ornery? I sent Ornery and Cassidy back to protect you."

"I haven't seen them. I didn't know there was a problem until I heard the shooting. You're bleeding hard, Cactus. We have to get that fixed, then we'll look for Ornery and Phineas." She ripped the sleeve off his shirt and saw the nasty wound. "What on earth happened?"

"Whoever that was in the barn hit me with something. I never saw the man or the weapon. Knocked the rifle right out of my hand."

She had it cleaned up, pulled the ripped skin together and used a tight wrap with some cloth to close the wound and said he would probably live. They were about to head out the door when Jack and Horseface came riding in at full speed. Jack's horse wasn't close to being stopped when he was out of the saddle and at a run for the house as Mims and Cactus walked out.

"What happened?" Jack yelled.

Cactus Jack told the story as fast as his Texas drawl would let him, and the four of them headed for the barn to see if they could find Ornery Pound and Phineas Cassidy. Mims was right alongside, and Jack motioned for her to get back to the house.

"The man's name is Hickory Slim Obregon," Jack said. "We've been chasing him from Skelton. That must be his horse lying in the dust back down the road. Rode him to death."

Mims didn't leave, heard the slightest whimper, and pointed toward the back of the barn where they found Ornery Pound in a pool of blood trying to help Phin Cassidy. "Cassidy's dead, Ornery. Let's see what we can do about your wounds while you tell us what happened." Jack got the man to his feet and with Cactus Jack's help, walked him to the main house and into a chair in the kitchen.

Horseface Hawkins stayed with Cassidy and took a long look at the wound that killed the man. "He whipped that quirt of his right at this man's throat and opened it better than a can of peaches," he muttered. Cassidy's revolver was still in its holster and his rifle lay next to him, not cocked.

"Those boys never knew the man was even here. Wonder why they came into the barn? Maybe this Obregon made a little noise and drew them in. He took out two men and never drew his gun."

"We rode up and tied off the horses and were gonna tell Mims that we were here when old Phin saw some boot tracks leading into the barn from the ranch road. We heard a noise down at the back there, and that's when those men attacked us."

"You mean there were two?" Cactus Jack looked around at the group. "I only saw one man, only one man ran from the barn."

"Had to've been two," Ornery growled. "Something slashed old Phin's neck open clean as you do a hog, and then it felt like I was either shot or something, and then I was knocked out. Had to be two men do all that."

"That Obregon is faster than most men I've ever seen," Horseface Hawkins said. "You saw him at Paddock's store, Jack."

"Yeah, I did. So, you followed the tracks into the barn and he lured you back, killed Phineas and knocked you out. That wound across your back and shoulders came from that quirt, probably on the backslash after slicing Phin's neck open.

"He rode his horse down getting here, so he must have been looking to steal one, not necessarily here to kill, rob, or steal anything else." Slater sat down at the table watching Mims clean and dress the wounds on Pound's back and shoulder. "You said Sheriff Connors was sending Reardon to Skelton, Hawkins?"

"That's what the wire said we were bringing you and Paddock. Reardon was bringing two deputies with him and was supposed to form a posse in Skelton to catch this Obregon feller." Hawkins walked to the stove and brought the coffee pot to the table and poured cups for everyone.

"There's a jug nearby, eh?" he chuckled, setting the big pot down. Jack pointed to a cabinet and Hawkins brought a jug of fine Kentucky bourbon to the table. "Need to keep our strength up."

Maybelle started crying and Mims flew to her room, grabbing her tightly. She held her close as she came back to the kitchen. "Our littlest one slept right through all the uproar, gunshots, and men talking too loud, me runnin' off like that," she said. There was a hint of snarl in her voice but a definite grin on her face.

"I'd like to mount up and chase right after that Obregon," Jack said. "But the smarter half of me says we would be better off waiting for Reardon and his posse. Anyone have a better idea?" Nobody spoke up and Jack emptied his cup. "Better take care of Phineas and that dead horse.

"He rode out of here on somebody's horse," Cactus Jack said, "and that's one more reason for that man to hang."

[10]

"Let's get you over to my office, Jimmy," Doc Fowler said. "You're hurt, but that'll heal up quick. Looks like the bullet went all the way through, so no broken bones to worry about."

"A couple of you men grab the outlaw and bring him with us if he's still alive after the beating Horseface Hawkins gave him."

"He's alive," Valley Paddock said, standing over Henry Coates. Coates was bleeding from many head wounds and holding onto his broken arm. "Get up, you miserable son of a coyote. We're gonna hang you after we fix you up," Paddock snarled.

"No, he'll get a trial, then we'll hang him," Delgado said to everyone's amusement.

Between gunfire and horses racing out of town, there was general hub-bub around Valley Paddock's emporium. "I need to get home," Robbie said. He was trying to manipulate his way through the crowd on his crutches. "Somebody help me up on my horse. Don't worry doc; I'll ride slow." Two men boosted the boy up, helped tie the crutches across the back of the saddle, and he was off. His left foot was in a stirrup, the other kind of hanging out to the side.

Jesse Winthrop let Jimmy Delgado hang on to him, Valley Paddock had Coates on his feet and under control, and they headed for Fowler's office. "Boy did we walk into a hornet's nest," Delgado quipped, sitting down with his wounded leg up on another chair.

"Better get him up on the table there, Jesse," Fowler said. He got Delgado's boots and pants off and started working on the leg. "Just what did that telegram say."

"Sheriff named and described this Hickory Slim Obregon as taking over the Jake Reynolds gang and said he believed Obregon was heading to Skelton to rob Valley Paddock's." He looked at Paddock with an ironic smile. "Guess he was right.

"Anyway, he said that Reardon and two deputies would be here today to form a posse and catch this Obregon and whoever was with him. It's a long ride, but I believe we'll see them before the day is out. Patch me up so I can ride, Doc. I intend to be in that posse."

"It's a nice clean wound, Jimmy. You'll be able to ride." Doc Fowler turned to Henry Coates who was just barely conscious. "You're lucky to be alive, mister. What's your name?"

Coates just looked away and grimaced as Fowler started work on him. "Doesn't matter, we've got a special section in the cemetery for unnamed outlaws. This is gonna hurt," Fowler said, applying some iodine to the open wounds. Jesse Winthrop and Valley Paddock had a hard time holding the man down.

"You did that on purpose," Coates howled.

"Sure, I did," he chuckled. "I'm a doctor. You don't want to die of infection, do you?" There were a few chortles in the office for just a moment or two.

"I can see the lights of town, Reardon," Deputy Tobias Sorenson said. "We're probably a half hour out." Reardon, Sorenson, and deputy Charlie Smith had made good time as they rode toward Skelton, stopping just twice to cool their mounts.

" 'Bout time. I could eat a bear," Smith said. "Think this Obregon fool will actually show up?"

"Don't shuck him off, Smitty. He's killed

more than one lawman and you saw what he did to Reynolds' face. Killer, outlaw, psycho? Yeah, for sure, but don't count on him being a fool. We'll find Delgado and get a rundown of what's going on, have a fine supper, and be ready for anything."

The three rode into Skelton at a trot and up to Delgado's dark house/office. Reardon saw no lights at the Alabama House Saloon either. "Might be riding into trouble, boys. Let's be sharp." They spread out and walked their horses slowly down the main street until they were hailed by Jesse Winthrop at the blacksmith barn.

"That you Reardon? Glad you made it." The Elko men tied off their horses in the barn and Jesse led them to Paddock's store, talking the entire way. He had the whole story told by the time he escorted the posse through the door. "We've got five men ready to ride with you," he said.

"Thank you, Jesse." Reardon was chuckling slightly at the thought of Horseface Hawkins beating the daylights out of Henry Coates, the big mean bank robber from the Great Salt Lake. "Must have been a sight."

Paddock had a large table with chairs set up toward the back of his store and invited everyone to sit down. He had a bottle of good whiskey out, the coffee was boiling away, and the lamps were lit. "Looks like Wild Bill knew what he was talking about," Reardon said. "Jesse pretty much covered what happened, glad you weren't hurt worse, Delgado, and I think our best bet is to ride out at first light."

"He went west, Eli," Delgado said. "Jack Slater and Hawkins were hot on his tail, but we haven't heard anything since they rode out. I don't want to put any kind of meaning to that, just that we haven't heard anything."

"Could mean anything, Jimmy." Reardon looked around the table, at his three deputies, at the townsmen, and continued. "To make a posse work there will only be one boss and that's me. I make the decisions and if you can't follow directions, don't ride with me." Reardon was a tough old law dog and would not stand for any nonsense. He meant to see to it that these men knew it. He also carried the reputation of bringing in his man and these men had heard stories. "We'll meet at Winthrop's barn at four thirty. Carry at least one side arm and a rifle. You'll need a slicker and bedroll."

"Do you want me to prepare a pack mule for you, Eli?" Winthrop asked.

"For three days, Jesse. Bare necessities. Coffee, beans, bacon, and flour. We'll ride mean and lean and capture one bad hombre. See you in the morning." He and his deputies left the store for the restaurant and steaks and beans on the county rub. Delgado went with them.

"That was short and sweet," Paddock said. "Everyone okay with what Reardon outlined?" Winthrop nodded his okay and Dick Riley sat quiet for a minute.

"Freddy Martin left right away. Suzy just had her baby and he can't leave for days at a time, and I'm not sure I can be gone for three days or more." Riley had a wife and young children and ran a leather shop. He did saddle repairs, built tack, and was very good at his leather tooling. Most wondered if the man had an aggressive bone in his body.

"You have between now and four in the morning to make up your mind, Dick. Reardon's a tough old bird but he is fair. We were hoping there would be five of us riding with him, and if you don't ride with us, there will only be three."

"I guess I was being a little selfish, Valley. I'll be there and ready to fight." His eyes were downcast as he said that, and Jesse Winthrop wondered if the man really would show up in the morning.

■ ■ ■ ■

Night was coming on fast when Obregon pulled his horse up under a stand of cotton-wood trees alongside a narrow spring-fed creek. He rode hard out of Slater's ranch and after fifteen minutes or so pulled the cowpony up to a solid trot, finally down to a walk to let him catch his breath. Obregon spent a lot of time looking behind him and never saw any dust, hoping he got away clean.

"If I can make Beowawe by tomorrow I can head north and not worry about any posse. Nobody'll catch me up there." He got off the main road after about a mile and spent the next several hours roaming the valley and hills leading west, never encountering a well-used trail or road.

"If they can follow that trail, I'll just give up," he chuckled. He tied the horse in some good grass after watering him and set about making camp. The pain in his hand never let up the whole day and he never stopped to give it any look-see. He had water boiling from the kit he found in Pound's saddlebags and pulled the bloody rags he had wrapped on.

"Oh," he simpered peeling the dirty rags

covered in dried blood back. "That's a mess that could very well kill this old son of Texas." He boiled some rags he found in the saddlebags and used them to cleanse both sides of the bullet hole through his hand. He could feel pieces of broken bone scraping when he put too much pressure on the rags and moaned with pain. The shot made his left hand and arm useless but allowed Obregon full use of that quirt and his sidearm. Firing a rifle would have to be one-handed, he thought, and then chuckled slightly, saying out loud, "I don't have one anyway." He gathered more wood and settled down for the night.

"One lousy lucky shot," he muttered. He had a good fire going, put a fresh pot of water on to boil and laid out the saddle blanket near the fire. "No food, no coffee, and no gold. I should have killed Reynolds and that whole gang of idiots and ridden off. I should make Beowawe sometime tomorrow."

Beowawe started out as a line camp when they were pushing the intercontinental railway through Nevada and was a railroad town that served the surrounding ranches and a couple of nearby mines. Obregon was very wrong if he thought he could make that ride in just one day. For a man not gunshot and with good food supplies, it would have been at least a three-day ride.

He might have been looked up to by other outlaws, but he was not trail wise nor was he fully aware of the vastness of the state of Nevada. Mountain ranges ran north and south, some very high, all rocky and filled with difficult terrain. Where the railroad came through mostly followed along the Humboldt River, but that was at least two days' ride north. He was in a bad fix and didn't know it.

Obregon was up at sunrise, drank a full cup of boiling water and filled his canteen with what was left, saddled the horse and headed almost due west. The trail he left meandered about the various valley floors, up into the foothills of each range he crossed, and hoped whatever posse might be following didn't have an old Indian tracker with them. The only tracks he saw were from animals of the desert, deer, antelope, rabbit, and coyote.

I might as well be hanging out signs along the way. I went this way. I think a blind man could follow my trail. I haven't seen another horse print. I gotta find a trail and get lost in other prints.

Mims rushed out the door when Robbie

rode into the large yard. He had a hard time getting off the horse but made it without taking a tumble. He fell into the dirt and grime when Mims rushed into his arms and the two of them went down. She wouldn't let go. She had her arms wrapped tight and hugged him, crying her eyes out.

Little Maybelle made her way down the steps off the porch and joined the gang on the ground. Robbie was doing his best to maintain some sort of dignity, Mims seemed to be doing her best to never let go of the boy, and Maybelle was having the time of her life, laughing and hugging both her mom and her new brother.

Jack was laughing trying to get the three of them on their feet. "Don't break his other leg, Mims." He got them up, untied the crutches, and they headed into the kitchen. "Was Delgado hurt bad? Anyone else hurt in that melee?" He asked.

"No one else was hurt, only Jimmy and that one outlaw that Mr. Hawkins whipped on. There's supposed to be a posse riding in from Elko later today and Jimmy and Mr. Paddock are trying to get some men from town to ride with it when it trails that guy that ran away."

Horseface Hawkins was chuckling as he listened to Robbie tell the story. "This old cane has proved itself more times than I can count, young'un. It's solid oak and weighs around ten pounds. That's what keeps me so strong, carrying it around."

"You're a kick, Horseface," Jack said. "But I'm sure glad you know how to use that thing. I'm glad Jimmy wasn't hurt bad. We had trouble here, too, son."

Jack took several minutes to tell Robbie what happened at the ranch with Obregon. "I'm sure the posse will stop here, and I will ride with them. Cactus Jack, I know you're pretty beat up, and Ornery, you too, but I want this place under armed guard starting this very minute.

"Pull men off the cow camps, Cactus. I don't ever want anyone on this ranch to fear an attack from any source, outlaw, Indian, or whatever.

"Sure wish I could ride with you tomorrow." Cactus Jack groaned just standing up and had an ironic grin on his face as he went for more coffee.

"Let's make some plans and then I'll get ready to ride with Reardon. That Obregon feller is going to die or wish he was dead when I catch him."

"You mean when we catch him, Jack," Hawkins said. "I don't carry a bed roll or trail kit on my horse most of the time. I'll have to borrow something if you got it."

"Horseface, you're a war party of one and you can have just about anything you want around this place." Jack slapped the old man on the back nodding to Ornery Pound to help get Hawkins set up. The two of them headed out the door, both talking up a storm, laughing, punching each other in the shoulder.

"There's a pair to draw to, Cactus Jack. Ornery and Horseface. Lordy I'm glad we don't have three of a kind."

After supper, Robbie was sitting in the living room quietly watching the shadows from the fireplace dancing across the wall. "Something bothering you, Robbie?" Jack asked. One of the walls in the large room was covered in books, almost floor to ceiling and Robbie had one of the books on his lap.

"Why do you have to go with that posse?" he asked. He was subdued, not his usual active self.

"That's the kind of question that sometimes is difficult to answer," Jack said. He took a seat in a large leather covered chair and lit a cigar, watching the smoke curl toward the open beam ceiling. "I believe that a man has many responsibilities in this old life we live. One of them is to help keep

139

the community he lives in safe."

"I thought that's what the sheriff was supposed to do."

"It is," Jack said. "Sheriff Connors and his force of deputies have been doing a fine job of keeping the people of Elko safe, but every once in a while, he might need a little help. This is one of those times. We live here, safe, warm, well fed, and comfortable. I feel that I have a responsibility to protect all that from ugly men like this Obregon feller."

"Is that how all the men in Skelton feel?" Robbie was fourteen years old, reaching puberty, on the one hand, still very much a little boy on the other, and working as a grown man around the ranch.

"Your mother had the hardest job in the world, living with a child in a strange community, not having deep ties in the community, facing disaster of every form at every turn. Raising a child alone, having to work long hard hours just to barely exist would crush many people.

"I'm sure we've told you this story many times, but Mims had a life even worse than your first several years before you and your mother came to live with us. You never knew your father, she never knew either of her parents. Children learn the concept of responsibility in many ways and from many people, not always parents.

"You had a strong sense of responsibility toward your mother, Robbie. You were ferocious in protecting her."

"I love mama and I miss her very much. You mean that you protect all of us and also want to protect those in the town?"

"If the town is safe, wouldn't that make it even safer here on the ranch? That man, Obregon, came to Skelton to rob Valley Paddock, maybe hurt or kill people in Skelton doing that. He ran away and did hurt and kill right here on our ranch. Do you understand now why it's so important for me to ride with that posse?"

"I think so." He turned his eyes down toward the floor, had a firm grip on the arms of the chair. "I don't want to call you Jack. I want to call you papa."

Jack stood up and took two steps to the chair, lifted Robbie into his arms and hugged him tightly. "I want that too, son." He put the boy down and sat back down. "You understand that people will talk, and not always have good things to say. I'm not old enough to be your biological father. I would have to have been ten for that to happen."

Robbie laughed at that, his eyes brighter than Jack had seen them for a while. "People have said bad things about me and mama for a long time," he said. "She said it's because they don't know any better."

"Sandra was a wise woman," Jack said. "The reality is, most of the people in this country are white. With your French and Spanish ancestry, you are slightly darker, thus, different. Ignorant people are afraid of anything that's different. Instead of trying to learn about what is different, they try to make it into something lower than themselves.

"Does that make sense to you? There is not one thing in the world wrong with being different, but to the ignorant fools, it scares the devil out of them. Don't ever let anyone try to put you down because of your ancestry. The French and the Spanish are fine people with brilliant histories. Be proud of who you are."

"I'm very proud to be your adopted son," Robbie said.

"No reason to include the word adopted, son. You're my son."

[11]

Nine men rode off the Slater place, grim in the face and determined in the heart, led by Elko County Chief Deputy Sheriff Eli Reardon. "With Obregon's background, he'll be a tricky one to follow. We want to watch for tracks that leave this road for no apparent reason. He's not a fool nor is he stupid in any way.

"And, gentlemen, first and foremost, he is a sadistic killer. If we find his trail and it leads toward a stand of trees or rocks, a deep gulch or gully, watch for an ambush. This will be a long slow ride, men. Don't let your senses get lazy."

Mims, Robbie, and Maybelle were on the porch watching the group leave. Mims couldn't see them but there were three Slater ranch buckaroos standing in the shadows of the barn, rifles in hand.

"They'll be okay, mom," Robbie said. "I'll take good care of you and Maybelle while they're gone. It's important you know, for a man to stand up to his responsibilities." He had a set to his jaw that made Mims remember Jack at that age.

I don't know where that came from, and calling me mom, too. This boy is going to be one fine man soon. "So, I'm mom now, eh? I like that. Have you and Jack been talking about things?"

"We had a long talk last night and then this morning we talked some more. Did you know that some men back east have built vehicles that can move without horses? Papa showed me a magazine article with pictures of a steam-powered carriage, they called it. He said I'm growing up in an amazing time."

"That's why it's so important for you to do your studies every day. You and Maybelle will be running this big old ranch someday and you need to know a lot more about the world than just throwing a loop or riding a fine horse. It takes a lot of work and a headful of knowledge to create something as amazing as a steam-powered carriage."

"Papa pulled out some books from his library and said he wants me to read at least once a week. And he said," his eyes wide open and broad smile on his face, "I can stay up later if I'm reading."

"It's our library, son," she chuckled. "Let's get this kitchen cleaned up. Those men ate every single biscuit and roll I cooked. That, Robbie dear, is not amazing, it's reality."

The posse picked up Obregon's trail an hour later when the outlaw left the main road and headed cross-country. "Looks like he might be thinking of Beowawe or hopping a freight at a water stop." Reardon knew Elko County like a man knows his barn and led the group along. It wasn't long before the trail turned north for an hour or so, and then back toward the west.

"I wonder what that's all about?" Deputy Smith picked up the change of direction turning the posse. "A change of mind?"

"No," Jack Slater said. "He'll be making turns like that, but always veering toward his ultimate goal. He's hoping that if someone is following they'll miss a turn or give up not thinking the trail is from a wanted killer runnin' for his life."

"He's forgetting something, Jack." Reardon looked all around the large valley west of the Ruby Mountains. "It's rare for anyone to ride out here, off the trail. He should have stayed on that main trail. The only hoof prints out here are his." That brought

145

laughter from several members of the posse.

They found Obregon's camp in the cottonwoods well before sunset and decided to continue. "He was pretty clever leading out of here," Reardon said. "He walked that horse in circles, headed off one way then another and then back to here. Let's stop right now before we destroy what it is we need."

He stopped off his horse and indicated that everyone should. "Toby, you've got the most experience tracking, ride out from here about half a mile or so and then make a long circle around the camp. Hopefully, you'll cross his real trail.

"If we find another camp before we find him, let's remember this." Tobias Sorenson rode out to pick up the trail. The man spent several months working with an army group trailing the last of the Bannock warriors that were plaguing the old Oregon Trail years ago and could read sign even when days old.

"Look here, Reardon," Horseface Hawkins said. "That man's hurt." He held up a blood-soaked rag that had been stuffed in the fire but didn't burn as Obregon hoped it would.

"That's something good to know. Cactus Jack said he was pretty sure he hit the man." Jack Slater looked at the rag and noted there was a lot of blood loss. "Maybe we'll get lucky and he'll die of blood poisoning."

"No, no," Delgado chuckled. "He's mine." He was rubbing his leg trying not to show any pain. "We gotta catch him before he dies."

Sorenson picked up Obregon's trail within fifteen minutes and the men were off. "He's not trying to hide it much. Only by wandering around through the sage and cedar bushes," Sorenson said. "Only other tracks are deer, antelope, and little critters. Hard to miss a big old horse's hoof print."

He'd gone two days without food, but had plenty of water to drink, continued not moving in a straight line toward Beowawe, but worried that maybe he better make for the railroad instead. His idea of riding into the little railroad town after just one more day never was thought of again. The only thing he knew for certain was the railroad main line was north and Beowawe was northwest.

"I can make Beowawe in two more days, but I can make it to the tracks by tomorrow afternoon." He was off by a large margin once again but found himself near a small water source on the side of a hill where the cottonwoods gave it away.

Obregon had the horse tied off in some good grass, dug out a small hole in the wet grass and let the spring water fill it up. A scrawny long-legged jackrabbit watched the activity and Obregon slowly pulled his pistol, took a long slow pull on the trigger and blew the rabbits head right off.

The horse panicked. Reared back and broke the leather on the headstall, fleeing the area at a fast run. Obregon went crazy, taking two shots at the racing horse. He cussed for a solid ten minutes before calming down and thinking about his situation. "All of this because Henry Coates got tangled up with those fool boys from Missouri. Now, I'm gonna die in this godforsaken desert with a bullet hole in my hand."

The reality made him more angry than afraid and he cussed long and loud, kicked broken cottonwood limbs, ripped the skin from the dead rabbit and cleaned its guts, flinging them into the tall grass. "I don't got nothin' now," he moaned, sitting down near the waterhole. "Even that pot and fire starter were still in the saddlebags. I hadn't even taken the canteen off that foul horse," he screamed at the dead rabbit.

It was pitch black dark by the time he was able to nurse a barely flickering fire and he quickly got it burning good. Using some rocks he found and his knife, he whacked sparks into the dried grass for half an hour before one caught enough for him to nurse a flame into life. "I've been alone before, been without more than once, but I better get myself under control if I'm gonna live through this," he mumbled. The understanding of his situation slowly crept in and along with it, fear.

He tied what was left of the rabbit to a broken branch, after mauling it several times in anger, and roasted it over the open flames. "It's food," he murmured. He dipped water with his good hand and got some to his mouth and curled up next to the fire to sleep.

Morning brought the true reality of the situation home to Hickory Slim Obregon, killer, outlaw, almost dead man. The rag tied around his wound was filthy with mud, dirt, and dried blood, and the pain was fierce. It hurt like all get out just getting the rag off the wound, and Obregon saw serious infection had set in. The wound was bright red and festering. His hand was useless, of course, and he had a difficult time trying to wash out the filthy rag.

Finally, he just got the rag sopping wet and wiped the wound with it, howling in pain as he did. "I'm not gonna die crying over a hurt hand," he screamed and tried again to wash it clean. "That's enough." He wrapped and tied the rag back on, using his teeth to draw the knot tight. He found the rabbit carcass and gnawed on the remaining pieces. It was morning, the sun was bright, and Obregon felt a chill down his back as he took a long look around him.

"I'm at least forty miles from the railroad and they ain't nothing between us but Nevada desert. If I stay here, I'll have water but nothing else. I've walked forty miles before." He set his course, picking a mountain peak out several miles for his first goal, and started out. The railroad ran east and west and if he stayed on a northerly course he was sure to hit the tracks, but men with no food and festering gunshot wounds usually can't walk a true course or make good time.

He refused to look back, only keeping himself on line for that mountain. It was late June and summer's sun was beginning to heat up the valley floor. It was about two hours later that he sat down in the shade under a juniper bush. "Not even five miles and I'm feeling it." Obregon was weak from loss of blood and very little food intake. He rested another ten minutes and started on, watching the mountain peak as it seemed to not get one foot closer. "I've got to find some water before the day is over."

"Sun's gonna be up in an hour, men, let's get up and ready," Horseface Hawkins bellowed. The old soldier had the fire going, coffee was brewing, and he was going to fry up some bacon for their breakfast. They found a camp, but no water the night before, and some of the men were not happy about a dry camp.

"You got no need to be all friendly and happy, Horseface," Dick Riley growled. Riley didn't want to be in the posse anyway, and a dry camp didn't help his mood. He would lose business at his little leather shop knowing his wife wasn't able to do the leatherwork and watch the kids, too. "How much longer are we gonna be on this hunt, anyway?"

"Till we catch the bugger," Jimmy Delgado said. He walked off into the sagebrush to relieve himself and was startled by some movement about twenty yards off. "We got company, boys," he said, pulling his revolver and cocking it. Horseface and Jack Slater were at his side in moments and both could see a shadowy form moving, could hear the bushes being moved.

Jack, bent over, crept up a couple of steps

toward the shadow, his gun drawn and ready, and stopped quickly. He stood up straight and slipped the Colt back in its leather. "It's okay boy, it's me," he said, creeping slowly up to Ornery Pound's horse, still saddled and bridled, but with the remains of a busted headstall. "Obregon either lost his horse or he's stolen another," he said, walking the gelding back to camp.

"Let me see," Jesse Winthrop said. "Saddled, bridle still on, but tied off. No, Jack, something scared this horse enough for him to break free. I'd venture to guess our man is on foot now."

"Let's hope that fool is afoot," Reardon said. "Grub-up, men and let's get back on the chase. I want him before the day is out."

"Yeah, and I want to get back to my saloon," Horseface said. He served up great slabs of fried bacon and pan-fried biscuits. The men wolfed it down and sloshed their coffee cups clean. "We've got a battle to fight, so let's get this squad formed and on the march." A couple of the men threw the old soldier a salute, moving toward their horses at a high lope. Reardon just smiled.

As the day wore on and the heat built, Dick Riley knew he had made a mistake making this ride. He rode up next to Jack Slater and wondered how the man could just ride off and leave his family at the ranch. "Why are we here, Jack? This isn't any of our concern? The man tried to rob Paddock, not me. I got no business being here."

"You're a free man, Riley. You can hightail it anytime you want. Ain't nobody holding you. But you're wrong about this not being any of my business. Obregon killed one of my men and seriously wounded two others.

"You don't have any business here? Yup, the man rode into town to rob Paddock, for sure. Who's to say your leather shop wouldn't have been next? He killed one of my good men, who's to say he wouldn't kill your wife or baby next? If you're not willing to stand up for your neighbors, maybe you shouldn't be here. Maybe you shouldn't be in Skelton or even Elko County."

Jack glared at the man for a long moment. "I believe some of the men in Skelton helped you build the leather shop building, and never asked a thing for their time and effort. I believe when we had the flu bug thriving in Skelton a couple of years ago, that it was town people took care of your baby when you and your wife were both down.

"You, my fine friend, you have every reason in the world to be riding with this posse and if you do head for home with your tail between your legs, don't ever speak to me again about what I should or should not be doing." Slater nudged his horse into a trot and rode up next to Horseface, leaving Dick Riley to think about things.

Late in the afternoon the trail they were following led to the small campsite where Obregon had spent the previous night. "We don't want to mess up his trail. Toby, see if you can pick it up. "Reardon stepped off his horse and saw the rabbit's remains, a small fire ring, and signs of an angry person. "Nice of him to dig out the springs a little bit. Let's cool the horses and let them have a drink"

Tobias Sorenson had Obregon's trail immediately. "He ain't trying to hide nothing, Reardon. In this heat, with a bullet wound hurtin' him, we'll have him corralled before supper."

"Don't get cocky, Toby, the man's not a fool. We really need to be on our sharpest edge from now on. He most certainly will attack anyone who comes near. When we leave here, we will want to spread way apart, off to the sides, staying back and apart from each other. We don't want to give him a good opportunity to take us out before we get him."

154

Slater kept his eye on Dick Riley as they got back in the saddle. *I would never have thought of him being a coward. I guess we really don't know about others until something like this happens. To want to run out on people who have helped you is more than I can imagine.*

[12]

The heat boiling off the desert floor was merciless as it drew every bit of energy from Obregon. There were no clouds in that broad open sky, only a few ravens worrying a dead rabbit, wondering if he would be their next meal. "Water," he mumbled as he searched the sides of the hills for something green that might indicate a small spring.

He wandered along, still holding the mountain in his sights as his goal. A stand of green meant a possible spring, and there was no green. He turned to look behind him, could still see the cottonwoods where he spent the night before, and something else caught his eye. A small cloud of dust several miles out. Thoughts of water vanished instantly.

"Men on horses riding up my back," he muttered. He shaded his eyes and counted. "Ten horses coming at a walk." He looked around, not in a panic yet, but he had to find a place to hide, a place he could defend. A small shelf of rocks, off a hundred yards or so caught his eye and he didn't hesitate.

He was panting hard when he fell behind the outcropping, sweat pouring across his brow, blinding him some. He slammed his wounded hand onto the rocks getting down and almost screamed from the pain. "No rifle, ruined hand, and ten cowboys coming to look for old Hickory Slim. You're gonna find him, boys, and die when you do." He had his revolver out, made sure it was fully loaded, and watched.

Obregon killed and wounded men more for the gratification than the necessity, and found his game reversed; he was the primary target. As was normal for the psychopath, he had to blame something or someone, as long as it wasn't Hickory Slim in the wrong. "If I live through this, and I plan to, Henry Coates is a dead man. He started all this. That old man in Skelton will have to die with Coates. Slamming my arm with that cane. Henry Coates first, though."

The heat was unbearable, boiling off the desert floor, blazing through an endless sky, and Hickory Slim Obregon sat counting what few bullets he had. "Six in the revolver and ten in the belt. A fresh box in the saddlebags of that run-off horse. Every bullet has to count," he said and counted them again.

"He's having a hard time walking a straight line, Jack." Eli Reardon and Jack Slater were in the lead riding with a ten-yard separation between them. "Bet he doesn't have any water or food."

"If I were chousin' a steer, looking at these prints, I'd say we're mighty close. Whoa, did you see that?" Jack was pointing at a slight rise in the desert floor off to the left and about a quarter mile in front. "A glint of metal from something."

"Yeah, something like a gun barrel maybe." Reardon chuckled and called the group to a halt. "Time to talk some serious stuff, boys," he said. "See that rock outcropping up on the side of that hill? More'n likely there's a man behind those rocks with a gun aiming down on us and we need to flush him out of there." He had half a smile on his face, but Slater saw a mean glint in his eye.

"I would much rather bring him back to Elko alive but if he don't want to cooperate, well, that's just the way it'll be. If it's him or us to die, we'll make it him. Horseface, you've faced something like this before, eh?"

"More'n oncet, Reardon." They had dismounted and were kneeling in the dirt looking at the rocks and chuckling at Hawkins' way of talking. "They's just one of him and nine of us but some of us would die if we just rode in on him. I'd send two men way out to the right and a little further along and let them sneak up as close as possible.

"Two more men go way off to the left and do the same thing. Don't line up though so that if the men on the right should fire they wouldn't hit the men on the left. The rest of the posse then should slowly creep up from front like, and he won't know where to shoot first."

"That's what we'll do then." Reardon had a nasty smile on his face wondering what might be going through Obregon's mind as he watched the posse deploy. "It's a hot one, that old boy probably ain't got no water or food, so we don't need to be in a hurry. Let him suffer some and he might be willing to walk out of there, alive.

"Deputy Sorenson, pick somebody and go to the right, and Deputy Smith, pick somebody and go to the left. I'll lead from the front. We'll be heading home within the hour boys, and let's not get shot taking this fool out."

Sorenson picked Horseface Hawkins who

159

had already determined that he would be in one of those groups. "You got good sense, deputy," he chuckled. "We'll put the fear of Alabama in that killer up there."

Smith wanted to take Jack Slater, but Reardon shook him off. "Take Dick Riley with you. You're both young and full of it, and that's a nice steep climb for you." Riley wanted to back out in the worst way but remembered the talk he had with Slater. He ducked his head, stared hard at the ground, and didn't say anything.

Reardon watched the four men spread wide and make their advance on the hillside, well out of range of whatever weapons Obregon might have. "When they start making their move toward that fool, we'll make ours. We need to spread out, at least three or four yards of separation."

"This isn't going to be as easy as Horse-face seems to think." Valley Paddock took a step or two forward, watching the rock outcrop several hundred yards in front. "There isn't a scrub brush big enough to hide a man between here and there."

"You're right on both counts," Jack said. "He will have to watch three sets of men as they advance on him. I'm sure there wasn't a rifle in Ornery's saddle gear, and I'm sure that feller only has the one handgun. We'll just take our time, move up on him and either kill him or capture him."

Slater had to chuckle thinking he was starting to sound like Horseface. *Been around that fun old geezer too much, I think. I wonder if he eats rattlesnake heads for breakfast?*

The five men, moving straight up the hill gave Obregon good targets and he leveled that Colt on the man wearing the star. "You just keep coming lawman. Another fifty feet and you're one dead man," he whispered as if someone was crouched next to him.

"He's getting ready to pop one of those men coming up from the front," Horseface said, bringing his rifle up. He and Sorenson had found a small gully to use moving toward Obregon from slightly behind him. "I don't think he knows we're here, Toby."

"Got a good bead on him?" Hawkins nodded, and Sorenson hollered out. "Obregon, this is the Elko County Sheriff's Office speaking. Throw down your gun and you will live. Resist and you will die."

Obregon whirled and fired the Colt at where he thought the sound was coming from. Horseface Hawkins fired his rifle as Obregon's round hit his leg. Hawkins let out a yell at the same time Obregon did. Both men were writhing in pain. "Quit yer jumpin' around, Hawkins and let me see," Sorenson said, pushing the older man down. "Aw, nuts, Horseface, it's just barely a scratch."

"Sure, you can say that. It's my leg what's scratched and bleedin' and hurt." Hawkins quit thrashing around and took off his neckerchief and tied it around the not very serious wound. "I'm gonna live." He snarled it out, grimacing as he scrunched down in the sand and dirt, expecting another shot at any moment. "I know I got him, too."

Hawkins rifle slug tore through Obregon's upper arm, and he dropped his gun in the dirt from the shock of the hit. He knew he was finished. "That's the end of it. One hand almost useless from an infected bullet hole, and now the other messed up from another bullet wound." The hand with the hole through it could hold a weapon but Obregon screamed obscenities at everyone and everything, finally standing up and pretending that he was going to shoot again.

Charlie Smith recognized that he didn't have a weapon in his hand, but Dick Riley didn't, and Riley pulled his rifle up for a shot. Smith knocked it aside just before Riley pulled the trigger. "What the . . ." he said, glaring at the deputy. "I had him dead."

"He's not armed, Dick. He wanted you to kill him. You were about to kill an unarmed man." He patted Riley on the shoulder and nudged him on his feet. "Let's go collect this ugly varmint."

Riley was shaking the whole walk to that outcrop where Obregon stood screaming at them. *I almost killed an unarmed man. Even if he was an outlaw, that's wrong. Why did I come on this posse? I'm not a killer, I should be home with my wife, with my business. Slater's wrong; I don't owe these people anything.*

Smith was talking to Riley as they walked up toward Obregon and the man was too self-absorbed to hear the warning. Smith held his rifle at the ready and told Obregon to shut up and stand still and put his hands on his head. "Do it now." He watched the man move the one hand up but not the other.

"Can't move that arm," Obregon whimpered. Riley took a step closer to turn the man and Obregon pulled a knife from behind his head, slashing back and forth with it. Smith fired the rifle, jacked and fired, once, twice, driving Obregon down into the rocks, dead.

Riley's face and chest took the brunt of the knife attack, and he was screaming in pain when Smith was able to get to him. Hawkins limped fast and Sorenson ran to the outcrop while Reardon brought his group at a run as well. Hawkins made sure Obregon was dead while Sorenson helped Smith get Riley's bleeding under control.

"It's gonna be a long slow ride back to Skelton," Reardon said when everyone got patched up. He motioned for Smith to take a little walk with him. "What was Riley trying to do, getting that close to the man?"

"I don't know, Eli. He almost shot Obregon, and while we were walking up, I explained how many men carried hidden knives and not to get close until we were sure he didn't have one. He just walked right up to the man."

"He paid for that stupidity with an eye and some serious wounds. We'll be tending those wounds for the next two or three days getting back. Good work on shooting Obregon. You did the right thing."

"How's that leg, Horseface?" Jack Slater asked, sitting down next to the old man. "Doesn't look too bad from here." Horseface was sitting at the fire with the intricately braided quirt Obregon always carried and used with such proficiency.

"Naw, it ain't bad, just hurts bad. Look at this beautiful work," he said, handing the

164

quirt to Slater. "For a man who had no use for the beauty of life to carry something with such intense beauty and artistry . . . well, I just don't know." Jack had never seen rawhide braided as that quirt was.

"Spanish in California do that kind of work, Jack. I've seen some fantastic work on headstalls and reins, and on reatas that would stretch out fifty feet." Horseface Hawkins was almost caressing the quirt.

"Riley's wounds are gonna slow us down," Jack said. "How about that leg of yours?"

"My leg? What's bad, that's my good leg." He cackled and continued. "That's the one what pulls the other one around," he cackled long and loud. "I gotta carve up another cane," he howled in laughter. "Two-cane Horseface is my new moniker, boys." Jack took the time to wash out the wound and wrap it properly, getting the man on his feet.

"You keep that quirt, Horseface, and display it at your saloon, and tell the story of the bad man Hickory Slim Obregon. You're the reason we caught him, you know."

Sorenson and Smith weren't having an easy time of it trying to take care of Dick Riley. The slash wound across his face was long and deep, right across the man's eye, and two slash wounds were also deep across his chest. "You lay back and quit jumpin' around, Riley," Smith had to say a couple of times. "You're gonna be in pain and miserable the whole way back so plan on it. I told you not to walk up to the man because he might have a knife and you walked right up to him. Now, look at you."

"Am I gonna die?" Riley cried out. "I don't want to die, not like this. What'll my wife do? My baby. Please, Charlie, don't let me die."

"You ain't gonna die but you are gonna hurt."

"Let's make up a camp and we'll light out at dawn," Reardon said. It had been a long hot day capped with about five minutes of incredible excitement. The fatigue was showing, and Reardon knew the men would need all their strength on the ride back to Skelton.

"We'll tie Obregon's body to that horse he stole, and Riley, it ain't gonna be easy, but you'll have to face riding back. How's our food holding up Mr. Winthrop? We gonna be okay getting' home?" Winthrop just nodded, sitting down in the sand, exhausted.

"I'd say bury Obregon," Hawkins said. "Ain't no use haulin' his dead butt back." He got nods of approval from just about everyone and Reardon took a minute before agreeing.

"I guess you're right. We all agree this is Hickory Slim Obregon and that he's dead?" Nods around again and Reardon told Sorenson and Winthrop to dig a grave for the outlaw. "He ain't getting' no special words from me," the chief deputy said.

"When do you think papa and them will be back, Cactus?" Robbie was mucking out one of the stalls in the barn. His leg didn't hurt at all, but the cast made it difficult to move around. The puncture wound was closed and healing nicely.

"Depends on whether or not they can find that guy. That's mighty big country out there. Man can get himself hidden easy if he works at it. This Obregon feller is hurt, though. I know I hit him with at least one of my shots." He took the rake from Robbie and helped the boy limp out of the corral. "How's that leg comin'?"

"It aches some but usually at night when I'm tryin' to sleep. My back hurts more than my leg. I'm a mess," he chuckled. "Let's go find something to eat." The friendship between fourteen-year-old Robbie and twenty-two-year-old Cactus Jack Faraday was about as strong as if they were brothers. "I almost said I'll race you, but I guess I won't," Robbie laughed.

"I'm glad Jack and Mims are gonna adopt you. Jack Slater's the finest man I've ever met, buddy. You've found yourself one fine man to be your pa."

"He's kinda strict, more than mama was." He had a little grin on his face and took a quick poke at Cactus Jack. "I'm all right with that. He gave me that Winchester rifle and helped me to shoot good with it. Said he wants me to be the wolf man for the next couple of weeks until Mr. Cassidy can be replaced. Will you ride with me, Cactus?"

"We'll make a circle right after we have dinner," Cactus Jack said. They trooped into the kitchen where most of the hands were already at the table eating. "I don't remember anyone ringing the bell," he said.

"Thought we'd get ours first before you two grizzlies got here," Ornery Pound said. That brought the table alive and the joshing and stories went on for half an hour. Mims had pork chops, mashed potatoes and gravy, and hot biscuits by the platter for the hungry crew.

"My goodness, you boys can put the grub away. For your information, I checked the peach trees this morning, and we'll be eating peach cobbler in just a few weeks. And the corn is making, so there'll be hot corn on the cob real soon too." It probably dated all the way back to when she was a little girl on the Jablonski farm in Dakota Territory, but she always felt like she had to make sure the men and boys had enough to eat. Jablonski used food, or a lack of it, as punishment and Mims did what she could to see to it that the boys got something.

It was during those visits to the barn late at night with biscuits and leftovers that she fell in love with Jack Slater. The memory flushed her face some and she turned quickly back to the stove with a broad smile splashed across her pretty face.

"Man gets a lot of work done when his belly's full," Cactus Jack chuckled. "Let's hit it guys." The men gave smiles and nods to Mims and headed out the door for the afternoon's work, already smelling something roasting in big cast iron kettles for supper later.

Cactus Jack held back for a minute. "Robbie and I are gonna make a quick circle around the ranch, Mims, but you'll have no less than five armed men around the place all afternoon. Ezra Jackson and Tater Thompson are gonna slaughter a hog for your salt barrels. They'll brine and smoke some hams, too."

"Thank you, Cactus. I guess we won't hear anything from Jack and the men until we see them." He just nodded to her and headed out to find Robbie and chase off some marauding wolves. Young steers, lambs, and pigs tend to bring the big animals down from the Ruby Mountains often.

Coyotes, wolves, mountain lions, and bears populated the Ruby Mountains along with deer, antelope, desert bighorn sheep, and mountain goats, and it was wolves that came down into the valley more often for snacks of baby cows. Almost every ranch had a wolf hunter, many of the small villages and encampments had hunters as well.

"Our calf losses have been very small this year," Cactus Jack said. "We'll work those eastern sections first and then drop down into the bottomlands." Both men carried rifles along with their sidearms and rode out on a pleasant late June afternoon. "If we do find some sign, you'll know where to start early in the morning."

[13]

"How's that leg holding up, Horseface?"
Jack Slater rode up alongside the old veteran. "That was a long ride yesterday, having any problems?"

"My problem ain't my leg." He gestured over his shoulder at the rider behind him. "That Dick Riley spent the whole day feelin' sorry for himself and makin' a fool of himself out of it. Damn fool walked up on a known killer and wants our sympathy. I'm gonna give him something but it won't be sympathy."

Jack chuckled, thinking what he'd give would be a cane thrashing to toughen the young man up some. "Look on the bright side, Two-Cane, we'll be home tomorrow sometime if we keep up this pace."

"Two-Cane," Hawkins guffawed. "Jack, you just made me day. When we stop for water or just a rest, you need to look at Riley's face wounds. He's been scratchin' at

171

'em and cussin', and I'd sure put some money on infection setting in. Who knows where Obregon's knife may have been before the attack. Up a skunk's behind, maybe."

Jack rode up to Reardon at the front of the group, still laughing when he pulled up next to the chief deputy. "Horseface thinks Riley's wounds might be getting infected, Eli. We'll need to stop soon and take a good look. I think there might be a waterhole about an hour in front of us."

"I want to ride on ahead to Skelton and wire the sheriff of Obregon's death and alert Doctor Fowler that he'll have wounded coming in. Will you be okay taking over bringing this group in?"

"Sure, I would, Eli. Wouldn't this be a good time to give Sorenson or Smith an opportunity at leadership? They've sure stood up well on this chase."

Reardon nodded with a little wry grin and hollered at Smith to join him, giving him the group, nodding to Jack again, and riding off at a fast trot. "What were you two talking about before he called me over?" Smith asked.

Slater told him about the possible infection and stopping at the waterhole near the cottonwood trees. "At this pace, we should

172

be there in an hour or so. We'd be about eight or nine hours from my ranch, so we could ride late today and get to Skelton by mid-day tomorrow."

"That's the plan, then," Smith said. "I'll spread the word."

"Looks like we're checking for wolves a bit too late, Cactus," Robbie said. They rode up on a half-eaten calf he thought wolves had dragged into a copse of trees. "This looks like this morning's kill."

"It sure does," Cactus Jack said. They dismounted, rifles in hand to inspect the kill and look for tracks. Robbie was still having difficulty mounting and dismounting with that cast on his leg. He floundered a bit, Cactus made a move to help, and Robbie shook him off with just the slightest grin.

"I'd like to use some language that Jack would not approve of," he joked. "Don't baby me Cactus, and much as I'd like you to."

"I'm not sure this is a wolf kill," Cactus said as Jack hobbled up to him. "You see how the carcass has been dragged into this deadfall? That's more the way lions work. Wolves will usually feast at the spot of the kill."

Robbie could see that the calf had been

dragged some distance. The kill had been made at least a hundred yards from where its remains were. "That old lion dragged the calf here, ate its fill, and tucked the leftovers under the deadfall," Cactus Jack said. "He'll be back tonight or tomorrow morning to finish it off. If we don't find that cat, we can use this carcass as bait and watch for that little kitty tonight."

"Don't get too many lions down in the valley," Robbie said. "With the spring crop of young deer, elk, mountain goats, and bighorn sheep in the Ruby Mountains, they got a pretty good table to choose from."

"Less, of course, they're old or sickly," Cactus Jack replied. Cactus knew a sick or wounded lion hungry enough to take on a three-hundred-pound calf wouldn't think twice about a couple of skinny buckaroos. The thought wouldn't go away, kept swimming through Faraday's mind as they looked for a sign. "You keep those eyes and ears busy, Robbie. Cats are quick and efficient killers."

"I've seen 'em walk right through Skelton in the winter." It hadn't rained for more than ten days; the ground was dry, and the grass was still springtime green. "Hard to see any kind of sign, Cactus. I can see where the calf was dragged, though. You got anything over there?"

"Looks like he ate his fill and moved off some to our north. Let's ride slow and easy toward that stand of aspen and cottonwood. There's a spring there that we dug out last year."

"I remember that," Robbie said, pretending he was bushed out tired from digging, but in reality, he was using that to hide how much difficulty he was having getting back in the saddle. "A big cat would eat, drink some water, and sleep off the day, wouldn't he?"

"Pretty much. Let's ride nice and slow and apart from each other some," Cactus Jack said. The grass thinned out some as they neared the trees and Faraday could see prints in the dirt. He stepped off his horse to take a close look.

"This animal's hurt, Robbie. Let's be as alert as we've ever been." He was on his haunches and could see one print clearly showing claws and puds missing. "Bet he walked into a steel jaw trap and broke himself free. That foot's gotta hurt like the dickens. That's probably what moved him out of the mountains. Easier hunting down here in the valley."

Trailing their horses, the two walked very slowly into the stand of trees, looking at

175

everything all at the same time. They had their rifles at the ready, taking one slow step at a time. "Gotta look in the trees, too, Robbie. A cat'll sleep in the branch crotches and drop on its prey. We don't want to be that," he chuckled.

The ground softened and was getting wetter as they neared the dugout spring, which was now about ten feet across and full of water. They could see where the lion walked up and took a drink, then walked off, still moving north.

"He'll get back in the soft grass and sleep or climb a tree. With that bad foot, I'm thinking sleeping in the grass under a deadfall or big bush would be his first choice." Sometimes called Puma, other times, Jaguar, and most often, Mountain Lion, the majestic cats roamed the continent and harried livestock everywhere. They were generally nocturnal hunters and weren't seen as often as coyotes and wolves.

"He went into that big stand of heavy brush, Cactus," Robbie said. He was pointing at tall, thick sagebrush at the edge of the trees. There was a rise in the ground behind the sage and would offer a safe place for the big cat to sleep off the day. "How do we get him out of there?"

"Not sure, pard." Cactus walked his horse

back to an aspen sapling and tied him off. Robbie followed suit and both men were standing, rifles in hand, looking at the side of the hill behind the sagebrush wondering if the cat maybe had walked on through. The answer came in a lighting fast rush from the brush.

More than one hundred pounds of big mountain lion leaped from the brush, took one bound, and hit Cactus Jack a solid cross-body block, claws digging in, teeth looking for giving flesh. When the cat hit, the two crashed to the wet ground and rolled a couple of times. Cactus Jack lost his rifle at the hit and was fending off those vicious teeth with his arms. The cat using those ugly claws on his back feet to try and rake the guts right out of the man's body.

Both horses were spooked bad by the attack but were unable to break free of their ties. Robbie was horrified at the attack but responded immediately. He had the rifle up and was trying to find a target. The commotion of a snarling lion, screaming man, and terrified horses kept him from finding a clean target. He sure as all get out didn't want to shoot Cactus. Cactus Jack was on top, the cat had one arm in its mouth and its rear feet were flailing away. Robbie saw a brief opening and fired, blowing a massive hole in the cat's head as the bullet entered just in front of an ear, blew through the brains, and exited in a mess on the other side.

Cactus Jack rolled off the cat, which was still jerking about in its death throes. He was holding his bleeding arm and had a hard time trying to stand up. "My guts are ripped, Robbie. Help me get on my horse, we gotta get back to the ranch." He was bent over, holding both his injured and good arm tight to his belly. "Quick now."

It was more than just a struggle as Robbie tried to get him in the saddle. Trying to half carry the big man, hobbled himself by a broken leg in a cast, and two horses in a panic to get away. It took long minutes to get him up and steady in leather, untied both horses and scrambled as fast as he could onto his, leading Cactus's horse. He kept the horses at a fast trot all the way back to the ranch house, hoping to find willing hands from the Buckaroos in the barn.

Cactus was getting weaker as they rode, from loss of blood, fear, and shock, and Robbie had to stop twice to get the man squared away in the saddle. "Come on Cactus, it's just another few minutes. Hang on, Cactus," he begged, trying to understand just how much damage that cat had done. "Stay with me, Pard, hang on tight. We're almost there."

Robbie was howling for help as the two rode into the big yard near the barn and corrals.

Reardon rode up to the ranch house porch, saw two men in the barn with rifles pointed his way and waved to them. "It's Reardon," he hollered. "Here to see Mrs. Slater." Ornery Pound walked out of the shadows, recognized Reardon and waved Ezra Jackson off.

"Ride on in Reardon and tie off. We're a little spooky around here." Pound walked up on the kitchen porch and held the door for the deputy. "After you," he said and followed in, poured the two of them a cup of coffee and said he'd find Mims.

Mims followed behind Reardon having been in the kitchen garden and saw him ride up. "I'm right here, Ornery," she said. "You're alone, Mr. Reardon?"

"The rest aren't too far behind me, Mrs. Slater. Young Riley is injured, and I want to alert the doctor in Skelton, also let the sheriff know we got our man." He smiled, took a long drink of hot coffee and continued. "Jack is fine, Horseface got a little nick, and we have the horse that Obregon stole

179

from here."

"That's my horse," Pound said. "He okay? That's one fine stock horse, deputy."

"He's fine, Mr. Pound." Reardon was about to say something else when there were loud voices near the barn. The deputy jumped to his feet and with Ornery and Mims right behind him, raced out of the kitchen.

"My God, what happened?" Mims saw Robbie and Ezra Jackson trying to ease Cactus Jack off his horse. Faraday seemed to be covered in blood, and they eased him down onto the ground.

"Lion," Robbie said. He was breathing hard after the fast ride in and helping get the big man out of the saddle. "His arm is tore up and the cat ripped his shirt and pants wide open. It looks really bad, mama. The lion killed a calf and we followed it when it attacked Cactus. We gotta get him to the doc's right away."

"Ezra, get the buggy ready, Ornery get Mr. Faraday in the buggy, and Robbie you help. I'll get Maybelle and we'll all go into town." She was on her knees next to Cactus Jack and saw the deep wounds across his chest, stomach, and upper legs. Faraday was conscious but not saying anything.

"We'll get you patched up, Mr. Faraday," she said.

Reardon and Robbie rode fast into Skelton to alert Doc Fowler and Ornery Pound drove the buggy with Mims trying to keep Cactus Jack from bleeding to death. Maybelle was sitting up front with Pound, laughing and telling the horses to "gitty-up". Pound let her hold one rein and he held the other. "You'll be a mule-skinner sure as I'm sittin' here," the old buckaroo laughed. Maybelle yelled "Get up there, Molly. Gee now, gee," and squealed in laughter.

The five miles to town were covered quickly and Doc Fowler had his surgery ready when Robbie and Ornery got Cactus Jack in and on the table. "I've seen lion attacks before, Mims. This one's bad. Robbie, you and Ornery get Maybelle out of here, and Mims, can you assist?"

Robbie had Maybelle's hand and they walked down the street to Valley Paddock's big store. Reardon met them halfway. "I wired the sheriff, so I'm going to get back out and bring Jack in at a gallop, Robbie. Is Faraday gonna make it? Did the doc say anything?"

"Only that it was bad," Robbie said. "Make sure papa understands everyone else is okay. He worries something fierce about all of us." Reardon had to smile as he rode off to find his posse, and Robbie found Paddock's boys in the store to tell them all the news. It was a long drive back to the ranch with too much time to think about too many things.

I love Jack and Mims like I've never loved anyone, but I miss my mother. Jack expects me to act like I'm a grown man and all I want to do is sit down somewhere and cry like a baby. But I won't. I'm not a crybaby, but dog-gone it, I'm not a big old grown-up man either. Those thoughts got mixed up with what happened to Cactus Jack, and little Robbie became big Robbie.

Cactus Jack is really hurt bad. Doctor Fowler and mama and even Mr. Reardon all said that he's alive because of me, but I was so scared I just did what had to be done. He sat straight up in the seat of the buggy as a slow smile spread across his broad brown face. *I just did what had to be done, and that's what Jack says is what it is that a man does. I want to crawl in bed and cry and men don't do that, men square their shoulders and do what has to be done, and right now, that means getting back to the ranch, taking care of mama and Maybelle, and seeing to it that the cattle are okay.* A little twitch on the reins and he had his team at a comfortable trot for the rest of the ride home.

Mims and Maybelle weren't allowed into this conversation with himself, they were in the back of the buggy. Mims was worried about Jack, worried about Cactus, and at the same time so proud of how Robbie responded to this emergency. *He's going to be one fine man. I've got a five-year-old daughter who thinks it's just fine to jump on a horse with her big brother and just ride off somewhere, and a new son who fights off mountain lions, and a husband who chases outlaws. My God, I've got the best that life could possibly offer.*

Ornery Pound was riding Robbie's horse for the ride back to the ranch wondering if all these excitements would ever slow down. *We've had an outlaw attack, a man killed right on the ranch, and now old Cactus Jack mauled by a mountain lion. Sure would be nice to just watch over some cattle for a few days.*

[14]

"We're gonna have to tie that boy up, Jack," Horseface Hawkins said. "He's too weak to stay in the saddle. That knife must have been filthy to bring on an infection this bad. And so fast." Hawkins found himself slapping that braided rawhide quirt gently on his leg as he talked, and remembered how field grade officers did the same thing with their swagger sticks. "Just look at me," he laughed. "You'd think I was some fool officer or something. It sure is pretty though, ain't it?"

Delgado was riding on one side of Dick Riley and Horseface on the other, keeping the injured man in the saddle. "It's a beauty, Horseface, and you probably should have been an officer." Jimmy looked over at Jack Slater and shook his head. "I don't think this boy is gonna last out the trip."

"We can't ride any faster than we're doing," Jack Slater said. "Going fast will kill him and going slow might. We'll be at the ranch in just a few hours and we can get him in a buggy or wagon and into town."

"I hope he stays with us that long," Paddock said, riding next to Jack. "I wonder what Dick Riley was thinking when he just walked right up to Obregon? That boy's a good leatherman but he ain't much of a thinker, never has been that bright. He has to depend on his wife to do most of the thinking in that family."

"The only conversation I've ever had with him was on this ride. I haven't been the least bit impressed," Slater said. "He takes help, but he doesn't want to give any back. Selfish little boy, in my mind. I'm sorry he got carved up, but there again, he just isn't with it.

"It's his wife and kids who will suffer, far more than him if he lives. Lives or dies, she's gonna carry a heavy burden for some time to come." Jack could see that with his injuries, Riley would be laid up for a long time and his wife would be the one to suffer.

They stopped near a stand of cottonwood trees to give Riley another rest and put a clean dressing on the wounds. "Sounds like a horse coming fast, Jack," Charlie Smith hollered from the side of the road. "Just one, I think."

Slater ran to see as Eli Reardon came into view from a rise in the road. "Glad to find you boys," he hollered. "There's been some trouble, Jack. You need to ride back to Skelton with me. Charlie, you've got the posse. Let's go, Jack, I'll explain on the way." Jack was mounted and the two lit out at a fast trot to Skelton.

Reardon spent less than five minutes telling Jack about the lion attack and Cactus Jack's injuries. "Important for you to know, Robbie did what would be expected of a full-grown man. He not only killed that lion, he tended to Faraday, and got him back to the ranch alive."

"He'll be a fine man soon, Eli. What did Doc Fowler say?"

"Faraday's a tough hombre, Jack, but those wounds in his belly were deep and if things got messed up inside there, well, belly wounds usually mean death. Only time is gonna tell us, I'm afraid."

"You go on back with your posse, Eli, I'm going to the ranch first, then into town. Young Riley's in bad shape. Bring him to the ranch and my men will see to it that he gets into town."

Reardon turned back to the posse and Jack rode at a fast trot all the way into the ranch. Sweat and foam covered the horse when they pulled up to the barn. He stepped off his horse just as Robbie limped out of the barn. "Am I glad to see you," Robbie called, trying to run hard to Jack's side. He threw his arms around the big man, sobbing out the story about Cactus Jack.

"He's the best friend I've ever had in my life, papa. That old lion was just ripping him to pieces and I couldn't find a good shot." The boy had held it in all that time, but when Jack Slater put his arms around him, all the emotions were set free. It's tough enough being a fourteen-year-old, half boy, half man, and then seeing a man you love and respect being torn to shreds by a wild animal, just about took him over the top.

Slater held the boy tight wondering just how long he had been holding in those tears. "It's okay, son. You did what had to be done and I'm very proud of you. Let's go have a cup of coffee and you can tell me everything Doc Fowler said. Then we'll go skin out that lion and you can hang the skin on your wall. There aren't that many men who would have done what you did."

They had many cups of coffee, got the lion skinned and stretched for scraping, and decided not to ride into Skelton until morning. "I think your mama needs to know that her two men are with her at the ranch, son. When you find a good woman, make sure she always comes first. I knew I loved your mama when I was your age, pard."

"We were planning to move some cattle into fresh pastures," Robbie said. "Cactus wanted to start moving them tomorrow."

"You take Ezra Jackson and Tater Thompson and move the cattle tomorrow. What else did Cactus have on the agenda?"

"We lost some fence and Ornery Pound and somebody else was working on that. I was supposed to be checking for wolves."

"Right now, son, you're the ramrod of this outfit. I'll spell it out when the crew comes in for supper, but you just got off wolf duty. This ranch needs a good hand running things and Cactus Jack has been training you for just that. Ornery Pound can be hard to get along with sometimes but that old man knows cows, knows water, and knows grass. Learn everything you can from him and you and I will keep this place running."

Robbie's heart was pounding, hearing what Jack said, and there was a touch of pride, then rampant fear set in. "I can't tell these men what to do," he stammered, watching Jack chuckle some.

"That's the pleasure of hiring good men in the first place, son. You don't have to tell anyone what to do. You will find yourself passing on to them what it is that I want done, and then you work right alongside them. You're a fine, honest, hardworking young man, Mr. Gomez-Slater, and this is your ranch, after all."

Robbie walked around in a dream for the rest of the day trying to figure out just how he would be talking to these men, so much older, with so much ranch experience. He thought once or twice that he could actually smell the fear he knew he could feel. *It would be so much easier if he just put Ornery in charge. How will they respond to all this? My God, what have I gotten into?*

Mims served up platters of pork chops and cobs of fresh corn along with hot biscuits and Jack outlined what happened to Cactus Jack. "I'm riding out in the morning to see the doc and that posse will probably be riding in and will need some help with young Dick Riley. He got carved up bad and his wounds are about as serious as it is possible and him still be alive.

"Robbie, you'll be honcho until Cactus Jack gets back with us. Ornery, I want you to work closely with Rob. We've got a lot of cattle out there, a lot of hogs to take care of, and sheep and lambs. We're gonna be shorthanded for a time, but we'll get through this."

"You'll be in Skelton all day, Jack?" Mims said. "Why not look for a hand or two. Find a good cook, too," she laughed.

Both Pound and Tater Thompson said, "No," to that idea. "We like the way you take care of us, Mrs. Slater," Tater said, almost blushing and getting a hurrah or two from the others.

"I'll see what I can do," Jack chuckled.

Robbie went out with the crew after their meal, hoping to have a chat with Ornery before everyone slipped into the bunkhouse, but it didn't work. "Glad it's you Jack picked to run this outfit," Pound said. "Old Ezra isn't up it, Tater couldn't handle it, and I'll tell you for sure I'da told Jack no. See you in the mornin' boss," Ornery Pound said, whacking the boy across the shoulders.

Now there's something I never would have seen coming.

"It's gonna be a long recovery, Jack, but your foreman's gonna live." Doc Fowler and Jack Slater were standing next to Cactus Jack's bed in the back room of Fowler's home/office. "That lion did some big-time damage to his stomach muscles, and they heal long and slow. There was some solid chewing on that arm, and those big teeth raked his head pretty good. Robbie surely saved his life."

"I'm glad to hear that. Sounds like you're in good hands, Cactus. You get well, old man. You'll always have your job, so don't give that a thought." Jack saw a slight smile on the Texan's face. "When can he come home, doc?"

"He'll need tending here for about a week, Jack. Those stitches across his belly won't hold if he's moving around. Everything else, it's just a matter of time, but that belly has to be carefully attended to. Maybe a week, maybe a bit more."

With both Paddock and Jesse Winthrop riding with the posse, Jack wasn't sure where to look for ranch help. He walked into Paddock's store to talk with one of the boys about help. "I could use a couple of hands. Anybody around town looking for work?"

"I'd like to take a job with you, Mr. Slater. I like Mr. Paddock, and he's done real good by me, but I don't want to work here the rest of my life." Tiny Howard was sixteen years old, Paddock has raised him since he was seven, after his parents were killed in a terrible fire. He's worked in the store all those years. The boy was big for his age but not in the best of shape and Jack wasn't inclined to hire him.

"You're a big boy, Tiny, but cow work is mighty hard work. Most of every day you'd be horseback and when you're not in the saddle you're fightin' a steer three times your size."

"I'd really like to try, Mr. Slater. I don't like working in the store." His eyes were pleading and his lip quivering when he said that and Jack almost chuckled, which would not have been appropriate.

"All right, Tiny, we'll give you a try, but don't be surprised if it doesn't work out. You clear it with Paddock and come to the ranch ready for work. Anybody else in mind?"

"I think Tony Sorrel is back in town. He's been working in Elko. He's got ranch experience and is pretty strong."

Jack walked over to the Sorrel home on the main street, near the Alabama House Saloon. "Morin' Mrs. Sorrel. Is Tony home? I'd like to talk with him."

"Is something wrong, Mr. Slater?"

"No, not at all. Why would you think something's wrong?"

"Well, usually somebody wants to see Tony, it means something's wrong. I'll get him for you. He's just getting up. Would you like some coffee?" she asked. They walked into the kitchen and Jack remembered that Mr. Sorrel was killed in a mine accident several years ago.

He sat at the table with his coffee, waiting for Tony. *Raised without a father and must get in trouble often,* he contemplated. *I should just walk out, get on my horse and go home. Tiny Howard probably won't make his first day, and I don't need a troublemaker.* His thoughts were interrupted by Tony Sorrel clomping into the kitchen, still tucking in his shirt.

"Good morning, Mr. Slater," he said. He didn't offer his hand, just walked to the stove and poured a cup of coffee. "What can I do for you?"

"I'm a little short-handed, Tony. Heard you have some ranch work in your background. Tell me about that."

"Been workin' in Elko. Just got back in town yesterday. Workin' at the Plus Two."

"Kind of a busy time of the year to be leavin' a ranch job. What brings you back to town?" Jack needed the help but didn't need a hand who would quit at this time of the work year. Spring, summer, and fall are busy times and he didn't need a slacker.

"Kind of personal, Mr. Slater, but I do need a job. How much?"

"Dollar a day and found. Bring your own horses and gear. Start tomorrow at sunrise, if you want the job. Thanks for the coffee, Mrs. Sorrel," he said. He wasn't smiling as he walked down the street to find his horse and ride home. "I just hired two hands, neither of whom will make the week. Good job, Jack old man. Good job."

[15]

It was close to the noon hour when Eli Reardon led the posse into Slater's ranch. "Took longer than we thought, getting here, Mrs. Slater. Dick Riley's in really bad shape. Can we bring him in before we try to get him into town?"

"Of course, Mr. Reardon. Of course." She held the door open while Jesse Winthrop and Charlie Smith carried Riley's unconscious body into the house. "Make him comfortable on the sofa, there," she said. She could see bloody bandages, ripped clothing, and Riley's extremely pale face. "Are you sure he's alive?"

Winthrop eased Riley down and heard him whimper some. "He's still alive, Mrs. Slater, but just barely."

Mims always kept a pot of water on the fire and brought it and some sheeting into the living room. The men helped her tear up the sheets into bandages, and Mims began cleaning Dick Riley's wounds. "Tell whoever's in the barn to get the buggy ready. His fever is higher than I've ever felt. Jimmy, bring me a bucket of cold water from the well. We have to get this fever down."

With hot water and soap, Mims had the wounds cleaned and dressed, and she started putting cold compresses on Riley's forehead and chest. The man's temperature was so high that the compresses got warm rapidly. "Buggy's ready, ma'am," somebody hollered from the kitchen, and Jesse Winthrop picked Riley up and carried him out.

"I can't ride in with you," Mims said. "Try to be as gentle as possible. He's lost so much blood and his temperature is so high."

"I'll see to it that the buggy and horse get back to you right away, Mrs. Slater," Reardon said. "Thank you for your help."

There was nothing more she could do or say and just stood on the kitchen porch, tears running across her ruddy cheeks, watching the men ride off. Jimmy Delgado was driving the buggy with his horse tied to the back Somebody had undressed Ornery Pounds horse and tucked it into a stall with fresh hay.

"It's about five miles, boys," Eli Reardon said. "Let's go nice and slow. The doc knows we're coming. There's no reason, Jesse, Valley, Horseface, to stay with the buggy. Deputies Smith, Sorenson, and Delgado will ride with me and we'll make it fine. Go on home and thank you for your service."

"The Alabama House Saloon will be open by the time you hit town, Eli. First drink's on the house," Horseface Hawkins said. "Have I got some stories to tell." Hands were shaken all around and the Skelton men rode off for home.

"I want to thank you men," Reardon said to his deputies. "You have done a fine job, we caught our man, and we've only had one incident. Charlie, what happened to Riley here was not your fault. I'll see to it that Wild Bill Connors is aware of how each of you handled yourselves.

"When we get into town, I'll send another wire to Connors, we'll have one cold beer with Horseface, and we'll ride back to Elko. Jimmy, you keep the sheriff informed as to Riley's condition." Chuckles about 'one cold beer' and thoughts of being home made the last couple of miles into Skelton go by quickly.

"I don't know why he's alive," Doc Fowler murmured, cutting away the bandages Mims had put on the severe knife wounds. Valley Paddock had ridden straight to Dick

197

Riley's home to tell Virginia Riley the bad news. She found a neighbor to watch the two young children and was with Doc Fowler when the group rode in.

"Jimmy, take care of Mrs. Riley. She can't be in here right now. Take her home and find someone to be with her," Fowler said. Virginia was sobbing, standing over Riley and Fowler needed to be standing there. "What was Paddock thinking, bringing her here."

The early summer sky was just starting to show some light when Jack Slater lit the stove in the big kitchen. Mims had lamps lit and was putting the first of many pots of coffee together. "Mornin' y'all," Robbie said coming in the kitchen door.

"You're up bright and early," Mims said. "And, what's with that kind of talk?"

"Cactus told me that the best cattlemen came from Texas and that's the way he talks." Jack guffawed at that and Mims just shrugged. "If I'm gonna be a good cattleman, I gotta learn to talk like one," Robbie laughed.

"Better not talk that way in front of Ornery Pound. He'll whup on you, sure as all get out," Jack laughed. "I have two men coming in this morning, Robbie. After you get the crew lined out, I want you to show 'em the place and then put 'em to some hard work. They both need to be shook out some.

"What did Doc Fowler say about your leg?"

"He's gonna take the cast off next week, finally. I'm awful tired of hobbling around like an old man. I'll have to learn to ride again, too, putting both feet in the stirrups." Jack nodded, and Mims gave the big guy a hug.

Mims walked out onto the porch and rang the big triangle to bring the crew in for breakfast. She had pounded some cuts of beef the night before and was frying it up to go with potatoes and eggs. Five hungry buckaroos spilled into the kitchen, freshly washed and ready for Mims' best.

"Biscuits and gravy comin' up in a couple of minutes," she said.

Little Maybelle waddled in and climbed up on Ornery Pound's lap, giving the old man a big hug. Before anything could be said, they heard a horse come in and stop near the kitchen. Tiny Howard walked in, dressed for work and a smile on his face. "Good morning, Mr. Slater," he said.

"Around here, I'm Jack, Tiny. I think you know everyone. Sit and eat. After breakfast,

Robbie will give you the tour and set you to work. See anyone on the trail?" It didn't surprise him that Tony Sorrel might be late showing up.

"Kinda dark when I left, but no, I haven't seen anyone. This certainly looks good," Tiny Howard said, filling his plate with breakfast. "Mr. Paddock wanted me to tell you that he would get even, whatever that means."

Jack chuckled thinking that sure as shootin' the man would think of something to get even with him for stealing an employee. Robbie spread the crews out, some with the herds, some on fences, and asked Tiny to walk with him to the barn. "If Sorrel shows up, I'll either be in the barn or out on the west range, dad.

"Better put your gear in the bunkhouse, Tiny." Robbie helped carry the man's bedroll and gear in and they walked to the barn. "We keep our working horses in the large corral there. How many did you bring?"

"I only have the one horse, Robbie," Tiny said. "How many will I need?"

"One will do for now, but when we move the herd, sometimes you'll find yourself changing horses mid-day. You'll need a good cow pony, a good horse to work when we brand, and a big strong one for our general work around here."

He spent half an hour showing Howard the corrals, stalls, hayloft, and corncrib. "We keep a good bunch of hogs, too, Tiny," he said and headed toward the pigpens. "Everyone does hog duty but it's Tater Thompson who's the honcho. It might be a bit smelly around the hog pens but come supper time you'll forget all about that."

Robbie was saddling his horse ready to take Tiny Howard out to the west pasture and introduce him to the herd when Jack called him in. He motioned Tiny to wait and headed to the house. A horse was tied to the kitchen hitching rail. "Caught me just in time, dad. Tiny and I are about to head out to the west pastures."

"Robbie, meet Tony Sorrel. He'll be working for us. Give him the tour and set him to work."

"Mornin', Tony," Robbie said. "I haven't seen you for some time. Welcome to the Slater ranch." He stuck his hand out and was ignored by Sorrel. Robbie slowly pulled his hand back, cocked his head just a bit, and glared at the man. Jack caught the look immediately and watched to see how Robbie would handle the situation.

"Some reason you won't shake hands with

me?" Robbie asked. He stood straight and tall, his legs slightly apart, his hands at his side, still glaring at Sorrel. There were several years separating the two, Robbie coming fifteen and Sorrel in his early twenties, but there wasn't much separation as far as size went.

Sorrel stood, cocky, eyes narrowed, staring at Robbie, and Robbie held a defiant glare back at the man. "We believe in good manners around the ranch, Tony," Robbie said, very quietly.

"Only shake hands with someone better than me, and you ain't one of them."

"Is that why you didn't shake hands with me yesterday, Mr. Sorrel?" Jack stiffened right alongside Robbie and was glaring at Sorrel as well. Sorrel didn't answer but walked to the table and poured a cup of coffee. Robbie had been slighted by arrogant men before and was ready to stand up to this fool.

Jack, on the other hand, could remember how men reacted to this type of behavior when he was in Deadwood. A confrontation like this often ended in gunfire and death. Jack wondered just what Robbie was going to do, but didn't have to wait long.

"Put the cup down, Sorrel, and walk yourself right out of this house," Robbie said. "You're far too prideful. Get on your horse and ride off. You'll never work for the Slater ranch."

"You can't tell me what to do, Mex. Mr. Slater hired me; I'm working here."

"No," Jack said. "I said to show up ready for work. You've just insulted my son, and he's the one who hires and fires around here. Be on your way, boy, and quickly." Jack took a step toward Tony Sorrel. The man turned in complete disdain and strolled from the kitchen. He jumped on his horse and whipped it something fierce as he rode from the ranch.

"Good work, son," Jack said, whacking Robbie across the shoulders. "It sounded like you two may have had priors."

"He's one of the men who said terrible things about my mother, called me a Mex or worse. It would have gotten ugly if he'd stayed." He stood quietly for a moment, looking almost forlorn. "Why do people have to be that way? Be mean and ugly to another person? He could have had a good job here. Instead, he tried to show that he was better than us. Why?"

"Ignorance, mostly," Jack said. "Ignorant and stupid people try to make up for that by acting superior, which actually makes them look even more ignorant. Along with his lack of education, his feelings of superiority comes from fear, fear that he will be found to be just as stupid as he acts, as he is. To make up for his lacking in life's skills, he tries to bring those around him down to his level.

"You crushed him by ordering him out of the house and off the property. There may be consequences from that, Robbie. How much of an enemy you've made won't be known until you two meet again. Be aware of that," Jack said.

"I was small when he called my mother those terrible names and couldn't do anything about it. I'm almost his size right now and he's been my enemy for a long time. No, papa, it's Mr. Sorrel who will need to be aware next time we meet."

Jack watched Robbie walk out to the barn to work with Tiny Howard. He had a slight smile on his face and nodded his head, pouring a cup of coffee. "That's one heck of a boy we've gathered in, Mims."

"Reminds me more and more of someone else I knew a long time ago," she whispered. "Do you think we should fear that Sorrel boy? His mother is afraid of him, and I remember Sandra telling me stories about him and some of the other boys in town making her cry sometimes."

"I doubt we'll see him again," Jack said. "He's just an ignorant little boy who thinks he's better than everyone around him and probably too dumb to really do anything that we should fear."

"You're not hitting the bull's eye on finding help," Mims laughed. "One boy, out of shape. You were looking for two buckaroos and a camp cook and got one store clerk." She was laughing hard and Jack was caught up in the situation, laughing right along with her.

"I talked with Irene at the café and told her that we needed a cook. She promised to keep her ears open for one. The people in Skelton all have jobs they're happy with. Maybe we need to take a ride to Elko. Maybe I can steal a hand or two from Ted Wilson," Jack chuckled.

"You've seen almost fifteen hundred acres of good pasture, Tiny, and lots of cattle. Now comes the work part of the day. Ride back to the barn and you'll find Ezra Jackson there doing some carpentry work. Work with him the rest of the day. You'll clean stalls and work with Tater and the hogs tomorrow.

"Over the next few days, you'll work with most of the men, mending fences, moving cattle, learning how to work with the cattle. You'll drag your butt at the end of the day, eat more than you've ever eaten, and feel better than you've ever felt." Robbie and Tiny had been friends for several years and he was looking forward to working with him.

"If you have any questions, now is the right time to ask," Robbie said.

"Mr. Slater doesn't think I'll be a very good worker, Robbie, but I know I will be. When Mr. Paddock took me in, I was not heavy like I am now. I know I'll hurt like the devil, but I won't let you down. Just tell me what to do and I'll do it."

"That's good enough for me, Tiny. Head back to the barn and we'll talk more at dinner." Robbie turned his horse to ride back to where Ornery Pound and one of the buckaroos were checking some wolf track they'd run onto.

"Looks like at least four in this pack, Robbie, heading toward the water hole where you and Cactus had the run in with that lion." Ornery Pound was standing in a patch of ground pointing out the large tracks.

"Let's ride 'em down, then," Robbie said. "Four hungry wolves is more than I want around our beef. That feller in Skelton's payin' two dollars a skin, so you boys can pick up some beer money."

Ornery Pound took a swipe at Robbie's shoulder, mostly in jest. "I need a new headstall, new spur leather, and a fancy hat band more than a beer, you young whelp," he snarled. That brought a guffaw from Robbie and the other buckaroo. "Go jump in a pond somewhere," he said and rode off to find the wolves.

[16]

"His fever is not responding, Mrs. Riley," Doc Fowler said. He was sitting at his desk, shaking his head and Virginia was sitting across from him. She had been wringing her hands for three days, crying every minute, and unable to eat or even think. "The wounds were very bad to start with," Fowler continued, "and when the infection set in, it was almost more than Dick's system could handle."

He looked into the saddest eyes he'd had the misfortune of seeing in more years than he could count. *This woman has been beaten down to a stub, her children are out of control, there isn't enough money or food, and now her husband is about to die on her. God help her because I fear no one else will.*

"He's never been a strong man," she whimpered. "Will he be himself? I've heard bad things about people with high fevers."

"Virginia, you must understand. Dick may

not survive."

"He has to, doctor, he has to. Tell me about what he'll be like when he survives."

Doc Fowler scowled just a bit then softened to the poor woman's plight. After all, it certainly wasn't her fault her husband attacked a man who was holding a knife "All right then," he said. "A high fever can have an effect on a person's mind," Fowler said. "We won't know until it breaks, until his wounds heal enough for his own system to work toward being well and healthy again. Right now, the question is whether the man will live through this day.

"If he survives this terrible fever then he will most surely beat the wounds. The facial scars will be very evident for the rest of his life and that could affect his personality. He will have to accept the fact that he is responsible for what happened, also. Only time will answer the questions.

"For right now, Mrs. Riley, the best thing for you will be to take good care of your children, keep your business operating, and spend as much time as possible with Dick. You'll have to be stronger than you've ever been, I'm afraid."

Virginia Riley was far more afraid than Doc Fowler would ever know, for she was aware that she was pregnant. Even Dick Riley hadn't been told. "When can I bring him home?" she whimpered. "I can take care of him at home, can't I?"

"Give me another day to get this infection fully under control and you can take him home, Virginia." *She simply won't accept the fact that this man probably won't make the day. I wish sometimes that I could simply say straight out, what people don't want to hear.* "I'll see to it that you have all that you'll need to care for him at home. Just don't expect a fast recovery."

Fowler prepared a list of things she would need, medicines, bandages, and potions and told her that Paddock's Emporium would probably have everything. She had no idea what she would use to pay for all that. Dick Riley's leather business didn't make very much money and he always had far more inventory than was needed.

Virginia Riley was thin, had been sick often in her life, had two children that she couldn't control and now a third one on the way. She needed Dick Riley to be the man she thought she married, and now, he would never even be up to what she needed. Her parents were dead, his folks never liked her, and she had no friends in Skelton. *If Dick wasn't so all-fired proud of himself, so ar-*

210

rogant and standoffish, we might have more friends.

She was trying to hold back the sobs when she walked into the emporium. "Good morning, Mrs. Riley. Have you been to see Dick?" Valley Paddock saw only misery in the lady's tear-stained face. "How about a cup of coffee? Here, have a seat." He helped her into a chair by the wood stove, even though there was no fire going.

"Thank you," she said. She handed him the list from the doctor. "Doctor Fowler wants me to get all of this, but I don't know how I would pay for it. We don't have any money, Mr. Paddock," and the tears flowed heavier.

"First thing is to get Dick Riley well, Mrs. Riley. What did the doctor say?"

"He's having a hard time getting the fever down and the infection under control. He doesn't know if Dick will live," she bawled. "Tell me what happened out there for him to get hurt so bad. Doc Fowler seemed to think that Dick was responsible for his wounds. How could that be? What am I to tell the children."

She had her fists balled up and pressed to the sides of her head, tears flowed, and her eyes pleaded for help. Paddock feared that the woman wouldn't hold up if Dick Riley

211

passed over, and the children would be left with no one. *I can't tell her what that fool did. How on earth can I tell her that her husband walked right up to a killer after being told by a deputy to be aware the man might have a knife?*

Paddock's eyes watered right along with Virginia Riley's as he looked over the list she handed him. "I'll put this order together, Mrs. Riley, and then you need to get home with your children. Is there someone there who can help?"

"No, we don't have many friends, I'm afraid," she whimpered. "I'm sorry for breaking down like this. We'll be okay, Mr. Paddock." He knew better and also knew that he wouldn't, couldn't say anything. It was a sad sight as he handed her the small package and watched her trudge out the door. Paddock couldn't understand someone like Dick Riley, a man who wouldn't take any suggestion offered, wouldn't say thank you for any kindness, and scoffed at the concept of friendship with neighbors.

"Live or die; it won't matter much to Virginia and the children, I'm afraid. He'll never amount to much because of that attitude, and won't be able to if he lives," Paddock muttered.

"Talking to yourself, old man?" Jack Slater

212

was chuckling, standing in the open door to the large store.

"Jack. Well, good morning to you. Let's have some coffee, shall we?"

"Came to pick up Cactus Jack Faraday and bring him home. I'm also in the market for a ranch cook. It's too much for Mims and there's no reason for her to have to do all the cooking for that gang we have. Got any ideas?"

"I have one, but you won't like it. Virginia Riley is gonna need a bunch of help."

"You're right, I wouldn't like it," Jack said. "Mims needs help and Virginia Riley and her two children would need more help than Mims would get. That won't work. You've known me since I was a teenager, Valley. I believe in helping people, I've been whupped on by more than one ugly citizen of this fine country for stepping in to help someone, but the plan here is to help Mims."

"I know that Jack, but Virginia Riley is going to be desperate and soon. You're right, too, I know. She has two young children she can't control, and you have a wife who's pregnant and is faced with a heavy workload. I'm afraid though that Dick's attitude is going to affect Virginia."

"Riley has never been accepted in this

213

community because he has never accepted this community, Valley, and you know it. And, yes. His attitude will reflect on Virginia, and that's just as wrong as his attitude. None of that has any bearing on why Virginia would not work out as our ranch cook." Both men were right and both men knew there would not be an easy answer to Virginia Riley's predicament.

"If you think of someone, send word. For your information, Tiny Howard's a good worker. I didn't think he'd make the grade, but the boy gets right in and is learning the art of cattle work."

"Your food bill's gonna go up," Paddock laughed. "I'm glad he's working out. I'll send word if I think of someone to cook for you. You gonna be here for all the doin's over the fourth?"

"We'll be in for the rodeo and feast. Ornery and Ezra have been working those calves half to death and plan on winnin' the team roping." Jack headed over to Doc Fowler's to get Cactus Jack.

"Gonna be a slow ride back, Cactus. You settle in and get comfortable. Instead of the bunkhouse, Mims has you set up in Sandra's room, so she can nursemaid you some. Don't get used to it." They laughed as Jack helped his foreman into the buggy for the ride home. "Still hurtin' bad?"

"No," Cactus Jack said. "Only when I breathe, talk, eat, or cough. Other than that, no pain at all. What did the dcc say about Dick Riley? I heard you ask but I couldn't hear his answer."

"Doesn't think he'll live through the day. That knife did some serious damage and the infection is now completely through his whole body."

"Gonna be tough on his wife and kids," Cactus said. "You ever meet them? I met her one day at Jesse Winthrop's shop. Nice lady, not a stuck-up jerk like Dick. Kids are a bit rowdy, but I guess that ain't all bad."

"Hey, Tony. You doin' okay?" Ron Desmond rode into Skelton to bring Sorrel his last pay from the Double Diamond. "It's only six bucks but that's better than nothin', I guess."

"Yeah, it is. Thanks." Tiny Sorrel was still hot over not getting on at the Slater place and being humiliated by that Mexican kid. "Anything else bring you down here?"

"My uncle is Dick Riley, the leather man. Guess he got carved up some trying to catch that killer, Hickory Slim Obregon. Riley made my gun belt and holster and these spurs I'm wearing. Kinda proud of himself, but he does good work. Note from his wife said he might die of his wounds, though."

"You'd never catch me ridin' in a posse." Sorrel spit some tobacco juice across the yard.

"No," Desmond laughed. "The posse'd be chasing you." They both laughed loud and long at that comment. "You still rope? There's a good purse for the team ropin' at the Fourth of July Rodeo here in Skelton," Desmond said. "I could use a partner if you're up to it."

"You get the head, I'll get the heels, boy," Sorrel yelled. "Darn tootin' and I could use the money right now. Let's practice some at the stockyards. You got a place to stay? Ma won't like it, but you can bunk with us. She's just old and grouchy."

"Sounds good to me. I'll drop this stuff off and then go see old Riley. I'll meet you at the stockyards in a couple of hours. Sven Youngblood and Tank Martin are gonna enter, but I think we can beat them. Anybody around here plannin' on bein' in the competition?"

"Yeah, a couple of the Slater hands think they're gonna win. I'd like to pound some sand into Slater's face. Slater adopted some Mexican kid after his mother died. Now he thinks he's some kind of big-time rancher.

I'd like to whup him down to size."

"Sounds kinda personal, Tony. You got backup, you know that."

"Always good to know, Desmond. Alabama House Saloon is open, let's have a brew or two. The goofy old man that runs the place will drive you nuts with his stories, but he does make good beer."

Sorrel helped Desmond get his gear stashed and they walked to the Alabama House. Horseface Hawkins was stoking the stove when they walked in. "Mornin' men, whatcha gonna have?"

"Just a couple of beers, old man," Sorrel said. Desmond stood at the bar, looking at the fine, well-braided rawhide quirt hanging over the cash drawer.

"That's a finely made quirt there, old man. You make that?" Ron Desmond, like his uncle Dick Riley, worked leather and rawhide, and he was more than taken with the work. "Never seen that fine a piece of braiding. Kinda reminds me of work I've seen done by the Spanish Vaqueros down in California."

"We just ketched the man that had that. He was a murdering fool named Hickory Slim Obrogon, and we chased him crosst this desert out there. He used it mean like, all the time, but something as finely made as that shouldn't be used mean. Don't think I've seen you, before."

"Been riding mostly in the Diamond Valley but come up to see my friend Tony Sorrel here, and visit my uncle, Dick Riley. I think Uncle Dick was on that posse you're a-talking about."

"Shorely was," Horseface said. "Got hisself knifed up good, he did. Walked right into it like he didn't care. Don't know if he'll pull through or not. That Obregon feller was a wily one, for sure. If Riley don't make it, he'll be leaving a woman and kids behind."

"Shame about that," Desmond said. "I guess I better get over to see uncle Dick before he passes." He drank the beer down, whopped Sorrel across the back and headed over to Doc Fowler's office, just in time to hear the doctor moan as Dick Riley breathed his last. Desmond saw the doctor pull the sheet up over Riley's face and bow his head for just a moment.

"What can I do for you?" Fowler asked, turning at the scraping of a boot heel.

"That's my uncle Dick under there," Desmond said.

"I'm sorry for your loss, son. He was bad wounded. Virginia will need to be told."

"I'll go over there right away. Is there an

218

undertaker in town?"

"I'll take care of that for you. Mr. Peterson is a good man. Be gentle with Virginia, she's very frail. It's good to know she has kin in the area."

"Well, not blood kin, doctor. She married into our family and has never really seemed to fit. I've only met here once. Don't recall much about her though." Desmond glanced at the covered body of his uncle and walked out of the office. *This is a fine mess I've come to. Don't like that woman, always pressing Uncle Dick to be something, to make more money, to sell more stuff. Man needs to have time to hisself not always bein' pressed.*

"Mrs. Riley? I'm Ron Desmond, Dick's nephew. I'm comin' from the doc's and I've got bad news for you," Desmond said. He had his hat in his hands, scrunching the brim around and scuffing his boots some. Two children were running around in the house, screaming at each other, and Virginia stood stock still, her eyes already red from several days of crying.

"No!" She screamed it out and fainted dead away. Desmond caught her up before she fell to the porch deck and carried her into the house. He set he down on a sofa mostly covered in coats, slippers, sweaters, and junk. He swept it all onto the floor when he put her down.

"Now what do I do?" he murmured. He picked up a couple of the sweaters and placed them over Virginia, had no idea what to do with the children and their screaming, and walked to the door, just because it was still open. A woman, about forty or so was coming up the pathway.

"Did I hear Virginia scream? Who are you?" She asked in quick order. Before Ron Desmond could answer, the woman swept past him and into the house, hurrying to the sofa. "What's happened?" she demanded. "What have you done?"

"Nothin', ma'am," Desmond said. "I'm Dick Riley's nephew and I come to tell her that he's gone and died. Down at the doctor's. And she fainted. I didn't do nothin' to her."

"Dick's dead?" She slowly stood up and looked at the long tall cowboy. "Are you sure?"

"Saw the doc pull the sheet up. Yup, he's dead. I come to tell Virginia. I gotta go now. I'm glad you're here, them kids are buggers," Desmond said, squared his big floppy hat and walked out the door. *I sure don't want to ever have to do that again. And I ain't never gonna have kids.*

■ ■ ■ ■

"Just a couple of days to the big Fourth of July rodeo and celebration," Jack Slater said. The ranch crew and family were gathered for evening meal. "You and Ezra planning to win the roping money?"

Mims noticed that it got very quiet at the table, that Ornery was spending a lot of time looking at his supper plate, and Robbie seemed to be squirming around in his chair. "Okay, you two," she said. "What's going on?" The only sound in that large kitchen filled with buckaroos was the quiet bubbling of the coffee pot.

Robbie looked up at Mims with a half grin on his face, then turned toward Ornery Pound, and finally gave Jack a half smile. "I guess we have to fess it up, Ornery," he said. Ornery just grumped some and Robbie chuckled.

"Confess?" Jack asked. "Just what have you two been up to?" Several of the buckaroos at the table seemed to have to cough some and none would look anyone else in the eye. "Must be pretty serious stuff here, gentlemen."

"Ornery hasn't been practicing the team roping with Ezra." Robbie said. "He and I are entered in the team roping at the rodeo."

"You can't do that," Mims said, loud and strong. "You have a broken leg. You can't be out there ropin' steers. I won't have it." She stood at the stove, her balled up little fists buried in her hips, and eyes blazing, first at Robbie, then at Jack. Ornery Pound started to scoot his chair back as if to leave the table.

"No, no, Ornery," Jack said. "You sit right on back down there. Let's start at the top, shall we? How long has this been going on?"

"Since that lion attacked Cactus Jack," Robbie said. "I realized after I got him up on his horse and we made the hard ride into the ranch that I had been babying my broken leg and asked Ornery to work with me to get all my strength back. We moved some cattle, did some roping and Ornery did the ground work." Robbie paused, took a long breath, and Jack continued.

"And you discovered that the two of you were a good team."

"Yup," is all Ornery said, still staring at his plate.

"I won't have it," Mims said again.

"Now Mims," Jack said in a low, quiet voice. "If these two have been doing this for a few weeks it's obvious there's no danger in doing it for another few days. Is that why you didn't want me around the branding?"

Robbie had that half smile plastered across his face getting positive signals from Jack. "Ornery doesn't miss those heels, and I'm pretty good on the heads, and between us we dragged a couple of hundred steers to the fire." Robbie turned to Mims, his eyes pleading with her.

"My leg is fine now. It doesn't hurt. Besides, Doc Fowler's gonna take the cast off next week anyway."

"All you boys at the table," Jack said. "You been watchin' all this?" Heads nodded but nothing was said. "Looks like the crew wants you and Ornery to represent the Slater Ranch at the rodeo. He'll be fine, Mims. After all, look what we used to do at his age."

"We didn't do it with broken legs," she said. Then she broke into a wide smile, walked over and gave Robbie a big kiss on the top of his head. "As for you, Mr. Pound, I'm holding you responsible."

There was not one word of argument at the table as everyone resumed eating with vigor.

[17]

Skelton was in a flurry, with the Fourth of July celebration just a week away, young Dick Riley was dead, and his funeral needed to take place, and there was worry over Virginia and the children. It was generally known that Riley died because he didn't listen to what Deputy Smith had told him, but still, he was in the posse and he should be buried with dignity and honor. Problems weren't limited to Skelton.

"Some of the busiest times of the year and my foreman is out of commission, I can't replace my ranch cook, my wife is pregnant, and now you want me to believe that we have ten beautiful steers missing? Cut right out of the herd?" Jack Slater was at the kitchen table with Ornery Pound and Robbie.

"Fence was cut, two men cut out the steers and drove them north, toward Elko." Robbie and Pound rode straight to the ranch house after the discovery of the loss. "There's a good trail. With some hard riding, we can catch 'em."

"Good," Jack said, downing the last drops of coffee. "Let's ride. Robbie, you're with me. Ornery, find Ezra Jackson and bring him, and follow us. There's lots of ground to cover and we've got to do it fast." He had his horse saddled in quick time and he and Robbie headed out at a strong pace. "Got any ideas, son?"

"If they swing east they can tuck those steers into one of the canyons leading into the Ruby Mountains. If they continue north, they're gonna run into ranches and people. And if they go west, they would have to have a place waiting for them, a sagebrush corral in a swale. But they'd need water."

"I'm pickin' east, then," Slater chuckled.

It was at least a half hour before they reached the cut fence and picked up the trail of the stolen cattle. "You're right, just two riders. Gathering range calves before branding is one thing but cutting fence and taking branded stock is entirely different. This is more than rustling some steers, Robbie. Somebody's making a statement of some kind."

"I don't follow," Robbie said. "Taking ten big fat market ready steers is flat-out rustling in my book."

Jack had to chuckle. "It is that. But more, too. Five men could have taken that whole herd and probably made a lot of money on the market. So why just two men taking ten steers." They were riding at a fast trot easily following the trail left by the small herd of steers. The cattle were not being driven hard and Jack motioned for Robbie to slow down some.

"A lot of mighty fresh droppings, Rob. We're very close and need to be more than ready for anything that might happen. You stay on the trail, nice and slow, and I'm going to skirt out, maybe ride up on that side hill, get in the trees, and see what I can see." He spurred his fine gelding off to the right and rode through some thick sagebrush toward a rise half a mile off. The flanks of the side hill were covered in Piñon giving him good protection.

Robbie moved along at a strong walk following the herd and trying to keep an eye open for Jack as well. "I think I know what he meant," he murmured. "Taking something from us because of a personal slight? Or just anger? Taking most of the herd would have been pure and simple rustling." He had a slight smile thinking about who might be angry enough at his father to do that. He hadn't gone two hundred yards when he heard voices not too far in front and pulled his horse up quick. He moved off the well-marked trail and into some heavy brush. Robbie sat still, listening.

We're very close to where they would be crossing the main road into Skelton. I wonder if that's why they stopped. Maybe have some help waiting for them. Hope Ornery and Ezra catch up quick.

Two men were milling about at the drag of the herd, letting them move at their own pace. "We ought to get a good price on these little boys," one of them said. "That sale paper you made up should be enough for a quick sale. That railroad feller gonna meet us at the corrals?"

"That's what he said. Let's see if we can move them a little faster. Somebody's sure to spot that cut fence. Get up there, whoeee, whoeee." The two buckaroos started moving the herd along at a faster walk.

Robbie felt he knew who that second voice belonged to but couldn't put a name to it, He waited a couple of minutes, to give the two outlaws a chance to get some in front of him before he spurred his horse into a walk.

Jack was tucked into a stand of pines and watched the herd from a high point on the side hill. He saw the two cowboys kick the herd up to a faster walk and rode back down to join Robbie, getting there about the same time as Ornery Pound and Ezra Jackson. Robbie held everyone up to tell what he'd head.

"You're sure he said railroad man?" Jack asked.

"Yes, that's what he said. I know that voice, but I can't place who it belongs to. I'll bet they have runnin' iron ready to change the brands, too."

"That was Tony Sorrel you heard, son. I recognized him immediately. This is how ignorant fools think they can get even when they think they've been slighted. We wouldn't hire the fool, so he rustles our cattle. But not this time."

"Take 'em now, boss?" Ornery asked.

"No, they're heading for a small canyon about five miles in front of us. Let's follow them in and find out who this railroad man is who buys stolen cattle." Robbie could see the anger in Jack's face and everyone could hear it in his voice. "Maybe this is why Sorrel came back to town, eh? Lost his job trying to steel someone else's herd.

"Okay, let's spread out wide and walk behind these fools nice and slow. I really want to know who that railroad feller is."

Robbie moved out far to the left and Ezra Jackson did the same to the right, leaving Jack and Ornery Pound to cover the middle, and they rode for what Jack figured would be about another five or so miles.

"I ain't never done nothin' like this before, Tony, and I'm not sure I like it. I've rode for some good brands, done some good work, and if anyone finds out about this, I'll never work again." Ron Desmond was a fine buckaroo and had ridden for some of the big ranches in California and Nevada and was having serious second thoughts about helping his old friend. "Tony, you said you made a deal for these steers, but now you're talking like maybe we stole 'em. Rustling cattle? They hang men for this."

"A little late for that kind of thinkin', isn't it?" Sorrel had a sneer in the comment and a snicker to go along with it. "Ain't nobody gonna catch us. We'll be at the corrals in an hour, brand out these ten steers, get our money, and be gone. We'll be drinking whiskey at the Alabama House tomorrow morning, in plenty of time for your uncle's burial." Desmond didn't laugh along with Sorrel and nudged his horse into a little faster walk.

The hour turned into an hour and a half

and the two men moved the small bunch of steers into a brush corral inside a shallow canyon. A single rider rode out from some pine trees to welcome them. "Right on time, Tony. I got some good coals nice and hot for your irons. Have any trouble?"

"Not a bit, Mr. Scruggs," Sorrel said, stepping off his horse. Desmond had the steers in the corral and Sorrel and Scruggs moved brush into the open space to close it off. "Got ten nice fat ones for you. You bring the money?"

"You bet, five dollars a head just like we said. Let's get started on those brands." Simon Scruggs already had the ten steers sold for six fifty each and wanted to get them moving fast. Scruggs was a laborer with the railroad but also dealt in many illegal activities, like selling stolen beef, guns, jewelry, or anything else of value. He was a slimy little dude, known to cheat at cards and sell watered down rye.

"Thank you for catching up my steers there, Mr. Sorrel," Jack Slater yelled as he and the three others rode down on Sorrel, Desmond, and Scruggs. Slater had his Winchester cocked and ready to fire, while Robbie and Ornery Pound rode to the left of the group and Ezra Jackson flanked Jack on the right.

"Drop your weapons, nice and slow. No reason to die on such a nice summer's day," Jack Slater had the rifle pointed in the middle of Tony Sorrel's chest and Simon Scruggs, standing next to the young outlaw grabbed for his puny little single shot pistol. Ezra Jackson reached out with the barrel of his Henry and smashed the man's arm. The gun tumbled into the dirt with Scruggs screaming in pain, his arm hanging limp and bending awkwardly from broken bones.

"That was more than stupid," Jack said. "Now, Mr. Sorrel, I want you to kick that little pea shooter away and help your partner with his arm." Ezra Jackson was off his horse, the big Henry staring Scruggs in the face. He picked up the small weapon and tucked it in his belt and moved Sorrel and Scruggs over near what would have been the branding fire. Jack picked up Sorrel's weapon.

Jack Slater motioned for Desmond to dismount and move to the fire as well. Desmond, looking down the barrel of Robbie's Winchester shucked his weapon and stepped down from his horse. There was a black cloud of doom in Desmond's face as he made the slow walk. Robbie gathered up his weapon, then gathered all the horses and got them tied off.

"Well, this is an interesting little group, eh?" Jack Slater had the men sitting in the dirt near the fire while Ezra Jackson and Robbie tied their hands behind their backs. Ornery Pound stood off a few feet with his rifle at the ready. "When we bring you in you'll be sent to the Carson City Prison where you'll be poundin' rocks for a long time to come."

"Heck no," Ornery Pound snarled. "String 'em up, boss. Rustlin' cattle's a hangin' offense. Some good trees right over yonder."

"He's right, boss," Jackson said. "No sense wasting any more time on 'em."

Jack sat down on his haunches with just a hint of a smile on his face. He took a quick glance at Sorrel and only saw blazing anger, not fear. "Introduce your friends, Sorrel," he said. Sorrel spit into the fire and didn't say anything. "Well, Ezra, I'd like to hang him, got no manners, ignorant and stupid, and ugly to boot, but I guess we'll just bring these fools into town.

"Robbie, you and Ezra drive those steers back to the herd and fix that fence, and Ornery, let's you and me drive these ugly and mean outlaws to Jimmy Delgado's little jail house. Git up, fool," Jack said, kicking sand at Tony Sorrel.

The three outlaws were boosted into their

saddles, hands tied behind their backs and their boots tied together under the horse. Jack rode in front with the three outlaw's horses tied off as if pack animals and Ornery Pound rode behind, that big Winchester resting comfortably in the crook of his arm. "Main road's about half a mile behind us, so we'll make good time getting back to town. Any of you boys feel like playing jack rabbit you might want to know that Mr. Pound there won the Christmas turkey shoot last year with that rifle."

Robbie had the small bunch of cattle lined out and, on the trail, back to the ranch, wondering just what it was that made Sorrel want to rustle cattle. "That guy's just stupid, Ezra, trying to run off some of our beef."

"That he is, boy. He gonna pay for that, too. Jack's lettin' him off easy."

"Going to prison doesn't sound like easy to me," Robbie said.

"Easier than hangin'."

It was a long slow ride back to the ranch. They let the small bunch graze along the way, stopped for a short break at a water crossing. They had the herd back in their own pasture, the fence fixed and were in the barn before sunset. "Where's Jack?"

Mims asked when they walked in.

Robbie told her the story as he and Ezra joined the rest of the crew already eating their supper. "Papa and Ornery will probably stay in town tonight. That Tony Sorrel was angry, and when papa wouldn't hire him, he said some bad things about us. He was never nice to me or mama when we lived in town. Even so, none of that is any reason to take our cattle."

"Jack says he's never been much of a man. Sometimes the world seems to be filled with bad people, I'm afraid. I've met my fair share, and so did your mother." Reflections of her bad times almost brought Mims to tears. She looked at her long and broad kitchen table filled with strong hungry men and thanked her lucky stars. "It's men like Jack that make it good to be alive. Jack is one of those men who are proud to be responsible for their actions. Men like Tony Sorrel will never be.

"You understand responsibility, Robbie. Sandra taught you right, and you know what Jack's talking about when he assigns chores and gives out his to-do lists." They had to chuckle over that. Jack sometimes had lists that took up more than two pages of paper. "It's just like today. You saw the problem brought it to Jack's attention and rode with him to save the cattle.

"Then, brought the cattle back and fixed the fence. It needed to be done, you knew that, felt a responsibility to get it done. Get 'er done, pard," she joked, bringing guffaws from the crew at the table. "I've got a Dutch oven full of peach cobbler and a pitcher full of chilled cream when you boys clean your plates."

It was a satisfied cow camp that night that heard two riders come in about ten o'clock. "Hope there's something left on that stove," Jack chuckled, unsaddling his horse. "What did you make of that young man who was riding with Sorrel. Just didn't strike me as a fool outlaw."

"He had cowman written all over him, Jack. I'd be willing to bet he got sucked into something he didn't want to be in. A big barrel of it. Gave me the impression he wanted to say something." The two put their horses in the corral and walked to the big house. "I could eat two chickens and half a hog right now, boss."

"I'll eat the other half," Jack laughed. "I think you're right, though. Young Desmond has probably been friends with Sorrel and got tricked into getting involved. That Scruggs feller, though, he's pure outlaw from his mama's teet."

■ ■ ■ ■

"Fourth of July weekend, Jack, and just look at this old town of ours. Flags, bunting, music, half beeves roasting in pits, and a rodeo about to take place." Horseface Hawkins had one of those half beeves roasting on a spit turned by big Tiny Howard with help from Tater Thompson. The parade through town would lead everyone to the livestock sales yards and the rodeo. One town-wide feast would take place immediately afterward.

"My heavens, I love a parade," the old veteran said. He was in full uniform, representing the First Alabama Volunteers, Confederate Army. "Did you know I was in the Union Army before the war, and then fought in the Indian wars in the Union Army after the big war. I wore the most stripes though in the Confederate Army," he joshed.

Rooster Murphy was standing alongside dressed in U.S. Army blue, both men showing the many stripes of high-ranking sergeants. They were about to lead the parade that would wind its way the full quarter mile of downtown Skelton, Nevada. Robbie and Ornery Pound would ride in the parade along with the other rodeo contestants, Mims was off at the community center helping the women put together all the trimmings to go with the roast beef, and little Maybelle had her arms wrapped around Jack Slater's neck, sound asleep in his arms.

"Anybody seen Jimmy Delgado this morning?" Jack asked.

"Probably sticking close to his not very secure jail with those cattle rustlers." Jesse Winthrop almost spit out. "That Sorrel boy never was worth much, but Dick Riley's nephew getting' involved sure caught me by surprise."

"There's something wrong with that picture," Jack said. "That's what I want to talk to Delgado about. See if either of them varmints have said anything."

"Your friend, Ted Wilson, is in town, Jack. He went to see young Desmond yesterday. Maybe you want to find him before you talk to Delgado." Winthrop nodded toward Paddock's big store. "He was at the emporium earlier."

Jack nodded thanks and headed toward Paddock's hearing Horseface starting a long discussion on how best to roast a big beef over open coals. "That man lives a full life," he muttered walking into the big store. "Hi, Ted, you marching in the big parade?"

"Jack, glad to see you. No, but I'm ropin' against that young boy of yours a little later. You here to buy me off?"

"Not enough gold in the world to buy you off. But, I do want to talk to you about a young man we found running off with some of my beef. I understand you know this Ron Desmond fool."

"Two days ago, I would have argued about you calling Desmond a fool, but he was caught red-handed. He's a fine cowman, Jack. Worked a couple of seasons for me and is currently riding for an outfit down in the Diamond Valley. I don't know what brought all this on. It simply isn't what I would have expected of the boy."

"I was hoping to talk to him before the parade got started. Join me?"

"I've seen nothing in that feller that says outlaw, other than the fact he had my beef. I just feel there's something we don't know," Jack said, and Wilson nodded.

The two walked the short half block to Delgado's office and jail shaking their heads in wonder. "Any chance of us talking with Desmond out of Sorrel's hearing?" Jack asked the young deputy. "Maybe sit out on your porch with some hot coffee?"

"He's pretty angry, Jack. You keep a good close eye on him. He's big, strong, and

238

ready to run."

"I'll be fully responsible, Jimmy," Jack said. The two cowmen brought three chairs out onto the porch and poured big mugs of coffee while Delgado went into the jail area to bring Desmond out. They were settled into chairs with one empty between them for the cowboy.

"Mornin' Ron," Ted Wilson said. "I think you've met Jack Slater. We need to hear your story, son. You've worked on my place; I helped you find that ride you've got now in Diamond Valley. What happened?"

Desmond had an ugly scowl on his face but accepted the cup of coffee and took a long drink. He glared at Jack, turned his eyes down to the porch planks, and sighed, almost gently. "I wish I knew, Mr. Wilson."

"What Slater explained to me isn't what I thought I knew about you. Why don't you start at the beginning and tell us what happened?"

Desmond looked up at Jack who gave him a nod and a gentle smile, then over at Wilson who did the same. Jack thought the young man looked conflicted as if he wanted to trust his old boss Wilson, feared Jack and felt wronged. He gave a long, almost tearful sigh and told his story.

"Tony Sorrel was fired from the Bar XO,

where I ride, and I brought him his last pay. We weren't really close friends, but I needed to come here because my step-uncle was Dick Riley who was killed riding with a posse. I wanted to be at his funeral, meet his wife and children. He and my step-dad are excellent leather and silver artisans, actually."

"That's something I would have expected of you, Ron. Keep going, please," Ted Wilson said.

"Tony said he made a deal to move some cattle from a large open pasture north of town to a buyer who was some kind of railroad man. It was when Tony cut the fence that I knew something was wrong, but he said the nearest gate was a couple of miles down the fence and he had been given the okay to do it."

"And you believed him?" Jack asked.

"He insisted it was okay, was so casual about it all, and seemed to know which ten steers were to be moved. He seemed to not care if some hand rode up or not. Yes, Mr. Slater, at that point I did believe him." Jack just shook his head, took a long sip of coffee and didn't really know what to say.

"Mr. Sorrel doesn't need to know we've had this conversation," Wilson said. "I'm going back to Elko in the morning and have a talk with the district attorney. Will you testify against Tony Sorrel? Corrigan might drop the charges."

"Are you as good a buckaroo as Wilson says you are?" Jack asked.

Desmond sat very still, holding his mug of coffee in both hands, looking back and forth at the two men. It took a minute, but he finally said, "Yes, to both questions. Tony lied to me, I would never steal another man's beef, and all I wanted to do was pay my respects to my uncle. I'll tell the district attorney or the judge the truth.

"In answer to your question, Mr. Slater, I think Mr. Wilson will agree, I am ready for my first job as cow-boss at some big spread. Something like this will ruin my life. I was raised moving cattle, been on big trail drives, can doctor, pull calves, and would rather sit in a saddle for twenty-four hours before sitting in a chair for ten minutes."

Jack and Wilson laughed at the comments watching Desmond blush some from the response. Jack Slater learned his way around cattle, the range, ranch operations from an old cowman when he rode in Wyoming and could understand what Desmond said.

"If Wilson can work this out, you come see me, Desmond. You won't start as cow-boss," he chuckled, "but a job would be there for you. I think you're in the middle of something that could ruin the rest of your life. You seem like an honest if very naive young man."

Desmond's stomach was churning, he was sure he would start crying at any minute and fought that as fiercely as he could. "I'm twenty-one years old, Mr. Slater. I've been working stock since I was fourteen. I'm sorry." He stood straight up, tried a couple of times to say thank you, just stammered, emotions finally getting the better of him. He collapsed back into the cane-back chair and held his head in both hands, fighting the losing battle to tears.

"I'll do my absolute best, Ron," Ted Wilson said. The two men nodded to Jimmy Delgado. "Keep him away from Sorrel until you hear from Wild Bill Connors, will you, Jimmy?" Delgado ushered the man back into the office, each carrying chairs.

[18]

"We might have got beat, Robbie Slater, but we gave them one heck of a fight. They didn't win 'till that last calf went down." Ornery Pound was wiping half a ton of dust from his pants and shirt as the two unsaddled their horses to head to the big feed in the community center.

"I thought we had it, Ornery," Robbie said. "How can you lose by one second?"

"You caught up that steer in nothin' flat, Robbie. I must've been a little slow catchin' those feet."

"That's nonsense, Ornery. Old Ted Wilson's gonna gloat a bit while we're eatin' I'm afraid. They sure were good. One stupid second," Robbie almost snarled and Ornery had to chuckle.

"I bet you'll think about that one second for the whole year until next Fourth of July," he cackled, and the two of them punched each other on the shoulders and laughed all the way to the community hall. "Even for second place we're gonna get fifty bucks, pardner," Ornery Pound said.

"Good show, you two," Jack Slater roared when they joined the family table. "That was some fine ridin' and ropin' out there. I thought you had it right up until they announced the time. I could see Ted Wilson's face and I bet he was sure he'd lost."

Ted Wilson and his heeler, Josh Higgins, walked up to the table, each sticking his hand out. "I thought it was yours, men, I really did. I think between the four of us we taught Elko County buckaroos how to head and heel today." There was some rowdy handshaking and shoulder punching, loud laughter, and it was the clanging of the dinner bell that broke up the melee.

It took Jack Slater a moment to realize that Robbie was as big as Ornery Pound, almost as big as the young buckaroo that partnered with Wilson and was drinking a cold beer from a large mug. "Whoa, there, cowboy," he joked. "You're a little young for that, aren't you?"

"No, he's not, Jack. One cold beer? For the way he was riding? Yeah, that boy is okay," Wilson laughed. Jack nodded to Robbie who coughed just a bit with each swallow of cold brew. His smile lit the whole community hall.

That is until Doc Fowler walked up. "I don't remember ever saying that a patient of mine could enter a rodeo contest wearing a cast. Young man, I want you in my office first thing tomorrow morning and heaven help you if you've destroyed any of the work I did to make that leg perfect again."

"He came within one second of being perfect, Doc," Ted Wilson quipped. Fowler just shook his head, glared at everyone, and joined the food line.

Ornery Pound drove the buggy with Mims and Maybelle, while Jack and Robbie trailed behind for the long ride back to the ranch. The road was busy with ranch hands and other families making their way home from the festivities. "I'll just walk these old boys home, Mims, so you and that pretty little girl have a nice nap. Might even sing you a little song along the way." Ornery had a bit of a raspy voice when he was talking or yelling at someone, but his entire personality changed when he sang, often strumming a beat up old mandolin he carried. Said he started singing when he was just a pup, riding on the Texas cattle drives.

"That would be very nice, Ornery. Maybelle always enjoys your singing. Just pretend we're a couple of nervous heifers on the Kansas plains," she laughed.

"I think I ate five pounds of Horseface's beef," Robbie said. He and Jack were about ten yards or so behind the buggy. "He sure was right about knowing how to roast a side of beef."

"It only works if you start off with fine beef," Jack said. "All the mop sauce in the world won't fix tough meat."

"Must have been one of ours, then," Robbie laughed. "I heard you and Mr. Wilson went to the jail this morning. That fool Sorrel have anything to say? I'll wager he'll be an outlaw the rest of his life."

"I don't wish that on anyone, but you might be right. We went to see Ron Desmond, not Tony Sorrel. I know you and Ornery were waiting for the parade to start but I wish you'd been with us. That young man isn't an outlaw, Robbie. There's not a criminal bone in his body."

"Well, he sure as the dickens stole our cattle."

"Do you know what the word coerced means?" Robbie nodded, and Jack continued telling what Desmond had told them and what Ted Wilson planned to do when he got back to Elko. Robbie listened carefully, nodded a time or two, but also shook his head slightly, a time or two.

"You think I'm wrong asking Desmond to join our outfit if the judge and district attorney agree?" Jack asked.

Robbie rode in silence for a few minutes chewing hard on what Jack was suggesting. "I'm still mighty young, just fourteen, probably the luckiest boy in the world having you and Mims as my parents, learning cattle work from Cactus Jack Faraday and Ornery Pound, and I can't picture me riding off with a friend after cutting someone's fence and stealing cattle." He rode quietly, shaking his head ever so slightly, glancing from time to time at Jack.

"That was well said, son," Jack said. "Unlike Ron Desmond, you're a thinker, not just a doer. Desmond is ten years your senior in age and five years your junior in thinking. The right word is naive. He simply believed what Sorrel told him without thinking, contemplating, understanding. You wouldn't do that, neither would Cactus, or any of our young hands."

"And you think he learned his lesson, as you like to say?" Robbie asked. He was chuckling some, giving Jack a slight prod.

"When I was just a year or two older than you, I was so naïve that I let an outlaw ride right into my camp, spend the night, and try to ride off with everything I owned the next morning."

"You lost everything?" Robbie hadn't heard this story before and couldn't imagine Jack being bamboozled by anyone. "Everything?"

"No, but I almost did. I literally woke up in time, shot the miserable thief and took his possibles. I learned my lesson, Robbie." Jack laughed and poked Robbie. "It took another lesson or two down the line, but I learned. I think Desmond's education began with one huge and difficult lesson."

They rode in silence for some time each deep in their thoughts. It was late when they turned down the lane that led to the Slater ranch house. "You know something, papa? I think now I know why mama says you're an amazing man. Every minute I spend with you, there's a lesson involved, and my life gets just a little more complicated because of it."

They were laughing loud as Ornery pulled the buggy up to the kitchen hitch rail and they rode into the barn. "Glad to hear that, son."

"Well, good morning Mr. Faraday," Jack said when Cactus Jack walked gingerly to

248

the breakfast table. "You must be feeling much better." Several of the hands jokingly disagreed with the boss.

"I've been working hard like old Doc Fowler told me to, and I think I can take over barn duty, now, boss."

"Working hard at hanging around the ranch house and eating all day," Ornery said to everyone's delight.

"Speaking of which, I'll just join you boys for some breakfast," Cactus said. "To be somewhat serious for a minute, though. I've been working on strengthening those stomach muscles that were torn apart by that cat, and I've taken my horse out a few times when no one was around. I'm feeling pretty good, really."

"Best news I've heard in a long time," Jack said. "Barn duty it is."

"If he's feeling that good he can take over the hog pens, too," Tater Thompson laughed.

"Where does that leave me?" Tiny Howard said. He looked like he might just cry as he said it. He was sure he was about to be sent back to Skelton and work in the Paddock Emporium. That, of course, would be considered a disgrace. Over the several weeks of ranch work his bulk had toughened up considerably, and he thought the Slater's were happy with his work.

"You'll be riding with us, Tiny," Robbie said. "No more barn duty for a while." Tiny's crestfallen face lit up like a lantern, and he had to control himself and not yell yippee or something equally stupid.

Jack and Cactus Jack led the hands out into the corrals watching the sky turn from morning reds to daylight blue. "Another hot one. Robbie, make sure all the water tanks are full and take this opportunity to introduce Tiny Howard to our irrigation systems. Ezra, you ride with them, too," Jack said. "Tater, grab two men and join me and Ornery moving the big herd into the far west range. By golly, it's a good summer."

Cactus Jack watched the men saddle up and ride off wishing he was going with them. Any buckaroo worth half his salt would rather spend his days in the saddle than on his feet. "I can almost feel that horse under me right now," Cactus muttered. As he walked back toward the barn, he noticed he was holding his hands as if he were holding a set of reins and had to chuckle some.

It took several weeks before the stomach muscles started responding to his exercise program and now that they were, he was fired up. Two hours of mucking out stalls and forking hay and Cactus Jack Faraday was ready to call it a day. He sat down on a bale of hay, wiping sweat and dirt from his face, the slightest smile spread across his long face.

"Glad old Jack ain't in here right now. I am about as weak as a ten-year-old boy on a bad day." The big mountain lion had ripped his stomach wide-open and right now Cactus Jack could feel every inch of every torn muscle. "If I live to be a hundred years old it won't give me enough time to thank Robbie for saving my life."

He sat on that bale for another few minutes, had a big drink of water, and walked out to the corrals, roped his best horse and saddled up for a short ride. Throwing the saddle up brought a loud groan from the Texan along with a smile knowing he got it up on the first try. Riding at a gentle lope is a fine way to keep the old belly in shape and he needed to get those muscles just as strong as they were when that cat hit him.

An hour later he flopped down in a chair at the kitchen table, sweat still streaming across his face. "I feel like an old man, Mims. Don't remember a time feeling this weak. Don't be tellin' anybody," he chuckled. "Getting' enough back-talk from those buckos."

"Can't do it all in a couple of days, Cactus. I even remember hearing the doctor telling you that," Mims said. "You do a couple of hours, take a break and do a couple more, and pretty soon you'll be doing a whole day. Eat a bowl of stew and go back out to the barn and try not to clean it bright and shiny in one day."

He was laughing as he asked Mims where Robbie was. "I haven't seen that boy all day."

"Went into Skelton early this morning to see Doc Fowler. He's really angry that Robbie was in the roping contest at the rodeo."

"That boy's got spark, Mims. He'll win that contest with the doc." Cactus chuckled all afternoon, raking, forking, moving bales of hay and straw, thinking over and over how Mims had given him a good old-fashioned 'mama' talk without breaking into laughter. He took several breaks during the day and was surprised when the first of the crews rode in for the day.

Even old Tater Thompson could have done what I did in four hours or so, but son of a gun, I put in a full day for the first time since that cat attacked me. He was wiping sweat from his face when he walked to the corral to help the boys unsaddle and wipe their ponies down. "You boys need to know I'll

252

be back riding herd on you-all within this next week. I'm feelin' pretty good right about now."

It was after supper when he was sitting on the porch with Jack that he admitted, "I about killed myself out there, boss."

"Mims told me you looked done in at the dinner bucket. I need you, Cactus Jack, back as my foreman, back as the best cattleman in Nevada. I'm gonna make a bid on Fred Meyer's place to our southwest, which means more hands, more work, and a strong foreman. I want to make Robbie cow boss. Can you bring him up to speed?"

Cactus laughed softly and rubbed his tender stomach. "Just as soon as I get myself up to speed, Jack. I've been working with Robbie all along with that idea in mind. That boy's got a good mind, has a good feel for what he's doing. He knows this country even better than we do," he chuckled.

"He's getting very good with the breeding program, those bulls we're holding back and the heifers you picked up to increase the breed are going to be fine, as well. Robbie will make a fine cow boss, Jack, and I'll be up to full steam in a week or so."

[19]

Jack Slater had nine men gathering the herds from the various pastures and ranges, getting ready to move the steers to Elko along with the separated cull heifers. It was a long process getting prepared for a drive like this. Along with all the animals that would go north with the drive, after separating they had to move the heifers and bulls into their late fall and winter pastures.

The summer had been a good one and as fall could almost be felt in the air, Jack had a satisfied feeling about his life. His foreman was back after the nasty ordeal with the mountain lion, his son was big, strong, and intelligent, and his wife's pregnancy was coming along nicely. "Bringing this herd in just about completes a good year.

"It's almost like a dance, Robbie," Jack said as they milled through a group of heifers. "Eventually everyone ends up where they're supposed to be but the first few steps are confusing."

Robbie had to laugh thinking about dancing with a cow and made like he was going to kiss one, bringing a guffaw from Jack. "Cactus said there's a whole new livestock operation in Elko. Where will our steers go when we sell them?"

"Two big markets will get most of them," Jack said. "The Virginia City, Reno, Carson City market is big, and the Salt Lake market is big. I'm glad you're studying breeding programs. You know, a hundred years ago cattle were raised for their hides. The meat was pretty tough. The hide market is still good but it's the meat that counts today, and breeding to that is what we want.

"Our steers eat sweet grass from the time they're weaned and finished at the livestock pens on sweet corn, and that meat is tender and juicy. That's your job, cow boss," Jack laughed.

"You said it's been a good year, dad, but what about all that trouble with that outlaw and the people that we've lost? Part of my year has been good, but I don't really think I've had a good year." Robbie would be fifteen by the end of the year, had lost his mother, had a broken leg, and was stabbed deep by a hay rake. He was also remembering the death of Phineus Cassidy and the rustling episode.

Jack had to sit back in the saddle and think on that comment. "Maybe you're right, son. May not have been the best year of my life, but I think it's been one of the good ones. We've lost some wonderful people, and that's never a good thing, but we've also made some fine gains in other areas."

They rode through the herd and toward the ranch house, continuing to discuss how life offers up challenges of problems at every opportunity. They ended the ride meeting up with Cactus Jack and Ornery Pound on the way. "We'll be ready to move 'em out day after tomorrow, boss. Close to seven hundred steers and about a hundred cull heifers and bulls. We've got a good crew and it's just a three or four-day drive. Not like moving them a thousand miles out of Texas. I grew up on stories about long cattle drives, searching for water, fighting Indians and rustlers."

"I could tell you some stories," Ornery Pound said. "I was about Robbie's age when I made my first ride on the Chisholm Trail."

"Those were long trails," Jack said. "We had our own yards right at the rails in Wyoming. Brought 'em down out of high mountain summer range and into boarding pens in one drive."

"No, sir, boss. We're gonna drive these critters nice and slow, let 'em eat when they're hungry, and bring 'em in ready for Horseface's open pit bar-b-que."

"Good, Cactus." Jack had to chuckle remembering all the stories about those trail drives and in one respect glad he didn't have to and on the other hand wished he had. "I'm gonna ride on ahead and make all the arrangements in Elko. Tell the boys they will have two days to blow their earnings and then they have to be back on the ranch if they want to keep their jobs. Mims and I are leaving in the morning."

Jack was driving the buggy with his saddle horse tethered behind. Mims and Maybelle were snuggled in a big blanket on the seat next to him for the twenty-five-mile ride to Elko. "I wish we could ride up Lamoille Canyon again like we did that one time," Mims said. "It's so beautiful, particularly this time of the year."

The canyon was a deep cut in the Ruby Mountains, extending for many miles into the high range of mountains. At the deep end one could look at rock walls extending a thousand feet up or more, and if one pursued the trail at the high end of the canyon, one would find a lake above ten thousand feet filled with golden trout. They only exist in lakes above ten thousand feet.

"There's no reason we can't on the way home," Jack said. "We won't have a herd to worry about, Cactus Jack will take care of the crew. Robbie will like it for sure. We'll do some fishing in the creek, maybe even bring home a big buck."

It was late evening when they checked into the hotel. "I'm awfully tired, Jack," Mims said when Jack asked where she might want supper. Jack arranged their gear, there was already a fire going in the wood stove, and he got Mims and Maybelle settled. "Our new baby is learning how to move about, and that old bumpy buggy ride didn't help any."

"I probably shouldn't have brought you," Jack said. "You and Maybelle go to bed. I'll have supper sent up if you like. I'm going out to see Ted Wilson in the morning. You and Maybelle stay in town, get some rest, do a little shopping."

"Just order me something light. Maybe hide some biscuits in the back of the barn." She giggled like a little girl to Jack's delight. "Maybelle needs new winter stuff. She's growing so fast, Jack. It's fun to watch her. Did you know that Robbie was taking her out on his horse once in a while? She adores that boy."

"He misses his mother very much, Mims, but almost every day he tells me how much he loves you and Maybelle. He's quite the young man. I'm glad you've kept up on his education, too."

"He does two hours in his room every night, Jack. He shows me every morning what he's been working on. He's much better with his numbers than I am. I think he's teaching me, and his reading has improved many times over. He got two books from the University of Nevada dealing with cattle and animal breeding."

"That was a brilliant idea establishing that university in Elko. It's been there since 1874, and now they're talking about moving it to Reno. I don't think that's right," Jack said.

"Sometimes I don't have any idea what Robbie's talking about in the morning. He's actually taking some kind of course by mail. He's growing so fast. Sandra was small, so his father must have been a big man. He's much taller than I am already."

"You get some rest and I'll send something up. After supper, I want to hear the latest market reports, so I'll spend a bit of time in the clubroom. I won't be late." Jack gave her a kiss on the forehead, tickled Maybelle and left the room.

"Herd's due in late this afternoon, Ted, but I wanted to find out what the outcome was on Ron Desmond's situation. Looks like you're a little late getting your gather underway."

"Some fool found some gold up north in Wyoming and me and other ranchers around here lost half our crews. Man's got a good job, gets fed good food, and runs off like an idiot at the word of a gold strike. When they come back with their tails between their legs they might not find me so welcoming.

"Cows will be in and safe well before the first big snows, though. Park yourself, Jack. I'll get the coffee pot and a couple of mugs and we'll talk about young Desmond." Wilson headed for the large kitchen and Jack found a big leather chair near the fireplace and made himself comfortable. "This looks like a hunting lodge instead of a living room, Ted. Did you shoot all these? The only thing you don't have stuffed in here is a jack rabbit."

"This was a different country when I got here, Jack. I've been on this old spread of mine for more than twenty years now."

"Even in the short time I've been here, there have been some big changes," Jack said. "I wonder what's in store for us in this bright new century heading our way. A conversation like this might take a week or more, Ted," he laughed. "Let's get back to Ron Desmond."

"As we talked earlier, Jack, you remember that the district attorney wasn't quite as receptive to our ideas as we were and wanted to prosecute all three men to the limit of the law. It took some heavy prodding from District Judge Emmitt Frazier to convince him the boy would be lost to society if he was jailed for his mistake."

"I remember Frazier," Jack said, "from that episode with the sheriff and the bank robbery. He was a tough old codger. Mellowed some, has he?"

"Not really. Word is he'd hang his mother if he thought she deserved it." They laughed at the comment and Ted Wilson poured some more coffee. "Fact is, Frazier spent several hours over a couple of days talking with Desmond and said about the same thing you did. The boy's just too willing to believe anything that's said to him and will help a friend at the drop of a hat.

"He had no more intention of stealing your cattle than he did of marrying your daughter. Naïve is not strong enough of a word to describe Ron Desmond. Our fine Elko County District Attorney stepped aside and said it would be up to the judge."

"How about Sheriff Connors? Wild Bill is pretty tough on outlaws. I would think he and the DA would want some satisfaction." Jack sat back in the big chair and took a drag on his cigar. "I was in favor of hanging all three, you might remember."

"Indeed, I do, but when you had a long talk with Desmond, you agreed with me that the boy was simply stupid, not a criminal, had no intent to rob you, was led into it by Tony Sorrel. Connors rode with Jimmy Delgado and Charlie Smith bringing the three here and had a chance to spend time with Desmond.

"Connors said he would go along with whatever Judge Frazier comes up with. Tony Sorrel and Simon Scruggs will face the judge the second week of November and Frazier's likely to send them to Carson City for five or ten years. Connors is holding Desmond as a trusty, working as a janitor in the courthouse. Absolutely no contact with Sorrel or Scruggs."

"That would be best," Jack said. "Even though Desmond had no intent to steal my beef — he did. What is the judge's final decision? Desmond must face punishment even if there was no intent. He has to face the fact that he did indeed help steal cattle. Am I being too harsh? I hope not because I really do feel like the boy's life can be saved."

"I think you and Emmitt Frazier are reading from the same book, Jack. That's almost word for word what he said just last week. Connors wants a minimum of six months jail time and the DA wants no less than one year in prison. Personally, I feel that both would be too strong, would hurt the boy's future.

"Ranchers don't like to hire men with jail time in their background. Buckaroos become close to the family, could influence other members of the crew. Desmond is a fine cattleman, Jack. He's looking at a long career on ranches all over the west. Going to jail could destroy the boy."

"We both agree on that, Ted. What does Frazier say?"

"He wants to talk to you before he makes his call. He knows you're here with your herd and wants to talk to you after the sale. Can we do that?"

"Sale will be tomorrow and Wednesday, and I'll need Thursday to wrap up my business. Will he meet with us Friday morning?"

"He said it was your call, so I'll meet you Friday morning at ten at the courthouse."

The two men spent the next hour talking cattle, weather, cattle, water, and the fool lawmakers in Carson City who seemed bent on destroying the cattle industry in Nevada. "I still think you should be in the legislature, Jack. I guess we'll never talk you into it, though. You have a good ride back to town, give my best to Mims and have a good sale."

"You were one of the first men I met when I arrived here, Wilson. I'm glad our friendship has lasted and grown. Even if I did steal Cactus Jack Faraday from you."

"You'll never be forgiven for that, Jack Slater," Wilson laughed.

Mims and Maybelle stood high on the porch of the Elko stockyards watching a cloud of dust slowly make its way toward them. Jack had ridden out to meet the herd and ride in with them. "You're watching your first cattle drive, Maybelle. I love this." Mims had the youngster sitting on the top rail of the porch and soon could hear the rumble of almost four thousand feet churning up the Nevada desert.

"Just listen to that, the cattle bawling, the men whooping and whistling, and the thunder of all those feet. That cloud of dust and deep rumble is what feeds us, little one, but we don't have to wear it. Let's go into the office while we can." She heard the tinkle of laughter from Maybelle as she lifted her off the railing and they scooted inside.

"Good job, Cactus. Looks like you made good time with these big boys." Jack was sitting straight and tall in the saddle with Cactus Jack Faraday on one side and Robbie on the other. "There are three buyers with gold in their pockets waiting to look at what you've got there. Bring 'em in strong and give 'em a good show."

"It was an easy ride, Jack. You plannin' to hire more help while we're in town or wait until spring? That new range you will be buying will take three or four more people to run depending on what you put on it."

"We don't have a lot of open range in that valley of ours and the west face of the Ruby Mountains isn't really conducive to grazing, as you know," Jack said. "We'll set up rotating pastures and also grow and cut good grasses and alfalfa for winter feed. It means a smaller herd but better beef in the long run. I've got something else cooking that we need to talk about as far as new men are concerned.

"When we get the critters corralled, let's

you, me, and Robbie go find some place to have a nice little talk."

"Some place with cold beer," Cactus laughed.

20

Even though the Elko Stockyards provided its own security, Jack had one man stay with the cattle and got the rest of the crew settled under some trees with fresh water available. Some of the men acted as camp cooks and between them figured on a skeleton crowd for supper with Elko's bright lights just half a mile away. "You don't show up in the morning, you don't ride for this brand," Cactus Jack told them after the cattle were in and settled and camp was made.

"We'll need every man-jack of you for the sale and you all have a job through the winter. Don't give that away for booze and broads." Robbie rode out with him to meet up with Jack for supper.

"What you said had some humor to it, Cactus, but I didn't see a smile," Robbie said.

"That was my foreman's face," he chuckled. "The men who work for you need to know when what you say is absolute law. There's a difference between a request and an order and it's often made in how you look when you speak." Cactus Jack was glad that Robbie picked up on his expressions because this ranch would be under his command in the not too distant future and he would need to know how to be a boss.

As a teenager, Robbie was also not always willing to accept what Jack Slater might say simply from natural rebellion, but coming from Cactus Jack, it was accepted almost as the gospel. Robbie also wasn't always fully aware that Cactus Jack and his newly adopted father were almost the same age. Jack Slater wasn't even ten years older than Robbie.

"The foreman is the manager, Robbie. A good manager doesn't do the job, he sees to it the job is done. A good manager doesn't manage by intimidation, a good manager leads, never follows. Now, my young friend, that's speechifyin', east Texas style." That brought on the laughter and a shoulder punch or two.

"You have any idea what Jack wants to talk to us about?" Cactus asked.

"Hasn't said anything to me. Tiny Howard did himself proud on this drive. He sure has toughened up from that first day," Robbie chuckled. "Tater Thompson looked glad not to make the ride."

"He needed to stay at the ranch along with that other young man. Barn animals, all those hogs, Mims' kitchen garden all need to be taken care of. Tater's gettin' old, and he likes working with the hogs. He'll complain about bein' left out, but not very loud."

"Did this drive hurt?" Robbie asked. "I didn't hear you complain any about your delicate little tummy." Robbie had to duck a quick backhand from the foreman, laughing hard as he did.

"My delicate little tummy is all healed up nicely, thank you, and another comment like that and you'll find yourself eating dirt and dust. I gotta say, though, I'm looking forward to a long quiet winter. Your skinny little leg bother you any?"

"Not a bit," Robbie laughed.

They followed the railroad track into town and spotted Jack standing with Mims and Maybelle in front of the hotel. "That herd filled those holding pens all the way, Jack. I left Shorty to keep an eye."

"Good job, Cactus. Let's find a quiet corner in the hotel lobby, maybe get them to bring a pot of coffee." He led them to an ornate setting in the lobby, dressed in

Victorian splendor. There were four large chairs around the table, which was lit by a hanging lamp festooned with numerous brilliant crystals.

Cattle ranchers in for herd sales were treated almost as royalty by the hotel and coffee, a decanter of brandy, and cigars were brought immediately. Both Cactus Jack and Robbie wanted cold beer and a gallon of cold water. Mims wanted to argue about Robbie getting beer but remembered he was doing a man's work, he should be treated like a man.

"I'm sure we all remember our little cattle rustling episode that Robbie discovered. Two of the men, Tony Sorrel and Simon Scruggs will be sentenced to prison later this week."

"Good," Robbie said. "Tony was always so mean, and for no reason. What about that Desmond fella? He seemed to know a lot about moving cattle. More than Sorrel. Wouldn't surprise me he was the honcho."

"That's why we're here," Jack said. "I had a chance to talk with Desmond on the ride to town that day, and Ted Wilson and I had a long talk with him on the Fourth of July. You're right, Robbie, Desmond is a fine buckaroo, knows cattle and can read terrain, but isn't the brightest candle you've seen. Sorrel was the leader and he lied to Desmond about what they were doing that day.

"Sorrel needed help stealing our beef and to put it right; he coerced young Desmond into helping him. Someone with a little more common sense would have seen through Sorrel's plans, but Desmond just isn't that bright."

Jack noticed that Robbie wasn't ready to buy that proposition, saw big questions in Cactus Jack's face, and continued his pitch. "Desmond worked for Wilson before moving west to the Diamond Valley, and we spent some time with him. Judge Emmitt Frazier has also spent considerable time with Desmond.

"The judge, and he's called the hangin' judge sometimes, is under the impression that Desmond had no idea at all that they were stealing those steers, and that if the young man were to be sent to prison his career as a cowman would be over."

"You're leading us up to something, Jack. What is it?" Cactus Jack Faraday sat back with a slight smile on his face, lit a cigar, and blew smoke toward the ceiling.

"Yes, I am. Wilson and I both have gone to the judge and asked for leniency, and I've gone one step further. Because of his arrest, the Diamond Valley ranch doesn't want Desmond back and Wilson wouldn't have room for him until late next spring. If he goes to prison it would be like that for the rest of his life. If he gets off with a slap on the wrist, ranch work will be available most of the time.

"The judge wants to give him two months in the Elko County hoosegow on a misdemeanor of reckless behavior, and then I would hire him for our operation. It will take the judge making that decision and you all supporting my idea."

"Ooh, Jack." Cactus let it out low and slow, looking Slater in the eye. "Put a man who rustled our beef to work on our range? That's a stretch, even for you."

Jack chuckled and looked around the table before he said anything. Robbie was almost as dumfounded as Cactus. "Ezra Jackson wanted to hang him, and you want to hire him?"

"And I know why," Mims said. She had been fascinated by the talk, by the way Jack presented the situation and could see Jack Slater written all over what he had said.

"An old copper in New York City kept Jack from being a street bum, a child criminal. A lady maintained a bank account in Jack's name when his parent's farm was

272

sold, giving Jack financial freedom when he turned eighteen. And a rancher in Wyoming taught Jack the cattle ranching business. There were others, big strong men, and women along the way that helped make Jack the man he is today.

"Jack, if you see potential in this young man who isn't that much younger than we are, then I vote with you." Mims was rocking Maybelle as she spoke.

"You see good in people, Jack." Cactus got up from his chair and poured coffee around, then walked around the table again, thinking what he would say next. "Hiring a known rustler is something I would never consider."

"Never is a long time, Cactus. Sorrel told a good story, one that you and I would never believe in a minute, Cactus, but one that Desmond took in like a bear would take honey. The judge calls him stupid, not criminal. I used the word naive, but the judge might have this round."

"When we rode up on those men, Scruggs wanted to go for his guns and Ornery Pound stopped that. Sorrel tried to run, and he was stopped. I saw Desmond slump and not make a move for his weapon," Robbie said. "What's the full plan and how will we convince the other hands?"

"The four of us have to be in complete agreement on hiring Desmond after his two months in jail. If we all agree and we're willing to work this out, the rest of the crew will either work with him or not. It isn't their decision. The man has a lot of experience on large operations and will be an asset as far as I'm concerned.

"Think about it. We'll have breakfast in the morning and I will want a yes or no. You know where I stand, Mims pretty much gave us her opinion, so you two need to give me an answer in the morning."

"I'll give you mine right now," Cactus Jack said. "Your ability to judge people has amazed me from the day we met, Jack. Look where I am today, you've adopted Robbie, and chased down the man who burned you out. If you feel this strongly about Desmond, then I will go along with you all the way."

"I was pretty sure you would feel that way but it's always best if we talk our way through a situation."

"If it was Sorrel, I'd say hire him, and then I'd shoot him," Robbie said, and there was no smile on his face. "I think I'm in the middle of a large learning experience here," and this time he chuckled, and looked deep into Mims' eyes. She gave him a grand smile and reached out for his hand. "I'm with you, papa."

"You're an amazing man, Jack," Mims said.

"You've had time to see the cattle, Mr. Slater has answered your questions, and it's time to exchange money for merchandise." Blackie Wellington was the stockyard grounds manager and had his big tally book opened, pen in hand. "Join me at my desk and let's talk money."

Prices were negotiated, and numbers had been determined. The cull heifers and bulls sold quickly to an Indian agent, and for a price that brought a frown to Jack's brow. "It's always better when there's several potential buyers. That agent just stole more beef than Tony Sorrel is going to prison for." Cactus Jack Faraday had to turn and walk away in order to chuckle for fear of being knocked about some.

"The good stuff is coming up, papa," Robbie said, stifling a chuckle. "I've heard some pretty good numbers being discussed. Our beef is special, you know." Jack didn't say a word and walked over to talk to one of the town men.

"I need at least three, maybe four more good hands and I sure could use a fine cook and housekeeper, Mr. Jackson. It's coming winter and some of these smaller spreads have surely turned some good men loose."

Jackson was one of those men one could find in almost any small town in the west. He seemed to know the answers to questions like Jack was asking. Yes, Mr. Jackson was a barman at the Cattleman's Saloon, and in the west if you wanted information, the local saloon barman would always have the answer.

He stood about five feet and ten inches but weighed in at a solid two hundred pounds. He enjoyed hoisting barrels filled with beer or cider, feeling the back and shoulders of his shirt rip wide open, his muscles, covered in thick black hair bulging with the effort.

"I can put five good men at your door within the week, Mr. Slater. I think old Puny Nordstrom's wife would be available if you could use Puny for something. He's no kind of buckaroo, but he can build just about anything that needs building."

"I'll be at the Stockman's, Mr. Jackson. Ask Puny Nordstrom and his wife to drop by this evening and send me five good buckaroos." They shook hands, a twenty-dollar gold piece ended up in Jackson's hand, and Jack ambled back toward the bidding table, which was loud and lively.

"The bids are high papa. By golly, we did good." Robbie was almost dancing in his enthusiasm and Jack watched, remembering times when he was about that age. Some of the most fun he had, and some of the most dangerous times he had, were in Deadwood and on that big ranch in Wyoming.

Henry Rupert taught me everything I know about ranching and cattle during those two years and I can see myself in Robbie right now. Robbie has had to grow up so fast, he's big, strong, intelligent, and willing. A son like that and a wife like Mims. My God, I'm the luckiest man alive

"You'll be fifteen soon," Jack said. "I was sixteen when I ran away from Jablonski, and that wasn't that many years ago. My folks taught me right from wrong, Seth Bullard in Deadwood showed me how right and wrong really work, and Henry Rupert taught me about life.

"You've had a couple of horrible experiences in your life, Robbie, and I can see a real man coming out. Mims tells me you're studying breeding and management at a higher level. How's that coming?"

Robbie's eyes lit up and he turned his full attention from the sale table to Jack. "There are some amazing things I've learned about how to breed to a desired product. I'm learning things about cattle that even Cactus doesn't know."

"And me, I'd bet." Jack laughed, thinking about what Robbie said. *Breeding to a desired product. He said that as if, well, as if he really knows what he's talking about.* "Maybe you could pass some of that information along to Cactus and me. Tell me about this breeding to a desired product while we walk back to the hotel."

"Don't you want to stay to the end of the sale?"

"No," Jack said. "It's too scary. Cactus is right there, so there won't be any nonsense going on and we'll get the full tally in the morning. I want to know what it is we'll be doing in the next few years with our herds, Mr. Cow Boss."

It was a long slow walk back to the hotel with many stops along the way while Robbie went into great detail about the breeding of various breeds of cattle to develop a strain that produced heavy animals with tender juicy meat. How bringing bulls with a specific background into the herd, how adding heifers with distinct backgrounds will build a fine herd.

"I've been taking these courses from the university right here in Elko and buying books from a university in the east. It's more than fascinating." Jack just shook his head remembering that he had gone out of his way to introduce the youngster to reading books in the first place.

[21]

"I'm meeting with Judge Frazier this morning, Mims. When I get back, let's discuss what we're going to do about that lady you met. Seemed friendly enough."

"Anna Nordstrom. Yes, I liked her, Jack. I think she would fit right into how we run our little place. She calls her husband Puny," Mims almost giggled.

"I guess that's the name he goes by. We'd have a puny and an ornery working for us. I guess he's good at carpentry and we do need some things built around that place, including a place for them to live. She'll need to be on the ranch within the next two weeks if you will be satisfied with her."

"She already said she could be there within three or four days. It's just too hard for me to do all the cooking and cleaning for our crew with the baby growing so big inside me. I wake up exhausted, Jack."

He held her close, rubbed her back gently,

gave her a kiss on the forehead and left for the courthouse. "I don't think this will take more than a couple of hours, Mims. Let's plan on leaving out early tomorrow morning. Cactus Jack has the crew rounded up and headed back to the ranch now, and Robbie wanted to ride back with them."

"Just you, me, and Maybelle for the ride home then." She had a big smile on her face. "And a ride up into Lamoille Canyon, even if it's just for one night under the stars."

Ted Wilson was waiting for Jack outside the Elko County Courthouse. "Word around town is you made a killing at the sale. Being the first in with a good herd to boot paid off, I guess."

"Those were hungry buyers, Ted. Seen the judge?"

"He just went in, said for us to come right up to his chambers. I think Wild Bill Connors is going to be there, too."

District Judge Emmett Frazier had everyone in a conference room adjacent to his chambers. Connors, Slater, Wilson, the judge, and young Ron Desmond. "Didn't expect to see Desmond here," Jack said as they got comfortable. Desmond was sporting a black eye and cut lip and was scowling when Connors brought him in.

"I was planning on a simple meeting between just the three of us, Mr. Slater. That is, you, me, and Mr. Wilson, but there has been a slight change as you can see." The judge was nearing sixty, Jack thought, with black hair sprinkled liberally with white, wore only a thin white mustache as facial hair, and had blazing black eyes that danced as he spoke, boring holes in whatever they were aimed at.

"Sheriff, will you tell again what you told me this morning?"

"As you know," Bill Connors said. He was scowling at Jack and the judge. "We were keeping Desmond from having contact with Tony Sorrel, and he was acting as a trusty here at the courthouse. Mr. Slater, I have a lot of respect for you, your background, how you've managed your ranch and your people, but I must question your judgment concerning Desmond.

"He has become a close friend to one Henry Coates. You're familiar with the name?" Jack nodded, remembering Coates was riding with Hickory Slim Obregon and was arrested following the attempted robbery of Valley Paddock's emporium. "My jailers broke up an attempted jail break last night involving Desmond, Coates, and two other prisoners."

"I certainly would not have expected that," Jack said. He exchanged glances with Ted Wilson and Judge Frazier. When he turned his eyes on Desmond, the young man was scowling right at him. Jack wondered what exactly had happened in the few short months since the attempted cattle rustling.

"You were joining these men in an escape from jail when you were already on your way out the door?" Jack's question carried its own answer to those sitting at the table. Desmond simply was stupid, not just ignorant. "I accepted your lack of understanding people, being incredibly naïve, but this is pure stupidity." He looked at Connors for more information.

It was Frazier who spoke. "I fear this man is one of those who will do what he's told to do without question. Desperately needs friends and will do just about anything to make and keep a friend. It isn't ignorance or stupidity, Jack, it's a complete lack of intelligence to begin with. I was flummoxed right along with you and Ted Wilson. Those who use people see a gem in Desmond.

"Coates saw how the jailers gave Desmond almost free rein around the jail and courthouse and took him in like a long lost first cousin. Sorrel did the same thing. He

283

has an extremely limited intelligence and can be manipulated by anyone. He wouldn't know how to manipulate a cup of coffee.

"I'm washing my hands of this entire case. He was initially charged with cattle rustling and those charges are still on the books." The judge was wagging his head slowly back and forth, staring at Desmond. "Now, additional charges of attempted jail escape, conspiracy to escape from jail, and assault on a law officer have been filed.

"I'm sorry we all had to go through this, but I'm also relieved that we found this out before the man could do more harm. Sheriff, please escort the prisoner back to your warm and hospitable jail. I'll arrange for a hearing on the new charges."

There were a few chuckles, and a snicker or two also as Connors jerked Desmond to his feet and handcuffed him. "He will not do well in prison, I'm afraid."

"That was as much of a shock as I want on a bright early fall morning." Jack and Ted Wilson walked into the saloon at the hotel for a cold beer and some smoked meats on fresh bread. "What an interesting situation."

"Well, Jack, we were almost right in our observation of the man. Naïve, but oh so much more so," he chuckled.

"I had Mims, Cactus Jack, and Robbie convinced that Desmond would be a fine hand and we should welcome him to the crew. I will be eating half a dozen crows for the next few weeks. Cactus is really gonna let me have it," Jack laughed. "At least I think we picked up a good ranch cook. Mims interviewed Anna Nordstrom for the job."

"She's a fine ranch cook, Jack. I guess you know you have to take Puny as well. He isn't worth much."

"I heard he could build anything that needs to be built."

"That is the truth," Wilson said. He quaffed half a pint of beer and nodded for another. "The problem is getting him to do it. He is one lazy old man and has cost Anna some good ranch jobs over the years."

"I'll just make Ornery Pound his boss." They laughed for several moments over that thought, and Jack headed up to his room to tell Mims the bad news about Ron Desmond.

"That's the saddest story I've ever heard," she said. "He's so young. I was angry to the point of saying something when that vulgar Tony Sorrel acted the fool in our kitchen and was willing to give Mr. Desmond the benefit of the doubt. What will happen to him?"

"It looks like many years in prison, Mims. Those are serious charges and there are many of them. I guess we're just lucky it happened now and not something after he was with us. Let's take Maybelle for a little walk and see if we can find her some ice cream."

"I'm glad we picked up that big wagon and those mules. It sure will make it easier when we're cutting grass. Have you ever seen a hay press, Cactus?" Robbie was more than impressed with the unit that was riding in the back of the big wagon. "Three men, one feeding, one handling the press lever, and one tying the wires. We can put up a winter's feed in a matter of a couple of weeks, Cactus."

"You picked up on that operation immediately, didn't you? You'll be running the grass and baling crew, Robbie, and teaching everyone how to operate all this fancy equipment. Did Jack buy that place southwest of us?"

"Signed the papers yesterday. We'll use that property mostly for hay and grains. Did you see that huge steam traction engine when we picked up the baler? That was a monster. Dad almost bought one."

"Personally, I'm glad he didn't. Baling the grass and alfalfa will be enough modern for me. All this nonsense about machinery replacing men and animals is just that. Nonsense." Cactus Jack was a traditionalist through and through, and he and Robbie had some lively discussions about how the modern world was unfolding.

"Dad hired five new hands who will be at the ranch over the next few days, and it looks like we'll have a new ranch cook."

"I hope she's half a good a cook as Mims," Cactus laughed. "What do you think of this idea of bringing Desmond into the crew?" Cactus didn't like it at all but knew that if that's what Jack wanted, he would do his best to make it work.

"I don't know if dad is right or not, Cactus. You might remember that I went along with Ornery and Ezra and wanted to string the bunch of 'em up right there on the trail. He was riding with a man who called my mother and me terrible names, went out of his way to hurt my mother and me, and I'm not sure I'm ready to work with or be friends with Desmond."

"I don't want to have to be a referee, Robbie. Jack's the boss."

"I know that, Cactus. But I still don't like it."

The Slater crew was strung out for half a mile on their ride back to the ranch, a couple talking here, two more discussing the fate of the world over there, and Ornery Pound riding at least two hundred yards in front of everyone. "Looks like Ornery wants to get home first," Robbie joked.

"Been sleeping on the ground for a week. All he can think about is his bunk and blanket. Me too." Cactus Jack chuckled softly, and he and Robbie stepped up their horses to join the old man in the lead.

"The problem with getting back to the ranch early like this is we will still have to cook for ourselves. Maybe we should have waited and escorted Jack and Mims back." Cactus Jack was joking, but the look on Ornery Pounds face told him he might just be right.

"I hope this Anna is a good cook. We've been spoiled by Mims, I'm afraid." Ornery Pound had worked some bare bones brands in his Texas days and relished a good bunk and three hot meals a day. "The best peach cobbler I've ever had," he smiled.

"Jack, you better ask Anna to come in," Mims said. She was in bed and Jack saw a strange look on her face. She had a stranglehold on his hand, and he felt her grasp it ever harder, squint her eyes, and groan slightly. "We're gonna have a baby very soon," she said, trying to grin.

It was the third week of November, the first real storm of the fall was screaming through The Meadows, bringing wind, snow, and cold to the ranch. "Hold on Mims," Jack said. "Should I get Doc Fowler too?"

"No, I think Anna and I can handle everything, but don't waste any time finding her," she laughed through a strong contraction. "Anna's been a midwife many times, she told me. Besides, who would want to ride through this storm?" She smiled and watched Jack scurry from their bedroom. The big man ran across the large

289

living room and into the kitchen where Anna was getting ready to bring the crew in for their mid-day meal.

"Mims needs you, Anna. It's time," he said. She grabbed some toweling and a couple of blankets that she had all ready for this occasion and walked quickly from the kitchen. She used her hands and arms to tell him he had to bring in the crew and get them fed.

Jack stood motionless for a couple of minutes. *We're gonna have another baby. I should be in there. No, I should ride and get Doc Fowler. No, I should feed the crew.* Jack Slater's mind was traveling fast and getting nowhere. He remembered that one cowhand at Rupert's ranch saying to him on a drive, "I don't have any idea where I am but I'm making good time." He laughed at the thought and tried to calm himself down.

He had to laugh even more because he simply couldn't get himself calmed down. He walked out onto the kitchen porch and rang the bell loud and long, bringing the crew at a run through heavy rain and mud. He got the Dutch oven kettles onto the table, already set, and just paced around the table two or three times.

"Aren't you going to eat, Jack?" Cactus Jack asked, watching the parade. "Where's

Anna?" The crew, some starting to serve, but most watching, had the same questions in their eyes.

"Anna's . . . that is, Mims is . . . We're having a baby," he finally managed to get out, and plopped down on a chair. "Good lord, I don't know what I'm doing."

"Should I send someone for Doc Fowler?" Cactus asked.

"Mims didn't think she'd need him, that she and Anna would take care of things." He sat quietly for a couple of minutes. "This storm would make getting the doc difficult, and he's difficult enough. I don't know. Where's Robbie?"

"He and Tiny are out taking care of the irrigation ponds." Cactus Jack said. "We're gonna have to flood some of the fields, Jack. Those ponds are filling fast and we sure don't want to have any dam breaks right now. Robbie has the irrigation ditches running full. I'm taking three men out after we eat to move cattle to higher ground."

"If we're lucky, it'll get cold and put a heavy layer of snow over everything. I'd sure hate to lose our good grass pastures." Jack saw the picture Cactus painted and didn't like it one bit. "Those fields are gold in the form of grass."

"We won't lose any, Jack. We'll control

flood them. It won't be like a raging dam break, but it must be done now. After we get some of the cattle out of the low areas we'll join Robbie and Tiny Howard and keep a close eye on the ponds."

Jack tried to eat some of the stew Anna had prepared and couldn't swallow a bite. A new baby was about to join the family, a possible disastrous flood was about to descend on the ranch, his son was out in this miserable storm fighting to keep the flood from happening, and he was sitting at the kitchen table, helpless. Jack Slater stood up, paced around the kitchen one more time, walked quickly toward his bedroom but stopped immediately, walked back into the kitchen, and looked helplessly at Cactus Jack.

"I gotta do something, Cactus," he said.

Cactus Jack was about to say something when Anna Nordstrom walked in. "Mims wants you, Jack."

"That's the last gate, Tiny. All the irrigation ditch gates are wide open." Robbie and Tiny Howard were soaked to the skin despite their slickers and frozen to the bone. "All we need right is for the temperature to drop four or five degrees and have this icy rain turn to snow." They were riding back toward the largest of the irrigation ponds, some ten or twelve acres in size.

"If that pond goes over the top of the dam, it will start eroding away the dam, and if it collapses, we'll have a cascade effect, taking out the three ponds below. We simply can't let that happen, Tiny."

They rode through the storm, heads down and bowed into the wind. Horses don't much care for high wind to start with, will turn tail to it at the first opportunity, and the men were having trouble keeping their mounts going into the wind. "If this gets any worse, we'll use our neck rags to tie around their eyes. This rain has ice crystals in it and is stinging the heck out of their eyes." Robbie was a far better rider than Tiny and was keeping a close eye on the man.

As they moved higher up the sloping hillside toward the main pond the rain was starting to fall as snow. "Come on blizzard," Robbie yelled into the face of the storm. The snow was wet, but it was snow. "Let's ride several hundred yards above the pond and see if we can dig a diversion ditch on the stream that feeds the pond."

The stream, one of many that started several miles to the east, coming straight out of the massive Ruby Mountains, was running high and fast. They rode into the trees that grew along the banks of the creek until they came to a slight bend in the flow. "This isn't going to be easy, Tiny. We'll dig away the bank where the creek takes its bend, and hopefully, the water will spill over and follow the terrain well to the south of the pond."

The creek in July furnished trout and a pleasant dip in cool mountain waters, but at the end of November, it was a raging torrent. Instead of being a few feet deep and just a few yards across, it was deeper than a man was tall and a hundred yards across, boiling down the hillside.

Each man carried a short-handled shovel tied off on the back of his saddle and the two rode their horses into a stand of aspen to tie off. "We want to start this ditch down and away from where the water's flowing, Tiny. That way we can work our way up to the creek and break the creek bank to start the diversion."

Tiny Howard had spent most of his young life working for Valley Paddock in that big store, and the last few months working the Slater brand had changed him in many ways. What was obvious to Robbie right now was the strength of the big fella. "We gotta change your name to mule or bull or something, Tiny. Slow down, you're slingin' mud like you're looking for gold." They both chuckled some but kept right on digging away the mud and creating a path for the water to follow when they opened a cut in the creek bank.

"This could get dangerous, Tiny," Robbie said taking a short breather. In less than an hour, they had a good trench several hundred feet long angling off south from the west flowing creek. "That water's moving awful fast, it's cold, and when we break through the bank it could come as a surge. It's okay if it does, but we don't want to be in the middle of it."

If the water followed the ditch they cut, it would flow at least a quarter of a mile south of the large pond they were trying to protect and would then begin to cut its own creek bed as it flowed toward the pastures, grass, and alfalfa fields below. Robbie stood on the creek bank, the rolling water just inches from the top, and sunk his shovel into the mud. There was no warning as the creek bank simply gave way and water surged into the cut, just as planned.

What wasn't planned was Robbie tumbling down that new ditch, being carried away by the bitterly cold waters in the fast-moving current. Dressed for the icy storm, his clothing soaked through, Robbie was fighting to keep his head above water. He couldn't get his feet under him, couldn't seem to move to the side to grab a branch or root, and was tumbled about as the water cascaded through the broken creek bank.

He'd never been as cold as he was, never been as frightened as he was, and fought desperately to survive. His legs were numb from the cold and wet, his arms felt like they weighed a hundred pounds each, and he cried for help at the top of his lungs. He was slowly losing the fight, he could feel nothing, not cold, not panic at dying, not afraid to take another face full of icy water when the loop of a buckaroo's reata flopped over his head.

It was a pure instinct that Robbie grabbed that braided rawhide rope and felt the loop tighten around him. He never was able to remember the cowboys grabbing him and jerking him out of the water, didn't hear some of the things said, wasn't aware of anything until he came to, wrapped in blankets and bundled in front of a raging fire in an aspen grove during a heavy snowstorm.

"What do you think we ought to do with him?" Ornery Pound said, throwing another large limb on the fire.

"Don't know for sure, Ornery," Cactus Jack Faraday said. "Ain't never caught a Slater Fish before. I guess we better just let him roast in those blankets for a while," he laughed, seeing Robbie's eyes trying to open through the fog of unconsciousness. "Welcome back young man. You sure picked a fool time to go swimming."

The buckaroos that rode for the Slater brand were more than aware of the seriousness of the situation, that Robbie would be dead if they hadn't ridden up when they did if Cactus Jack hadn't made a perfect loop, if Robbie hadn't been able to grasp the rope. Humor was the only way they could face what they did, what didn't happen.

Tiny Howard had been knocked aside by the surge of water and despite being covered in icy mud was able to help Cactus and Ornery pull Robbie from the muddy water. He was wrapped in a blanket and was sitting next to Robbie, tears running down his face. "I thought you were gone for sure, Robbie. Thank God for Cactus Jack."

"You picked a strange way of doing it, pard, but it looks like your diversion is gonna save that big pond. Good work. We'll get you dried off and back to the big house, Robbie. You probably have a new sister or

297

brother waiting for you."

His teeth were chattering so much he couldn't speak but his eyes told those standing around everything they needed to know. It was a long slow two-hour ride back to the ranch, the wind howling, snowflakes as big as a ten-dollar gold piece flailing through the maelstrom, and bitter cold gnawing at bones and skin. The good news was that everyone lived.

[23]

Jack barreled toward the bedroom fearing the worst and dreaded the moment. He had heard stories from a few people but had never been around pregnancy, never in all his dealings with children and life situations had he been around childbirth. More than once during the last several months he had spent hours discussing what to expect with Mims.

She teased him and chided him, reminding the big man how many calves he had helped bring into this world, how many horses had foals because of him, and just how many lambs have been able to run around the big ranch because of him. "Ain't the same," he'd say, feigning anger and she'd give him a big poo-poo back.

"I've been a big brother figure almost from the time my parents were killed, Mims," he said just the week before. "I've helped young children face terrible times, I have two children that I've legally adopted, but I've never been close to what we're about to have happen. I've been frightened by things that have happened in my life, but never as frightened as I am right now."

"For heaven's sake," is all she said, and to give it a little more emphasis went, "Moo," and then laughed for a full five minutes. He just sulked off.

As he reached for the doorknob he heard some serious squalling coming from the other side and froze in place. "Oh, my God," he mumbled. He finally gathered his courage and slowly opened the door and found Mims sitting, propped up by several pillows, nursing a big baby boy. "About time you got here. Look at the size of this monster," she giggled.

Jack walked slowly to the bed and carefully sat down, his eyes wider than Mims had ever seen, a smile spread across his big face, and didn't say a word. He sat for minutes just looking, first deep into Mims' eyes, then at his newborn son. "At least say hello to the gentleman, Jack," she said.

Jack couldn't say a word, just sat very still looking back and forth at the two. Finally, he reached out and brushed his fingertips softly across Mims' cheek and bent down and kissed her as gently as if she were a mist. He carefully lifted the heavy baby from her and wrapped huge arms around him. Mims saw tears rolling down his face as he kissed the boy's head softly.

He held the boy for long minutes, rocking back and forth, seemingly saying something but not out loud, and never taking his eyes from Mims'. He very carefully laid the child back in his mother's arms, kissed her again, and quietly stood up and walked from the room. He walked through the house, across the broad kitchen and out into the raging storm, stood in the middle of the ranch yard, spread his arms wide, and howled like a wolf for a full minute.

The men in the barn, those near the hog pens, and all the chickens could hear him howl, "It's a boy, I have another son, It's a boy!" Wet snow pelted him, driven by high winds and he didn't even know he was soaked through. It was Ezra Jackson who took him by the arm and led Jack and all the buckaroos back into the kitchen.

Anna Nordstrom had a goodly fire going, a full pot of coffee boiling, and headed back to be with Mims. The men grabbed cups and sat at the table, but Jack found himself walking around the big table, stopping at each man to say, "I have a son." Ezra

301

couldn't help himself and was laughing loudly.

Ezra stopped suddenly and walked toward the kitchen door. "Riders coming hard," he said and grabbed his slicker, joined by the rest. They were all standing in the storm when Cactus Jack Faraday led the group from the irrigation crew in at a fast lope. They reined up at the kitchen porch, and all but one baled off their horses quickly. That one was slumped, almost unconscious in his saddle.

"Let's get him in by the fire, boys. Get some coffee boiling." Cactus Jack grabbed Robbie from his horse and Ornery Pound grabbed the boy's legs as he came down. The two of them hustled inside and sat Robbie in a chair, still wrapped in blankets, by the fire. "He fell in the creek, Jack."

The euphoria of childbirth was quenched instantly by the fear of a child's accident. Jack knelt next to Robbie and slowly pulled the blankets away, allowing the heat from the wood stove to do its work. Robbie's eyes opened as the heat began to penetrate the ice. "Dad," is all he said, throwing his arms around Jack.

Anna came in and took control of the situation. "You come with me, Robbie Slater," she said and walked him into his bedroom, keeping the men in the kitchen. She got the wet blankets off, then his iced and wet clothing off him. She quickly tucked him in his bed and went back into the kitchen.

The men stood quietly and watched while Anna took two small cast iron frying pans from the stove and wrapped them in towels and went back to Robbie. She put one towel wrapped pan on one side of the boy and one on the other side. "Now, young sir, you sleep. That will get you warm and keep you good and alive." He smiled, barely awake, and squeezed her hand.

While Anna was busy with Robbie, Cactus Jack told the story to Jack and the other men. "Another few seconds and he would have been lost to us, Jack. He and Tiny Howard saved the irrigation ponds, saved the ranch from a disastrous flood, but came within a gnat's eyebrow of dying." Cactus found he was shaking as he told the story and had to sit down.

"Thank you," is all Jack could say. And he said it over and over. It was a full two pots of coffee before any kind of calm could be noted in the kitchen. Cactus, Ornery Pound, and the others that rode with them thawed out, dripping great puddles in Mims' kitchen, and Jack was finally able to tell the crew there was an addition to the house-hold.

"He's really big," Jack said, stretching his arms wide to the delight of everyone.

"Whatcha gonna name him, Jack?" Cactus asked.

"Two men taught me more about life than you can imagine. Seth Bullock in Deadwood and Henry Rupert in Wyoming. Mims and I have decided to name this noisy critter Henry Seth Slater," Jack laughed. "Young Henry Slater arrived on a fast blue norther."

Anna had to come in and quiet the boys. "Gentlemen," she said in her quietest voice. "There's a baby trying to sleep that-a-way, and another young-un trying to sleep that-a-way. You might be more comfortable in the barn if you keep howlin'." There was instant quiet in the Slater kitchen.

"I'll have supper in an hour if you boys can find somewhere else to be."

Cactus Jack led the buckaroos back to the bunkhouse through snow starting to ac-cumulate and Jack Slater walked into Rob-bie's room to sit with the boy. He was surprised to find him awake. "How are you feeling?"

"I'm sick to my stomach," Robbie said.

"You probably sucked in a lot of that

304

muddy water. Getting warm, though?"

"Yeah. Those pans that Anna shoved under the blankets were really hot."

"I've got some good news for you. You now have yourself a little brother."

"Wow," was all Robbie could say. His eyes were bright, and he had a smile for the first time in hours. "A brother. I've always wanted a brother. I love Maybelle, and she and I have a lot of fun, but I've always wanted a brother." He grimaced as pain shot through his gut and Jack grabbed the chamber pot, just in case.

"I'm going to ride into Skelton in the morning and bring Doc Fowler out. He'll need to see young Henry and he'll give you a good going over, too." Jack gave Robbie's head a good rubbing and walked back to the kitchen, feeling pretty good about things. *Young Henry. I like the sound of that. Maybelle, Robbie, and Young Henry. Things seem to happen fast around this old ranch.*

[24]

"This is my fourth winter here in Nevada." Jack Slater sat at the kitchen table surrounded by cowboys and family. It was the week before Christmas and Jack wanted to make sure the ranch and stock were ready for a long cold winter. Jack took this time to let his crew know just how much he appreciated their hard work. "This is a fine brand we're riding for, and it's that way because of all of you.

"We've had a more than an interesting year so far, with more excitements than are really necessary." That brought some chuckles, some grumbles, and many nods and wry smiles from everyone. "Now we're being attacked by old man winter, too."

Cactus Jack Faraday's wounds from being attacked by a mountain lion were healed, Robbie's stomach problems after swallowing muddy water were over, and there hadn't been any other injuries or sicknesses.

"This winter looks to be one for the books."

He had to laugh gently. "The whole year has been one for the books so far. Between outlaws, injuries, and death, this old ranch has taken a beating."

Young Henry was growing fast and making as much noise as a heifer looking for its young while Maybelle had taken it upon herself to be his constant companion. Only one problem continued to bother Jack Slater, and it was minor in nature. How to get Puny Nordstrom off his fanny and out on a job.

"I'm sure there've been harder winters, but this is the most winter I've seen. That snow is gonna keep our cows busy trying to find feed, and that means we're gonna be haulin' feed out to them at least every other day. How does our supply look, Jack?"

"We cut and stacked a lot of hay last summer. We'll make spring with no trouble even if we have to feed every day. The best thing we did was bring that herd down from the higher pastures and into these lower sections. That could backfire on us too, come spring thaw." He sat at the table wagging his head, not wanting to think about even more flooding down the line.

"The wagon and mules Robbie picked up will be fine for the feeding job. I'm sure glad he's feeling better. Puny has some time working with mules and I've assigned him to see to it the teams are hitched every morning and the wagon filled with feed. He and two men can then drive through the fields distributing the feed."

"That's good, Cactus. Very good," Jack said.

Robbie ingested a lot of mud when he was swept into that raging current and it took a long time for his system to cleanse itself. He had intestinal problems for most of November and well into December. Doc Fowler taught Anna how to make a vile tasting concoction that helped cleanse everything from one end to the other.

"Robbie's eating like a bear in the fall, Cactus," Jack laughed. "Let's set up a feeding schedule for the cattle and the crew, so everyone gets a shot at freezing out there. Most of those beautiful girls are pregnant and if these storms keep coming we're gonna have our hands full come spring. Several hundred calves coming with several feet of snow on the ground trying to melt. We better be ready."

Anna poured another round of coffee and brought the third pan of biscuits from the oven. "I want to take a couple of minutes and talk about what I think we'll be looking at this next year," Jack said. "We have those two new sections of land to our south that will need lots of attention, we have at least six new hands, and we're going to increase our hay and grain production, and the size of our herd."

"I like working for a busy brand," Cactus Jack laughed. "Bring it on Jack Slater. You've got a fine crew here." He got some rousing, almost rebel yells from the crew on that comment.

"Riders coming," Ornery Pound said. "Looks like three men." Jack strode to the kitchen door, picked up his rifle, and walked out onto the porch. The crew, almost to the man was armed, moved Mims, young Henry, Maybelle, and Anna out of the kitchen. Mims hurried back and handed Cactus Jack her shotgun.

"Everything's fine, it's Jimmie Delgado," Jack yelled back at the men. The kitchen filled with the sounds of big revolvers being shoved back into warm leather. Delgado and two others after riding through heavy snowfall all the way from Skelton, rode right up to the ranch house, stepped off their iced horses and hurried into the warmth of the kitchen. "You boys have been riding hard," Jack said as they crowded around the hot stove.

Elko County deputy Jimmie Delgado, blacksmith Jesse Winthrop, and saloon owner Horseface Hawkins all nodded, crowding even closer to the wood cook stove. "It's a cold storm, Jack," Delgado said through bouts of shivers. "I've got bad news. You remember Henry Coates?"

"Yeah, he rode with that Reynolds gang and was with Hickory Slim Obregon at Paddock's place. He on the loose?"

"Worse than that," Horseface Hawkins snarled. "He, Tony Sorrel, and Ron Desmond killed two deputies, wounded the sheriff, and escaped."

Before he could continue, Delgado jumped in. "Sorrel has vowed to kill you and Robbie and burn you out as well."

"I thought they were sent to the Carson City Prison?" Jack said.

"Desmond's trial just ended, and they had to keep Sorrel in Elko for his testimony. Coates's trial hasn't even happened yet. Delays on top of delays." Delgado was pacing around the kitchen. "Wild Bill Connors is angrier than I've ever seen him. Reading the wire he sent seemed like I could hear him bellowing like a bull set free."

It was silent in that large kitchen as Delgado's words echoed through each person's mind. Mims was crying softly, sitting at the

310

table holding young Henry, Anna made herself busy fixing another pot of coffee and adding wood to the stove, and Jack sat mumbling serious words about Sorrel's background.

"There's more, Jack," Horseface said. "Sorrel also promised to burn Skelton to the ground."

"When did this happen, Jimmie?" Jack asked. "If they're coming this way the storm is sure to hinder a fast approach. Cactus Jack, make sure every man on this ranch is armed at all times and understands the situation. Set up a guard plan like we've discussed. No one moves around outside a building alone. Two or more people if you're outside a building."

"I got the word on the wire this morning Jack," Delgado said. "Must have happened late last night or early this morning."

"That at least gives us time to prepare a good defense. And Desmond is with Sorrel?" Jack said. "He sure had me, and old judge Frazier bundled up tight. Well, okay, Cactus leave one man here in the house with us and you and the crew set up your defenses.

"Robbie, you, me, and whoever Cactus leaves will protect the house. What are your plans for protecting the town? Sorrel's mother lives there and Desmond's aunt, Mrs. Riley, lives there with young children. Are those men capable of killing their own family?"

"Remember that Coates was a part of the Reynolds gang and they were the ones terrorizing the ranches in the county last summer," Delgado reminded the men. "I warned Mrs. Sorrel about Tony's escape and she was worried sick, but Virginia Riley, still out of sorts following Dick's passing, is terrified."

"Bring her and the children here, Jimmie," Mims said. "We can't let that poor woman be alone now, not with two small children and no husband. You bring her and the children here." She bumped her little fist on the kitchen table to make her point, and Maybelle sitting next to her did the same thing.

Jack had the slightest smile as he listened to her. He hadn't heard Mims be that firm since she was a little girl giving old Pete Jablonski the what for in his own kitchen.

"We have men and guns, Jimmie Delgado, it's almost Christmas and we can't let that woman be alone and afraid. In fact, if there are other women in town who are afraid of this Tony Sorrel, you bring them out here, too." Mims was standing with little Henry in her arms and Jack almost had to laugh at the memories the scene brought back. He could see her standing in that kitchen, a Dutch oven in one hand and her little fist knotted up resting on her hip.

"I'll escort them out myself," Horseface Hawkins said, "if you'll let me borry your wagon and team, Jack."

"Puny, go hitch your mules to the big wagon and take it to Skelton with Horse-face. Get that wagon filled with whatever Virginia Riley and the children need, and hurry back here with them. Be quick now," Jack said. "And take your rifle with you."

"I'll help you, Puny," Horseface said. "We'll be back as soon as we can, Jack."

The main road into Skelton from the north was covered in at least three feet of fresh snow and the storm was showing no let up as the three men eased their horses into a stand of winter-bare aspen trees. The creek was running high and cottonwood trees were mixed in with the aspen. "If we can get back far enough into these trees we can light a fire that won't be seen from the road." Henry Coates said. He could almost feel the warmth of a fire just talking about it.

"I could go for a good fire," Ron Desmond said, "but we're only about five miles from town and a warm house to be in."

"Ma won't like it, but we can just hole up at my place until the storm quits. There's plenty of food and wood for the fireplace," Tony Sorrel said. "I think we should keep going."

"Whatever posse might be following us can't go any faster than we're going," Coates said. "I guess you're right. We'll have the advantage if we are in a warm house when they get there. A good firefight will make it a lot easier to burn out that big store and the rest of the town." He was almost laughing thinking of burning old Valley Paddock out.

They had run their horses hard getting out of Elko and plowing through heavy snow for many hours after that and the men had to walk them slowly. Five miles through the storm with high winds and heavy snow made for a long hour and a half ride. The three were covered in snow, their beards and faces iced over when they rode into the darkened town. Nightfall brought bitter temperatures to the little town nestled at the base of the towering Ruby Mountains. "I figger it to be probably well below zero," Desmond said.

They tied their horses at the back of the

Sorrel cabin and only Ron Desmond took the time to unsaddle and unbridle his. Tony Sorrel led them into the unlit and cold house. "I wonder where ma is?" he murmured.

"Sure ain't the warm cozy house we talked about," Coates snarled. "Get a fire lit and some lamps going, Sorrel. Desmond, find some food." Coates was carrying a shotgun he took from one of the deputies they shot and stormed through the small cabin making sure they were alone.

"Where would your mother go?" Coates snapped coming back into the kitchen. "She gonna give us grief?"

"It's not like her not to be home. Fire will be hot shortly." Sorrel had a lamp lit and on the kitchen table and Coates could already feel the heat coming from the wood burning stove. "Desmond is lighting a fire in the fireplace, so we'll be warm shortly." He was shaking his head mumbling about not understanding why his mother wasn't home.

"You have guns around? I have this shotgun and you have the pistol you took from one of the deputies, and that's all we have. We're gonna have to fight our way outta here, you know."

"Yeah, Coates, I have guns here. I'll get

315

'em," Sorrel said ambling off toward one of the bedrooms. He returned with two rifles and three revolvers and several boxes of ammunition. Coates grabbed a handgun and rifle and left the shotgun on the table. Sorrel had a revolver tucked in his waistband and took the other rifle. "Desmond can have the shotgun and pistol."

"I could eat a bear right now," Desmond said coming in from the living room. "Where's your ma keep the meat?"

It was an hour or so before that, that Horseface and Puny drove the mules and wagon into Skelton and pulled up in front of Valley Paddock's large store. "Slater wants us to bring Virginia Riley and her children out to his ranch for protection, Valley." Horseface was half frozen sitting on the seat next to Puny. "Any other women folk in town that would rather be out there?"

"When I told Mrs. Sorrel about the jailbreak, she almost fainted. She's inside now, sitting by the stove, scared half out of her wits. She said Tony would kill her for sure." Paddock helped the old veteran off the high wagon while Puny tied the team off. "Come on in and get warm and we'll see what we can do about Virginia Riley. That poor woman doesn't have a friend in the world."

"She's got one in Mims Slater," Horse-face laughed. "If those idiots busted out of jail yesterday, they could be here any minute, even with this monster storm howling at us. Let's not waste time. Send one of your boys up to Mrs. Riley's place and tell her to get packing. Where's Mrs. Sorrel?"

"You're still wearin' those sergeant stripes, eh?" Paddock laughed. He motioned over toward the stove where Beulah Sorrel was sitting in a bentwood rocker and hollered for one of his boys.

"Mrs. Sorrel," Horseface Hawkins said. "Mr. and Mrs. Slater said that if you're afraid, you would be more than welcome to come to their ranch until this all blows over." Usually as rough as any cob, Horse-face Hawkins was also a son of the south and as such, was pure gentleness when dealing with women.

Beulah Sorrel moved west with Mr. Sorrel in the 1860s when life in Missouri became more and more dangerous. Mr. Sorrel, as she always referred to him, was stick skinny, mean-tempered, and couldn't put in a full day of any kind of work. He died about a year after Tony was born and Beulah hadn't had a full meal at any sitting since.

"Thank you, Mr. Hawkins, that's very kind of them. Tony scares me sometimes and if what Mr. Delgado said is true, you know, about burning down the town, I'd feel safer with the Slater's. I better get to packin'," and she got up slowly from the rocker.

"Would you like some help?" Horseface asked.

"No, thank you," she said. "I think I'd like to sit here by this stove for another few minutes and then I'll just throw some clothes in a basket and hurry right back here." She would never tell Hawkins, but she was so weak from hunger that she hadn't even lit a fire that day. It would take her at least a half hour to make the short walk to her little cabin but she was just too proud to accept that saloonkeeper's offer of help.

It's bad enough that all of Skelton knows my son is a murderer and is coming here to burn out the town, and now I have to have help from the Slater family, I'm not going to tell Mr. Hawkins that I can't even pack my own bag or light my own fire. Horseface stood with the woman for a minute or two and watched as she slowly made her way out of the store.

"Okay, Puny, let's get them mules up to the Riley place and bring Virginia and the children down here. Anyone else you can think of, Valley?"

"I don't think so, Horseface. Just be careful out there in this foul weather."

[25]

"Where's Mrs. Sorrel?" Horseface said. He eased himself down from the high wagon seat. The wind was still blowing hard, driving great waves of snow through the streets of the village. "She said she was just gonna put a couple of things in a basket and come back here."

"Haven't seen her," Valley Paddock said. "Oh, dear. She's so frail, we better check on her right away. If she fell, she could already be under half a foot of snow. Come on, Horseface, let's get Mrs. Riley and children inside and warm."

The two were back on the street in minutes, burrowed deep into their winter coats and scarves and heard shouts from about a hundred feet in front of them. The snow was so thick they couldn't see who was hollering but hurried forward toward the noise. The wind was whirling as a dervish through the streets, between buildings, and it carried blinding snow along for the ride. It took a couple of minutes to make such short progress.

"Who's that hollering?" Horseface Hawkins yelled out.

"That you, Horseface?" a voice answered back. "Come on and hurry. Mrs. Sorrel is half frozen here." Horseface recognized Jimmie Delgado's voice and he and Paddock fought to move through deep drifts to reach them.

"She must have slipped and couldn't get up. Her house is right there, across the street. Let's get her inside and get her warmed up." Delgado and Jesse Winthrop had just arrived and found Beulah Sorrel as they started to tie off their horses. "Miserable weather, Horseface. Miserable ride back."

"We have Virginia Riley all packed. Puny is with her and the children now, and Mrs. Sorrel was going to the cabin to pack some things for her stay at the Slater ranch."

Jesse Winthrop had no trouble lifting the frail woman and the men battled their way across the narrow street to the Sorrel cabin. "You think maybe we should take her to Doc Fowler's instead?" Delgado asked. "I'm not sure she's even breathing."

"She's alive," Winthrop said. "I think the

doc is the better place for her right now."

It took a full ten minutes for the men to plow their way through the heavy snow and Horseface pounded on Doc Fowler's door. "What is this?" Fowler said when he got the door opened and the three men and Mrs. Sorrel moved into the warm front parlor.

"She fell in the snow and couldn't get up," Delgado said. Winthrop carried the unconscious woman into Fowler's Room #2 and laid her out on a bed. "She's terribly cold, Doc," Delgado said.

Doctor Fowler couldn't imagine what the woman might have been doing out in this weather but didn't say anything as he piled wool blankets on top of her. "There are some bricks under the cook stove, Horseface. They should be good and hot. Bring as many as you can get in the coal-scuttle. We'll put them under the blankets and she'll be toasty warm shortly."

He looked around the room and finally couldn't keep his curiosity under control for another minute. "You all look like you've been out in this storm for hours. You're dripping gallons from the ice you're carrying. Just what is going on? Why would you men be out in the middle of this maelstrom with Mrs. Sorrel?" He was looking back and forth at the men just shaking his head in

322

confusion. "Why?" He asked again as Hawkins came back with a scuttle full of hot bricks and some towels he found on the sink to wrap the bricks.

Delgado chuckled, helping put some bricks in the bedcovers. "It's a long story, Doc."

An hour and two pots of coffee later, the men sitting around Doc Fowler's kitchen table noticed a change in what the storm sounded like. "Wind's easing off," Winthrop said. He got up and walked over to the window, moving the curtain aside to look out. "Just a light snow falling straight down. We better get back to Paddock's and make sure Puny and Mrs. Riley are still packed and ready to go."

"It's best if Beulah stays here," Fowler said. "She's in no condition to make a wagon ride out to Jack Slater's place. It's probably zero or less out there right now and when the sun goes down, it's gonna get real cold." He chuckled at his comment and only Horseface chuckled along with him.

"Her place is almost next door, but you said she was afraid that rotten son of hers might want to kill her. Well," he said with a smile, "she'll be safe here with me. She's so frail I worry about pneumonia setting in from her exposure out there. I'll keep her warm here. You boys go on and take care of Mrs. Riley and those children of hers.

"I don't know if you're aware, but Virginia Riley is very pregnant. She hadn't even had the chance to tell Dick before he died. Take care of her because I don't think she can take care of herself. Neither she nor Dick Riley had an ounce of common sense."

Winthrop, Delgado, Paddock, and Hawkins bundled up and stepped out of Doc Fowler's place into a winter wonderland. Drifted snow with peaks and valleys sparkled in bright sunshine and nothing was moving. There were no tracks out on the street, and the only thing moving was smoke rising from the many chimneys and stovepipes above the homes and businesses.

"Beulah Sorrel said she hadn't even lit a fire, Valley. Remember?" Horseface was standing still looking over at the Sorrel cabin. "Ain't that smoke comin' from that chimney? Somebody's inside her cabin."

"It's gotta be Tony Sorrel," Delgado said. "He would have Desmond and Coates with him." He shook his head and mumbled something, then said, "My rifle's on my horse."

"Mine too," Winthrop said. "Let's just walk over to the horses like we haven't seen

324

a thing and get them."

The four men strolled through the deep drifts to the hitching rack and Delgado and Winthrop slipped rifles from their leather. "Anybody see any movement over there?" Delgado asked.

"Curtains are drawn tight," Winthrop said. "It's gonna be some time before that posse gets here. It's just us, I'm afraid." Winthrop and Delgado each had rifles and side arms, Horseface had his big cudgel and a Remington tucked in his pants waistband, and Valley Paddock was unarmed.

"According to the wire from Reardon the men took guns from the guards and I'm sure there were guns at the Sorrel cabin." Delgado hunkered down on his haunches looking at the building, seeing smoke from the living room chimney and the kitchen stovepipe. "Valley, you head back to the store and get Puny on the road with Mrs. Riley and the children, get some weapons and a man or two if you can find them and get back here.

"Let's tell those fine upstanding citizens hidden away over there that we're here, and they ain't going nowhere." Paddock took off, doing his best to make good time through the heavy drifts and Delgado sent Winthrop around to scan the back of the

Sorrel cabin. "I don't want those fools sneaking out the back door.

"I'm gonna put a round through the living room window there and holler at those fools hidden away all safe and warm. They are insane madmen who have already killed more than one person. Let's not be stupid."

"Bring 'em on, Jimmie, I'm ready," Horseface chuckled. "Never been a time in my life I wasn't ready for a good fight." His eyes were shining, his jaw was set, and he had that old Remmie out and cocked. "Let er rip," he howled as Delgado put a round from his rifle through the window.

"That would of woke the dead," Horseface laughed, and they heard two quick gunshots reverberate from behind the Sorrel cabin. "Jesse's got some action," he said.

"They won't try that again," Winthrop hollered out. "I think I hit one of them as they scurried back inside."

"Let's put another couple of rounds into the cabin, Horseface. Maybe they'll quit."

"Sorrel and Desmond are too dumb to quit, and that Coates feller is the one I hit with my cane at Paddock's place. They won't quit, Jimmie Delgado, we gots to kill 'em all to get this over. Of course, a smart man wouldn't be in that position in the first place, eh?" He laughed hard and put two bullets through that front window. Delgado waited a few seconds and then put two through a kitchen window.

Within the time it takes to take in a big breath of air, return fire erupted from the cabin. "See? I told you so," Horseface laughed, putting two more slugs through that window.

"Unless you've got a box of bullets with you, we better go easy on the shootin', Horseface." Delgado was about to say something else when he heard hollering from inside the cabin and heard Puny letting the mules know who was boss as he turned the big wagon west and left town with Virginia Riley and the children.

"At least they're riding in the sunshine and there's no wind," Horseface said. Delgado motioned for him to be quiet, so he could hear what was going on inside the Sorrel cabin.

"They're either fightin' with each other or somebody's hurt pretty bad in there. Let's see if we can make 'em feel some serious heat," Delgado said. He raised his repeating rifle and put four slugs into the cabin while Horseface Hawkins emptied his revolver of its remaining rounds. Delgado had a big smile on his face when he heard heavy rifle fire coming from where Winthrop was hiding.

"That was a pretty strong message there, deputy," Valley Paddock said, slipping down behind a water trough near the two shooters. He had two rifles and boxes of ammunition with him. "Brought one for you, Horseface, and we got lots of stuff to make much noise."

There hadn't been any return fire after the last volley and no sound was coming from the cabin. "Look," Horseface said, pointing at the broken kitchen window where smoke could be seen drifting out. "The cabin's on fire."

"Be ready for a breakout, Jesse," Delgado hollered across to Winthrop. "They set the cabin on fire. Start shootin' now and drive them our way."

He didn't have to say that twice. Winthrop pumped five fast shots from his rifle into the back end of the cabin and followed it up with six from his handgun. While he was reloading Horseface emptied his rifle into the cabin, and Valley Paddock followed up with his.

"Hold your fire now and let's see what happens. Make sure your weapons are fully charged, gentlemen." Delgado had his rifle up and ready to fire as he spoke and saw heavier clouds of smoke coming from that broken kitchen window. "Be ready for a dash, and they'll come out guns blazing. They haven't done much shootin' so far."

"You're fidgety, Jack, what's wrong?" Mims was sitting at the kitchen table, little Henry on her lap and Maybelle sitting next to her. "The storm's let up quite a bit."

"No, it's not the storm. There's something wrong, Mims. Puny and Horseface should have been back some time ago. I'm going to go find out what's wrong," he said, putting on his heavy wool coat.

"I'll ride with you, dad," Robbie said, jumping up.

"You and Cactus Jack grab your gear. It's gonna be a cold ride. Ornery, you need to stay here with Mims and the children. Bring Ezra in also. I don't know what it is, but I can just feel there's something wrong. Keep your rifles handy, we'll be back just as quick as we can."

They wore heavy winter blanket coats as they broke through high drifts to get to the barn and saddle up. "It's probably the storm, Jack," Cactus Jack said. They're having trouble getting through all this snow." Robbie moved out first and hollered back at Jack. "I'll break trail for a while and you two ride behind, then we'll switch when my horse tires some."

It was a long five miles from the ranch to Skelton, Jack knew, but even with all this snow and storm that brought it, Puny and Horseface were late getting there. "Even if Virginia Riley and those kids gave them trouble, even if Beulah Sorrel threw a fit, they wouldn't be this late." Jack had an entire conversation going but only with himself.

Cactus Jack Faraday had seen this in Slater many times over the past couple of years. *That man feels he is responsible for every single thing that happens or doesn't happen. That's why I tease him so often about learning how to have fun. Maybe all of this is his way of having fun.* Nobody heard the quiet little chuckles as Cactus Jack nudged his horse some.

They were out about half an hour when Robbie pulled his horse up to a halt and pointed down the road. "Looks like Puny coming now, dad."

The bright late afternoon sun on fresh snow was blinding and Jack spotted the wagon in the glare. "I don't see Horseface," Jack said. The mules were plodding their way through the heavy drifts and staying a true course on the roadway. It took minutes for the group to get together.

"There's trouble in town, Jack," Puny hollered as they closed on each other. "Horseface stayed with that deputy. I heard lots of gunfire as I was pulling out. Woman and children are okay but cold. Me too," he laughed.

"Glad you're safe, Puny." Virginia Riley and the children could be seen in the back of the wagon, wrapped in heavy blankets. "I don't see Mrs. Sorrel."

"I think that's part of the problem. Something about her son. Mr. Paddock was pretty upset when he sent me off."

"Okay, Puny. You get these people back to the ranch and get 'em warm and fed. All right, you two, let's ride into town and help Delgado and Valley." He spurred his big stock horse into a good trot, following along the trail broken by the wagon and making good time. They were about a quarter mile out when they saw heavy smoke coming from one of the cabins on the main street.

"That's Sorrel's cabin that's burnin'," Jack said. "Let's not ride into a gunfight, gentlemen. If Tony Sorrel, Desmond, and Coates are already in town, we need to be careful." He turned his horse toward Paddock's store and lifted his rifle as he stepped off. "Let's cross the street and move toward Doc Fowler's place."

Jack could see tracks moving north on the west side of the street, the Sorrel cabin, burning hot on the east side, just a lot or two north of Fowler's office. Doc came to the door and motioned the group in as they neared his place. "Tony and Desmond are holed up there," Fowler said, pointing toward the fire. "There's a third man with them."

"Where's Mrs. Sorrel?" Jack asked. "If she's in there . . ." and his thought trailed off.

"No, no, Jack, she's right here. With me. It's a long story, but she's well and warm, now. Jimmie can use your help. He's got those fools trapped in that cabin and now it's on fire. Go help that man."

Jack didn't need any urging, and he motioned Robbie and Cactus Jack to follow. He headed right back out the door and into a volley of shots coming from the cabin, aimed at Delgado and company across the street. Jack caught the deputy's attention and waved at Delgado to let him know he had back up. Jack led the group through the snow, around behind Fowler's and north to join with Jesse Winthrop.

"Glad you're here, Jack. All the action is coming from the front of the cabin right now. There's three of 'em in there, and I think at least one is wounded. That fire's getting mighty hot, Jack. They're gonna have to either give it up or try to break out soon if they want to live."

"There'll be no living if they try to break out," Jack said. He had been scanning the area all the time Winthrop was talking. "Robbie, if you can get behind that old tree over there, and if I can sneak around behind the well, we might be able to convince those fools to give it up. You stay right here with Jesse, Cactus, and we'll be able to put some heavy lead into the inferno."

"You mean fill the cabin with hot lead first," Cactus snickered, getting a nod from Slater. Robbie didn't wait, just pushed off and ran two steps diving into the snow behind the tree. He didn't draw a shot, which caught both he and Jack by surprise.

"They've forgotten you're back here, Jesse. Worried about Jimmie and his bunch out front." Jack hunched down and moved as quickly as he could through the snow, dropping behind the well, hidden by the thick timbers holding the ropes and pulley.

He motioned to Jesse, Cactus and Robbie, brought his rifle up, and the four of them put three rounds each through the back windows of the cabin.

"We hit somebody," Robbie yelled. He was the closest to the building and was sure he heard screams from inside.

"You men inside," Jack yelled. "We have you surrounded. There are fifteen of us and three of you. You're about to be roasted alive. Come out, one at a time, hands high, and you'll live. If you don't, we'll keep you bottled up until the cabin burns to the ground and you with it. Your choice."

The old and dry wood of the Sorrel cabin was tinder, the flames danced through the roof and the heat back where Jack crouched was fierce. One section of the roof, probably over the kitchen where the fire started, crashed to the ground sending a fury of sparks and flame flashing through the air.

"Better make up your minds, boys. That's not a friendly way to die, roasted over open coals like a dead steer." Horseface Hawkins could be heard all over Skelton, yowling at the outlaws. "I got some good mop sauce but it's best on a steer," he cackled.

Jack was still chuckling when he saw the back door of the cabin begin to open. "Come on ahead," he yelled. "Nice and

335

slow, hands high, and no weapons." Ron Desmond was first out, his hands up and empty.

"Sorrel's wounded. Can't walk," he said.

"Drag him out slow," Jack said. "What about Coates?"

The answer came from the end of a shotgun as Coates flung Desmond aside and he and Sorrel came out the door, firing wildly. Jack shot Coates dead and Jesse Winthrop killed Sorrel. Desmond stumbled once and fell face down in the snow, bleeding hard. Robbie was closest and ran to Desmond to make sure he was unarmed. "Better get him to the doc's pretty quick," he said.

"They used Desmond to get out knowing he was so badly wounded he couldn't help them. Rotten people, that's what they were," Doc Fowler said after they brought Desmond in. "He'll live long enough to be hung, Jack."

Fowler started work on Desmond and told the rest to get out. "Horseface, take this bunch over to your saloon so I can get my work done. Beulah, you stay here and help me. As soon as I'm sure this fool will live, we'll be over to join you."

Slater nodded, jerked his head toward the door, and the bunch trooped out, headed for the Alabama House. "I'll stir up the fire and have this place warm as toast," Hawkins said. "Beulah and John looked mighty tight in there," he cackled.

"We took her into his office when we found her unconscious in the snow," Jesse Winthrop said. "She was as light as a sack of feed, Jack. Just skin and bones."

"You boys might remember that Doc had big eyes for Sandra Gomez before Jack kidnapped her out to his ranch." Valley Paddock chuckled some. "He's getting' pretty good at that." Jack didn't say a thing.

It was less than half an hour later that Doc Fowler and Beulah Sorrel came into the saloon, cold and tired. "We lost him, Jack. Bullet went in under his armpit and ripped open major blood vessels. Couldn't stop the bleeding.

"How about a cup of that coffee, Horse-face, and lace it with the best brandy you've got back there."

"Everything I owned was in that cabin, John." Beulah Sorrel was sobbing quietly, holding onto Doc Fowler's hand as tight as she could.

"I know, Beulah, I know," he whispered. Jack, Valley Paddock, and the rest were sitting around cocktail tables with Fowler and

Mrs. Sorrel. Robbie had ridden back to the Slater ranch to make sure Mims was safe. Horseface Hawkins was behind the bar mixing drinks in his Alabama House Saloon.

"It was while I was trying to get Beulah warmed, and we were talking that we discovered how much we have in common, Jack." Doc had seen all the eyes trying to pry their way into what was taking place between Beulah Sorrel and himself. "She's an amazing woman, driven almost to despair by circumstances over which she had no control." His eyes were filled with warmth, he patted Beulah on the hand lightly, and sighed a deep and warm sigh.

"He said he's gonna make me a fat and happy doctor's wife," Beulah Sorrel chuckled. For many in that little saloon it was the first time they had heard Beulah laugh or chuckle. "He said he didn't want to put his arms around a bunch of bones." She was blushing, and Doc just sat there smiling. "Imagine me, a fat old woman?" That brought the house down.

"Now there's a part of Doc Fowler I've never seen," Horseface chuckled. He brought a tray filled with glasses, a bottle of his own bourbon, and a bucket of ice he broke from massive icicles hanging from the roof of the saloon. "Do I see an opportunity

338

for a party in the near future? The only thing better than a good fight is a good party, I've always said."

It took some prodding from Horseface and Valley Paddock before Doc Fowler, a bit red in the face, finally said, "Yes, you buggers. Beulah and I will be driving the buggy to Elko when this snow allows it and getting married, proper like."

"I need to buy a fat steer from you, Jack," Horseface said. "We'll have us a southern style roast, with a side of beef, a hog on a spit, and as much whiskey and beer as can be consumed in one or more sittings. I feel a hounds-a-howlin' party comin' on."

Laughter and conversation lasted well into the night, and it was a bitter cold ride back to the ranch that night for Jack Slater and Cactus Jack Faraday. They found all the lamps lit at the ranch as they rode in, and most of his crew still in the kitchen, the table still filled with food.

Virginia Riley sat quietly at the table, surrounded by buckaroos trying their best to make her feel welcome, her two rowdy children were playing with the two rowdy Slater children in the middle of the kitchen floor, and Mims and Anna were at the stove taking pans full of sweet rolls from the oven.

It took well over an hour for Jack to tell

the story of the standoff at Beulah Sorrel's cabin, about Doc Fowler getting ready to run off to Elko and marry Beulah Sorrel, and the party that Horseface Hawkins was already planning for the wedding reception. Buckaroos drifted off to the bunkhouse, led by Cactus Jack, Anna got Virginia and children properly taken care of, Robbie kissed Mims goodnight and whopped Jack on the shoulders, and Jack led Mims into their bedroom.

"Day after tomorrow is Christmas, Jack, can you believe that? Where has this year gone?"

"This has been the longest year of my life, Mims. Incredible trouble with a county full of outlaws, ranch hands being killed, losing Sandra like we did, floods." He just shook his head slowly, wrapping his arms around Mims. "Just missing famine, I guess," he chuckled.

"There's been a big bowl full of love, too, Jack Slater. We adopted Robbie, we have Henry, Maybelle is growing like a weed, and we have our health, our warm home, and most importantly, each other."

"The good outweighs the bad by a considerable amount, my lady. I've never been happier in my life. All of this, Mims, because my parents were killed in an accident, a big old mean cop gave me over to the Children's Society and they sent me to you. Jablonski just got in the way is all."

They fell asleep laughing at how Jack told their story. "How can anything in the rest of our lives beat what we already have?" He asked.

"I'm sure you'll find a way," she murmured.

ABOUT THE AUTHOR

Reno, Nevada novelist, **Johnny Gunn,** is retired from a long career in journalism. He has worked in print, broadcast, and Internet, including a stint as publisher and editor of the *Virginia City Legend.* These days, Gunn spends most of his time writing novel length fiction, concentrating on the western genre. Or, you can find him down by the Truckee River with a fly rod in hand.

Gunn and his wife, Patty, live on a small hobby farm about twenty miles north of Reno, sharing space with a couple of horses, some meat rabbits, a flock of chickens, and one crazy goat.

Printed in the USA
CPSIA information can be obtained
at www.ICGtesting.com
JSHW020240311024
72664JS00008B/8